THE WARRIOR PRIEST

AN AFTER THE RIFT WORLD NOVEL

C.J. ARCHER

WWW.CJARCHER.COM

PART I

CHAPTER 1

I first met Rhys Mayhew when he plucked me out of the path of a runaway horse with one hand, a half-eaten apple wedged between his teeth. He told me later that he could only spare one hand because he didn't want to put down the tankard of ale he held in the other. He didn't spill a drop during the rescue, nor when he shoved me behind his three companions standing side by side near the entrance to the inn. The first and only drop fell when my pursuers arrived. I watched through the gap between two burly men sporting the symbol of the warrior priests' order on their belted, knee-length brown tunics as Rhys pointed the tankard in a southerly direction.

He removed the apple from his mouth. "He went that way."

"Thank you, Brother," one of the constables said as he ran off.

The fatter constable stood with hands on hips, his chest heaving as he sucked air into his lungs.

Rhys handed him the tankard. "You look like you need this more than me."

The constable gulped down the contents with the same enthusiasm he'd shown for pursuing me. He gave the tankard back and swiped a gloved hand across his mouth. "Merdu bless you, Brother." The constable set off.

Once he and his colleague were out of sight, I turned to run.

Rhys grasped me by the back of my doublet again. The leather was so thin, the seams so old, that it began to rip.

"Let me go, oaf!"

Rhys released me to the sounds of his priest brothers chuckling. He gave me what remained of the apple. "Walk with me. I have a business proposition for you that will put an end to your need to steal. It'll even put a roof over your head." He gave his friends a look and they wordlessly entered the tavern.

I fell into step alongside my savior, although I suspected he shortened his strides so I didn't have to trot. His offer intrigued me. More than that, I knew what it could mean—a way out. When a warrior priest made you an offer to end your starvation, you took it. Famous for their discipline, sacrifice and rigid adherence to their oaths, including celibacy, I felt safe assuming he didn't want me for my body.

I greedily ate the apple, hardly swallowing one bite before taking the next.

"Slow down," he said. "You'll give yourself a stomachache."

I didn't slow down. I finished it, core and all.

We turned the corner and I realized we were in the inn's courtyard. A groom led a horse into one of the stables while its rider strode to the rear door of the inn, a worn leather satchel under one arm. Another groom swept the cobblestones, while a third sat on a bale of hay, watching a boy struggle to roll a barrel across the uneven ground. No one paid us much attention. Our conversation wouldn't be overheard.

"What do you want me to do?" I asked.

"A little spying here and there."

"Why?"

"Because you rarely make a mistake like the one you made today."

He was right. Today had been different. I'd seen my mother's uncle for the first time in almost a year. While I was confident I'd done enough to change my appearance since then, seeing him again had brought back ugly memories. Panicked, I'd fumbled then dropped the carrot I'd stolen from the costermonger's cart. He'd noticed and shouted "Thief!", drawing the attention of constables who'd happened to be passing by.

I studied the priest. He was classically handsome with his tanned skin, short brown hair and clear blue eyes, but it wasn't merely his face that would have the women of Tilting lamenting he'd chosen a life of celibacy. Tall, even for a Glancian man, and broad across the shoulders, I would have guessed he'd be capable of wielding a sword even if I hadn't seen his order's badge on his tunic.

Yet it wasn't his good looks or impressive physique that made my heart flutter. There was something else, something I couldn't quite define. The spark in his eye and tilt of his lips made it seem as though he went through life in the best of humor, as if nothing troubled him and never would. For someone like me, whose life had shrunk to living in dank sewers and stealing scraps to survive, Rhys was magnetic.

I learned later that he was only twenty-four when we met. That age never quite felt right. It seemed too old for the mischievous, youthful air that clung to him, and too young for the responsibilities that would one day burden him. But I didn't think about that until much later.

"You've been watching me," I said, a challenge in my voice.

"You're quick and nimble. I've seen you steal a bag of nuts at the market without the stallholder noticing, or some ells from a man's pocket, also unnoticed. You have light fingers, and being small helps you slip away easily, or simply to blend in. Despite your poor attempt at a disguise, people usually take you for exactly what you want them to see—a boy."

I resisted the urge to touch my cropped hair and instead settled my feet further apart, as I'd seen lads on the cusp of manhood do. "I *am* a boy."

"You must think I'm an idiot to fall for the girl-disguised-as-boy trick."

I gave in without a fight. For some reason, I wanted him to know. "In my defense, people usually are idiots."

"'In my defense?'" he mimicked. I'd never quite been able to lose my upper-class accent, and with him I'd barely even tried to hide it. "The child speaks like she just stepped out of her tutor's schoolroom."

"I'm not a child. I'm seventeen."

He scoffed. "Nice try. You're thirteen, fourteen at most. Tell me, why is an educated girl living on the streets as a boy?"

"None of your business." It was a pathetic response, but it was all I could think of at the time. He'd unbalanced me with his assessment. He was right—I was educated, a girl, and living on the streets disguising myself as a boy. He only got my age wrong. I *was* seventeen. Perhaps if he'd studied my figure more closely, he'd have noticed, but he kept his gaze firmly fixed on my face.

"What's your name?"

"Jac."

"Short for Jacqueline?" When I didn't answer, he said, "My name's Rhys Mayhew. I'm a brother in the Order of Merdu's Guards." He tapped the badge depicting a sword crossing a blazing sun stitched into the tunic at his chest.

"I noticed."

He removed a small pouch from his pocket, tossed it in the air and caught it. The clinking of ells had me salivating. The apple had been my only food that day. "An advance payment." He dropped it onto my outstretched palm. "There'll be more if you meet me back here tonight when the temple bell strikes eleven."

I stared at the pouch. "How do you know I won't run off with your money and not come back?"

"You won't."

"But how do you know?"

He smiled, revealing a dimple in each cheek, and signaled to the ostler to bring his horse.

Weeks later, Rhys admitted that he hadn't known, he'd simply gambled on me being desperate enough. Once again, he was right. Even though my thieving kept me from starving, I was tired of always looking over my shoulder, tired of living in squalor, and sleeping with one eye open and my back to the wall. His offer was the best thing to happen to me since I ran away from my great-uncle's home. I had no choice but to accept, if I were to survive.

Before the ostler could bring out Rhys's horse, the two constables walked past the entrance to the yard and just happened to look through the archway directly at us.

"There he is!" shouted one, pointing at me. "Brother, you've caught the thief! Thank you. Now hand him over."

Rhys regarded the advancing constables as if he didn't have a care in the world. In truth, he didn't. It was me who'd be thrown into prison if I were caught, not him. All he had to do was reassure the men that he had indeed caught me and was about to take me to the sheriff's office. He could claim I escaped on the way. The lie would keep his reputation pristine and me free.

Instead, he spoke to me under his breath. "I feel like having a little fun. Do you, Jac?"

The constables strolled toward us, swords still in their scabbards. They weren't worried about me attacking them, and they were entirely unprepared for Rhys working against them. "If your idea of fun is saving me, then yes. Do you have a plan?"

"Of course." He clapped me on the back, grasping a fistful of my jerkin as he did so, and marched me toward the constables.

My stomach plunged. He was apprehending me, after all.

Although I didn't say a word, he must have felt me tense beneath his grip. "Have faith, Jac." The laconic drawl defined the carefree twenty-four-year-old Rhys Mayhew. His words, however, would one day haunt me.

Faith would tear us apart.

"Slip past them while I distract them," he went on.

"*That's* your plan?"

"You underestimate how distracting I can be."

"Ha! Nobody underestimates that."

His grip loosened. "Good sirs! The lad is a slippery fish, but no one outwits a brother of Merdu's Guards." He angled us between the constables and the exit, then released me. "Here you go."

I ran.

Behind me, I heard the constables shouting at me to stop, then at each other to go after me, then at Rhys for blocking the way. "You're obstructing us on purpose!"

I didn't hear Rhys's response, or perhaps he didn't give one. The next moment, as I sprinted down the street, he drew up alongside me. "Turn left," he directed. "Get lost in the market."

The market was always busy, and it was easier to disappear as long as you darted around carts, stalls and people without knocking anything over. Easier, that is, if you were small and nimble. Rhys was surprisingly fleet for a large man, but he wasn't in the least unobtrusive. Everyone noticed him.

I risked a glance behind us. "They're still following."

"Surprising. I thought they'd run out of steam by now."

He leapt over a wooden crate while I darted around it, only to have a wheelbarrow full of cabbages thrust at me. I wasn't sure if the cabbage seller did it on purpose or if it was an accident, but it slowed me down as I lost my balance.

Rhys grasped me around my waist before I fell, and tucked me into his side, lifting my feet off the ground. Not only was it an ungainly position, he would have felt all of my feminine curves, what little curves my undernourished figure had.

"Put me down! I'm not a sack of potatoes."

He glanced around and finally released me. "Down that lane," he ordered. "We need to get out of the market. Coming here was a bad idea."

"I could have told you that *if* I'd known your plan," I tossed over my shoulder as I ran.

"It would have been a good plan, if you'd avoided that wheelbarrow."

"How was I supposed to avoid it when it was shoved directly at me? I don't have legs like a giant leaping spider," I said pointedly.

"I've been compared to a few creatures before, not always favorably, but never a spider." How could he sound so calm? My heart thundered in my chest, not only from fear but also exertion. I was used to sneaking, not running for my life.

I dared another glance back at the pursuing constables, only to trip over the uneven cobblestones.

Rhys once again grabbed my jerkin, causing the beleaguered seams at my shoulders to finally rip apart. "You're good at thieving, not so good at escaping."

"I don't usually need to escape," I spat out between labored breaths. "Today is not a good day."

"Cheer up. It's about to get better."

"Why?" I followed Rhys's gaze.

He looked directly ahead where a brick wall loomed. The lane came to an end. The only exit was behind us, where the constables were still in pursuit.

"How is that better?"

He flashed a grin. "Change of plan."

"*What* plan?"

He stopped and linked his fingers together, forming a cradle. "Up you go."

I looked up. The building was the only single-level one in the entire lane. With Rhys's help, I could escape across the roof. But could he climb up without any assistance? There was nothing for him to stand on to give him a boost.

"*Now*, Jac." It was the tersest he'd sounded throughout the entire escapade.

I glanced along the lane. The constables had slowed, but

there was no way to get past them out of the lane. "What about you?"

"Don't worry about me. I've been in stickier situations than this and got out of them."

"With Merdu's warriors at your back," I said as I placed my foot into his hands. I grasped the roof tiles and hauled myself up. Rhys made it easier, pushing me as high as he could.

Despite a niggling doubt, I wasn't too concerned about him. Constables wouldn't arrest a warrior priest.

Below me, the constables drew their swords and faced off against Rhys. They were alone in the lane. There were no witnesses. They could attack him with no one finding out what they'd done. Rhys had to rely on his own skill with the sword, and two against one weren't favorable odds.

But he didn't even draw his sword. He simply ran at the wall below and leapt. Using the wall as leverage, he stretched up to grasp the overhanging roof. Swinging his legs, he managed to get half of his body onto the roof. But one of the tiles broke under the weight. He slipped.

"Rhys!" I grabbed his shoulders. The pendant around my neck emerged from beneath my shirt as I leaned forward.

I doubted I played much of a part in saving him, but somehow he managed to keep both arms on the roof while his body dangled down. Seeing an opportunity, the two constables leapt at his legs.

At that moment, Rhys swung them up again. This time, the tiles held, and he pulled himself onto the roof. He lay on the sloping tiles and grinned at me. "Don't look so terrified, Jac. I won't let anything happen to you."

I tucked the pendant back under my shirt. "Merdu and Hailia, you're mad! Why didn't you just give yourself up? Or will you be thrown out of the order if your master hears of this?"

He sat up. "Never. I'm his favorite." He stood and peered over the edge of the roof, just as two hands suddenly gripped the tiles from below. "Isn't that interesting."

I scrambled to my feet. "What is?"

"They're still going. I'd have put money on them giving up by now. Come on. We'd better get a head start. You're going to need it since you don't have legs like a giant spider." He indicated I should go up the roof ahead of him, much as a gentleman signals to a lady to enter a room first.

To the tune of grunts coming from the two constables as they tried to get onto the roof, I used all fours to balance as I scrambled up the tiles. "If you get me killed, I'm coming back from the afterlife to haunt you."

"Our religion doesn't believe in ghosts."

"Then it's lucky I don't believe in religion."

The ensuing silence felt heavy after the lighthearted moments we'd shared during our escape, but I needed to concentrate on my balance as I navigated the roofline, so gave it no further thought.

I came to a stop as the building butted up against a taller one. We'd need to repeat our climb if we were to continue that way. The only other way out was down the sloping roof on the other side then dropping into what appeared to be a courtyard surrounded by buildings. In other words, we would be easy to trap down there.

I turned to face Rhys. "I don't fancy going up again."

"Afraid of heights?"

"No. I'm tired of being chased."

He glanced over his shoulder. "Do you have a plan?"

One of the constables was on the roof, although he looked unsteady on the steeply sloping tiles. He was calling down to his colleague, instructing him on the best way to get up.

"Unlike you, yes."

I was glad to see the humor return to Rhys's eyes. I wasn't sure why it bothered me that he'd been offended by my heathenism. All I knew was that I preferred his mischievousness.

"I have some skill with a knife," I said. "I presume you have some skill with a sword. If we work together, we might have a chance."

He chuckled. At the time, I had no idea why. Later, I would witness Rhys's skill for myself. Even with his eyes closed and a hand tied behind his back, two bumbling constables would offer no opposition. If I'd known that then, I would have found his actions even more baffling. Why didn't he just fight them then and there?

Perhaps he didn't want to harm them. Or perhaps he was simply enjoying himself.

"I have a better plan," he said.

"It's about time," I scoffed. "What do you propose?"

He looked down at the courtyard.

"But we'll be trapped!" I said.

"I told you, Jac. Have a little faith."

"Fine," I ground out. "Do I go first or do you?"

I'd not even finished speaking before he was on his way down the sloping roof. He hung onto the edge and swung himself down to the ground, landing deftly on his feet. He held his arms up to me. "Jump. I'll catch you."

I stared at him, open-mouthed.

Behind me, the constable stood on the ridge of the roof. "Got you," he snarled.

I jumped.

Rhys caught me effortlessly. He didn't set me down immediately, however. With his hands at my waist, I was pinned against his body. The cloth of his tunic and the shirt underneath hid nothing, not the ridges of muscles across his chest, rising and falling with breaths that had suddenly become ragged for the first time. Could he feel the contours of my body through the layers of my disguise? Was that why his gaze suddenly heated as it locked onto mine?

Eye to eye, chest to chest, I could easily kiss him. I *wanted* to kiss him. It was as if a madness had come over me, taking control. I'd never felt this brazen, this much desire and need.

Rhys consumed my thoughts, even to the exclusion of my own safety, and I hadn't even known him an hour.

I reached up my hands to bury them in his hair, when he suddenly lowered me to the ground.

That's when I heard a door behind me crash back on its hinges. I suddenly turned to see the second constable barreling out of the house and into the courtyard. He drew his sword. "You should be ashamed of yourself, Brother."

Rhys put his hands in the air. "Let the lad go. He's just a hungry child."

"I thought you had a plan," I hissed.

"Who says it's not going how I wanted it to?" he hissed back.

"You *wanted* this to end in our surrender?"

"Not ours. Just mine."

"I'm not letting you do that for me."

"All will be well. Nothing will happen to me, Jac. You can still escape through the sewers. I'm standing on the grate. When I step off, open it quickly. Climb down the ladder then continue left. Always go left. Eventually, you'll come out at the river."

"I know the way. You're not coming with me?"

"I'll stay up here and keep him busy. Don't worry, I won't let him follow you."

I glanced up to where the constable on the roof was carefully navigating his way down the slope, arms out for balance, his attention focused on each slow, cautious step.

Rhys stepped off the grate. I bent down and wrapped my fingers around the bars.

"Stop!" The constable in the courtyard advanced.

Rhys moved to block him, his hands still in the air. "I said, let the lad go."

The constable, however, thrust his sword point at Rhys. "Move aside, Brother."

Rhys glanced at me. "What's taking you so long?"

"It's stuck," I said.

"Pull harder."

"Easy for you to say."

He grunted, conceding that he must have miscalculated. He swore under his breath, and the fingers of his right hand twitched, as if he wished he held his sword. For the first time since the pursuit began, he seemed rattled.

The constable ordered Rhys to step aside. Rhys hesitated before complying. The constable drew in a relieved breath then came for me.

I pulled out the iron grate and swung it at him. It hit his arm, and he lowered the sword with a grunt of pain.

I sprang up and ran past him, grabbing Rhys's hand as I did so. "Your plan needed a slight modification."

To the shouts of both constables, we raced across the court-yard. Just as we were about to enter the building, the constable on the roof cried out. I glanced back to see the constable on the ground look up at the same moment his colleague rolled off the roof. He dropped his sword in order to catch the man.

Both tumbled to the cobblestones in a tangle of limbs and curses.

Rhys and I ran on, out through the building and back down the lane. We reentered the market briefly before turning down another street then another. More twists and turns later, I was quite out of breath.

Finally, Rhys stopped when we reached the river. It was then that I noticed we still held hands. As if he'd just realized, too, he released me. I bent over double in an attempt to catch my breath.

After several moments, I straightened. Rhys's eyes were bright, his lips curved with his smile. He wasn't in the least out of breath. "I told you I had a plan," he said.

"*That* was *not* part of your plan."

"Wasn't it?"

I narrowed my gaze at him, no longer sure if it had been or not.

He started to laugh, and I couldn't help laughing along with him. Perhaps it was the danger and excitement we'd just shared, or perhaps it was because he made me feel safe, but in that moment, something exploded inside me. It was heady and all-consuming, and it awoke every part of me in such a way that I was utterly and completely absorbed by the feelings coursing through me.

Rhys made me feel wonderful, alive, special.

If I made him feel that way, he didn't show it. As his laughter faded, he simply pointed upstream. "You can find your way home by following this until you reach the crooked house, then go right, then left at the high fence."

"Oh," I managed to say. "Right. I mean left. Right." *Hailia, stop me.*

Still smiling, Rhys sauntered off, one hand resting on his sword hilt. "Don't forget: tonight at the eleventh hour."

I watched him walk away with an overwhelming sense that my life would be different from then on. A believer would say that Merdu, the god of change, had me in his sights. I was no longer sure if I believed in the power of the god and goddess. Like Rhys's, their plans seemed poorly considered.

All I knew was that meeting Rhys would be just the beginning.

CHAPTER 2

*T*hree years later, I peered out of the window in a room where Rhys used to take his lovers. According to Mistress Blundle, the old woman who rented rooms on the ground floor, Rhys had a string of them before he became a priest. I discovered he hadn't stopped when he became one of Merdu's warriors, however. He simply became more discreet.

Not discreet enough, though, and I told him so after I overheard two women discussing him in the street as he passed by. He'd assured me that liaison had ended and he never took women to our secret meeting room anymore. From the way he avoided my gaze, I wondered if he still had lovers but just took them elsewhere. I decided I didn't want to know, so I didn't try to follow him and find out.

There was very little I couldn't find out. That was why Rhys hired me. I found things out for him, and sometimes for myself. Sometimes I found things out *about* Rhys, like Mistress Blundle's offhanded mention of women. Her comment intrigued me enough to investigate the ownership of the secret room. A little nocturnal excursion to the Glancian property office revealed the entire building had been owned by Rhys's father until his death when Rhys was aged just thirteen. I knew Rhys had been raised by the order after he became an orphan, then taken his priestly vows once he reached eighteen, the legal age of majority. According to the records, the building's ownership had been formally transferred to the order at that point, no doubt along with any other belongings Rhys possessed. The second-floor room had been left vacant, however, and Rhys continued to have access. I wondered how many brothers in his order knew.

After the first time he employed me to undertake a little spying, we changed our meeting place to that room, and we've met there on and off for three years. If he wanted to speak to me, he lit a candle and placed it on the windowsill, and I did the same if I had something to report. The central location of the building meant it wasn't out of our way to walk past and look up.

What began as sporadic meetings whenever he had a job for me became more frequent. Then they became daily. Sometimes we discussed a task he needed me to do, but usually we just talked or watched the stars in silence from the balcony. He was my friend—my only friend—while I was just one of many to him.

I watched him stride across the street, his cloak billowing behind him like a sail. Even in the poor light cast by the flickering torches, I could make out Rhys's brown hair, a little darker than the blond of most Glancians, and his impressive physique. Once he was out of my sight, I counted slowly from one so I was ready for him to enter when I reached nine. As usual, he'd taken the steps two at a time. For someone who possessed patience in abundance, he had a distinct dislike for the slowness of stairs.

He removed his cloak and tossed it over the back of the armchair, one of the few pieces of furniture in the room, then placed his gloves on top. "Rain is in the air. You should stay here tonight, Jac, instead of going home."

"A little rain doesn't bother me."

It was an old argument that he repeated every time bad weather struck Tilting. Rhys paid me enough so that I no longer had to live on the streets, but even if I didn't have a roof over my head, I would refuse his offer. If I stayed in the same place where he and I met to exchange information, Mistress Blundle and the other neighbors would grow suspicious. Rhys may have owned the house once, but he didn't anymore. The master of his order might put a tenant in if he found out Rhys met a woman here, even if she was just his information gatherer, not his lover. That's if they realized I was a woman. I still passed myself off as a boy.

Rhys was nothing if not persistent. "But it's cold tonight."

"Stop whining, you big baby. Put on an extra hair shirt before bed if you're cold."

He crossed his arms over his chest. "Only zealots wear hair shirts, and I don't get cold. My muscles keep me warm." He flexed his arms, to prove the point. "You're skin and bone, Jac. Still. That reminds me…" He dug into the pocket of his tunic and produced a slice of honey cake wrapped in a cloth. "It was the cook's special treat after dinner for the celebrations." He handed me the cake.

It was rare for the priests to be given treats. All of the orders, whether dedicated to the god or goddess, had rules that required their priests and priestesses deprive themselves of worldly goods. I would argue that delicious food wasn't a worldly good, it was a necessity, but my argument would fall on deaf ears. If Rhys's friend Andreas was to be believed, Merdu's Guards dined on gray sludgy gruel twice a day. Then again, Andreas was prone to exaggeration.

I accepted the cake. "Thank you."

"Don't thank me, thank Rufus."

"He knows I like honey cake?"

"I stole it from his plate when he wasn't looking. You don't expect me to give up my own honey cake, do you?" He ruffled my hair.

Ruffled! He still saw me as a child. Sometimes I think he also still saw me as a boy. If my mother was alive, I'd be dancing at balls and playing the pianoforte, wearing pretty dresses with my long blonde hair elegantly arranged. Yet here I was, sitting on a windowsill, eating honey cake brought to me by the man I loved, who treated me like a fourteen-year-old boy.

I ate the honey cake as the first drops of rain splattered on the windowpanes, and tried very hard not to dwell on something I couldn't change.

Rhys built a small fire in the fireplace then warmed his hands by it. "You were at the parade ground this morning. Did you enjoy our display?"

"I did. There's nothing more exciting than watching oversized men with oversized opinions of themselves pretend to fight each other with wooden swords."

He shot me a wry smirk over his shoulder. "Blame the master for the swords. I wanted to use real ones for authenticity, but he thought drawing blood while the king, governor and high priest all watched on was a bad idea. Can't think why. What do they expect from the protectors of the faith?"

"You had all the ladies swooning."

"*Andreas* had them swooning."

I rolled my eyes. I wasn't sure if Rhys was truly unaware of the effect he had on women, or whether he was just being modest. "How did you see me? Half the city was there, and I had my hood drawn low."

"I didn't." He sat in the armchair, stretched out his long legs, and smiled slyly. "You just confirmed it. You're a good spy, Jac, but don't get caught. Your captor will have the truth out of you before you're aware you're being interrogated."

"This is hardly an interrogation, and I had no need to keep my presence at the parade ground a secret from you."

His smile faded. "Just don't get caught when you're spying."

"I'm too good to be caught."

"You're forgetting how we met."

"I've gotten better at escaping since then." A lot better, thanks to Rhys teaching me how to balance and use my small size to my advantage. "Besides, I was distracted that day."

He arched his brows, waiting for me to tell him what I'd seen that I'd found so distracting. When I didn't respond, he added, "Promise me you'll be careful, Jac. Don't get complacent."

"I promise. What's brought this on?" It was nicer than I thought it would be to have someone worry about me, particularly when that person was Rhys. Perhaps he'd always worried about me, just never expressed it.

He crossed his legs at the ankles and stared into the flames. The light flickered across his face, highlighting the strong angles of his jaw and cheeks and giving his eyes a moodiness that wasn't natural on him.

I got up and stood between him and the fire. "Rhys? Do you have a new job for me?"

"You're good, Jac, but I think I'll ask someone else." He shrugged without meeting my gaze.

"For Hailia's sake, just tell me about the job. If I feel it's beyond me, I'll reject it, but don't pretend there's someone else you can ask because there isn't. I'm your best spy."

After a moment, he lifted his gaze to mine. "And you accuse me of having an oversized opinion of myself."

Despite my irritation, I couldn't help my smile. "What's the job?"

"I want you to look for a document in the governor's office."

I went very still.

Rhys missed nothing. "What is it?"

I shrugged, dismissive. "What's the document?"

He narrowed his gaze. "A declaration giving Tilting's governor the power to make decisions without the agreement of his council."

"That can't be allowed! He'll change laws to his advantage, assign contracts to businesses linked to his own interests... It's dangerous to give a man like him so much power."

Rhys's gaze narrowed further. "That's why we need to know if it's just a rumor or not. If the document exists, I want you to find it. I don't need to see it. I just need to know what it says. The governor can't be given more power. He already pays the magistrate and sheriff to do his bidding. This will be disastrous for the city."

"The king won't allow it."

"King Alain has other things on his mind. Things that involve his kingdom, not its capital city."

"Such as?"

"Such as the fact he's dying and has no heir. If he dies soon, which is looking likely, there'll be a power vacuum. Filling it will keep the nobles busy fighting amongst themselves and possibly fighting off the king of Vytill."

He was right, although I'd never given it much thought. The ruler of our neighboring kingdom was a distant cousin of King Alain's. Glancia would be swallowed up by Vytill unless we went to war with them and chose a new king from one of Glancia's dukes instead. The problem was, which duke? If they both wanted the crown, it could result in a civil war between their factions.

I knew nothing about the dukes, but I did know that Glancia couldn't afford to go to war, either with its richer neighbor, or with itself.

"I'll go tonight," I assured him.

He put up a hand. "Slow down, Jac. There's a lot of security at the governor's office. It requires preparation to learn the guards' movements—"

"The cleaners arrive as dawn breaks, just before the guards change shifts. The guards will be at their sleepiest and won't notice an extra cleaner, and if they do, they'll simply see a youth blackened by chimney soot."

He rose without taking his gaze off me. He never studied me with such intensity. It was unnerving. Yet it warmed my insides, too. "How do you know when they change shifts? Or when the cleaners arrive? I've never asked you to break into the governor's office before, so this should all be new."

I shrugged.

"And why the hesitation when I mentioned the governor?"

"I didn't hesitate."

"You did. You also showed an uncommon interest in the existence of such a document. You've never shown an interest in knowing the implications of any job I've tasked you with before."

"That's because they've always been petty or dull or both." It was mostly true. I never took an interest because the jobs didn't directly affect me. The machinations of noblemen and rich merchants mattered nothing to my day-to-day existence.

This was different.

I might as well not have spoken. "Why, Jac? Why the interest this time?"

I crossed my arms, but when I realized that made me seem defensive, I lowered them to my sides. "You're mistaken. I'm not interested."

"Merdu, Jac, are we not friends?"

I flinched at the vehemence in his tone. "We are."

"Then why don't you trust me? I trust you."

"It's easy to trust me because you know I owe you. I'd be in prison if it weren't for you, or dead."

It was his turn to flinch. "I had no idea I was just the source of your next meal. But then, I have no idea about anything when it comes to you. You tell me nothing, no matter how many times I ask."

"You haven't asked in a long time."

"Because you wouldn't tell me anything!" He stormed off toward the door, snatching up his cloak and gloves, only to stop before opening it. He lowered his head, and his shoulders slumped. "I thought we were friends, Jac," he said again, without turning to face me.

"We are. We *are*, Rhys." I surged toward him, only to stop myself before I pressed my palm to his back. "I do trust you. I was annoyed just now because sometimes I hate that you can read me so easily."

He half turned and watched me through his thick dark lashes.

I *could* trust him. I knew that in my bones. It was time to tell him. "You're right. There is something about this particular task that affects me, more than any other you've assigned."

He faced me fully. He didn't speak. He hardly seemed to be breathing. His intensity, so unlike his usually carefree self, was unnerving.

It was why I blurted out my confession in a rush. "The governor is my uncle."

Rhys slumped back against the door. He stared at me. "*You're* the governor's niece!"

"Great niece," I said. "He's my mother's uncle."

His brow furrowed. "I remember when you were abducted. The entire city was looking for you, including me and all of the other brothers. Merdu and Hailia…you weren't abducted, were you? Otherwise you'd reveal yourself and return home. You ran away. You didn't want to be found."

"I hid in the sewers while the city searched for me. None of the other homeless vagrants and orphans realized I was a girl after I cut my hair and changed my clothes." I fingered the short strands at the nape of my neck. Sometimes, even now, my reflection startled me when I caught a glimpse of it. I looked nothing like that long-haired innocent sixteen-year-old who'd believed her uncle had her best interests at heart. "If they had, they would have turned me in for the reward."

"The search was called off when your burned body was found after a fire in a warehouse at the docks. The sheriff claimed the investigation revealed the building was used by child abductors who hid them there until they had an opportunity to transport the children out of the city by riverboat. Everyone assumed you'd been one of their victims."

"That fire was a stroke of luck for me, although sadly not for the real victim."

"Or the so-called child abductors. The governor was so upset he tortured them when they were caught."

"They were indeed child abductors, according to some of the children in the sewers. If there's one good thing to come out of this, it was their capture."

"The governor was brutal, so I heard."

"Not because he was upset over losing me. He wanted something of mine. He must have tortured them to find out why it hadn't been on the body, and what they'd done with it." I removed the blue-green cabochon pendant on the end of the silver chain I kept around my neck.

Rhys barely even looked at it. He couldn't stop staring at me. "Is it a family heirloom?"

I nodded. "It's been handed down through the female line over many generations, so my mother said. It's the one thing that was truly mine, and the only thing I had of hers. Yet my uncle wanted it."

"You ran away from a comfortable home because he wanted your necklace?" He shifted his feet and finally his gaze slid away. "Or was there another reason?" He suddenly and violently shook his head. "No, you don't have to answer that. You don't have to tell me anything if you don't want to."

"It's not what you're thinking. He never touched me. To the outside world, it looked as though he took me in because he was my only relative. But in truth, he only gave me a home to get his hands on this." I held the pendant higher, wanting Rhys to take a closer look, to marvel at the stone that I'd marveled at for many years. "All my parents' worldly goods, including me, were given to my nearest male relative, Uncle Roderic. My mother had gifted me this stone on my sixteenth birthday, shortly before she died. She called it a talisman, and claimed it held power put there by the sorcerer himself. That power could be drawn upon by the one who possessed it. Family legend says it must be passed down the female line. My mother didn't know how to extract the power or even what it does—the details were lost long ago—but she made me promise to always keep it on my person. It was that power my uncle wanted for himself. Within minutes of me moving into his house, he asked to see it. When I refused to hand it over, he spent the next few weeks alternately trying to trick me into giving it to him or attempting to take it from me. When he realized I wouldn't give it up and couldn't be tricked, he ripped it right off me. Then he locked me up."

"Clearly you stole it back."

"My first theft. My mother may have given me this pendant, but my father gave me a few skills that he thought might prove useful one day."

I smiled, remembering those lessons. My father had died when I was ten. It was just my mother and me for another six years, until she caught a fever. It had happened so suddenly she'd never been able to make alternative arrangements for my upbringing. Either that, or she hadn't known how cruel her uncle could be and thought he'd make a fine guardian. He'd hidden his true nature from us. From everyone. He still did.

Rhys continued to stare at me, not the stone. Nor did he seem to have taken in what I'd said about the pendant's power. He probably thought it was nothing more than an old family tale, passed down from mother to daughter with a wink as they bonded over something that all wished was true but couldn't possibly be. After all, women held no power in Glancia. Indeed, none of the kingdoms on the Fist Peninsula recognized women as having legal rights when they had a male relative to control them. I wasn't sure about Freedland, that republic full of rebels at the very southern end of the peninsula, but I doubted it was different. My uncle's desperation to get his hands on the pendant was the first clue the story about its power might be true. Since then, I'd wondered how it would work, if it were. If it held power, I had no idea how to unleash it.

With access to the old archives at his order's library, Rhys might be in a position to find out. Even if he couldn't, I didn't regret telling him. I did trust him, and I wanted him to know that.

I held the pendant higher and finally he took notice. He picked it up by its chain. "It's pretty."

"Hold it to the light and you'll see a star in the center."

He angled it toward the fireplace. "So there is. It's as if it shines from within." He went to pass it back to me but stopped. He held it near my face. "The stone is the same color as your eyes."

I was thankful for the poor light when a blush infused my cheeks. I took the pendant and lowered my head as I put it back on. "My mother had the same color eyes, as did her mother and hers, and so on, according to family lore. I liked to think that an admirer of one of my ancestors found the stone while out walking one day and noticed it matched his beloved's eyes, so he had it polished and gave it to her as a gift."

"It's a nice story, and more realistic than the one about a sorcerer putting power into it for some unknown reason then giving it to your ancestor, also for some unknown reason."

His response was hardly surprising. I didn't really believe it myself. "You don't think it could even be remotely true? Not a shred?"

"No, Jac, I don't. I believe in Merdu, Hailia and the minor gods and goddesses. To admit the existence of a sorcerer is blasphemous. Not that I would admit it, because I don't believe sorcery exists."

I tucked the gemstone back under my shirt. It was warm against my skin from Rhys's touch. "The Zemayans believe in a sorcerer."

"Some do. Most don't. They tell their children stories about the sorcerer to scare them into behaving. Nowadays, most believe in the gods and goddesses that we do here on the Fist, led by Merdu and Hailia." A gust of wind rattled the windowpanes, catching his attention. "I should go. I've changed my mind about breaking into the governor's office. I don't want you to do it. It's not worth the risk. All will be officially revealed sooner or later anyway."

That may be true, but it would help Rhys to know in advance. Or, rather, his order's master. I presumed that's who ultimately employed me, since Rhys had no money of his own to pay me. Merdu's Guards might not be responsible for catching criminals who broke the law—that was the job of the sheriff and his constables—but they could be called upon to quell unrest that threatened the city's peace, since Glancia's high priest lived here in Tilting. It made sense to be aware of potential conflicts before they arose.

Rhys made to leave only to stop again. "I'm sorry you had no one after your mother died, not even the man who was supposed to protect you. I can't imagine what it felt like being all alone."

"You were younger than me when your father died, and you had no other family."

"I had the order. Master Tomaj was my father's good friend and took me in without question. The brothers became like real brothers to me. We're a family. Thanks to them, I've never felt alone."

I wondered if that was why he'd joined their ranks when he turned eighteen, because he wanted to stay close to the men who'd become his family. But that wasn't a question I felt comfortable asking, even if he was my best friend.

He rested his hand on the door handle. "I'm glad I found you, Jac. Now you have brothers, too." He slipped out and closed the door softly.

My vision blurred as tears welled. He was right. His friends had become my friends over the last three years, and I was extremely grateful for them. But mostly the tears welled because an ache had settled into my chest. I didn't want Rhys to feel like he was my brother. I wanted him in an entirely different way. One that his religious order forbade.

CHAPTER 3

I waited in the room awhile after Rhys left. I usually did, to ensure we weren't seen leaving together. Sometimes I left via the main door, too, and other times I exited through the balcony doors and climbed down the thick vine that grew up the external wall of the building. But for once, I stayed. I slept in the armchair until I awoke just before dawn. The secret room was closer to the governor's office than my home and I was feeling lazy enough that I didn't want to walk the extra distance.

Before I left, I smudged my face with soot from the fire and ran my fingers through my hair. I rubbed more soot over my clothes with a sigh. It would be hard to remove later. Borrowing a brush and hand shovel kept in the cupboard, I crept downstairs on my toes, past the tenants' room on level one, and Mistress Blundle's on the ground floor. I drew in a deep breath as I passed her closed door. It always smelled of herbs outside her room, day or night.

The rain had stopped but everything was damp. The clouds had kept the night from freezing, but it still felt icy. I made my way through the quiet city where only the lowest of the low stirred—vagrants in search of warmth, night soil men taking away cartfuls of stinking excrement dug out of the pits of noblemen's houses before they awoke, and the cleaners.

I waited in the shadows of a building on the square, then when the cleaners arrived, I simply joined their train. A yawning guard asked for identification while another watched on, holding a torch. When it was my turn, I showed my identification card that proved I was a Tilting resident, given to me long ago by Rhys who'd obtained it from Merdu knew where. I'd left mine behind at my uncle's house when I escaped. The guard barely glanced at it before waving me through.

None of the cleaners raised the alarm. Either they didn't care or they presumed I was one of the regular youths employed to clean out the chimneys. With sooty faces, it was hard to tell them apart.

Getting into the building was the easy part, however. There were guards roaming the halls, these ones more alert as they patrolled in pairs. We split into groups and dispersed into the rooms across the two floors. I quickly swept out the fireplaces, moving from room to room until I found the one that must be the governor's office. It was the largest, but it also smelled faintly of woodsmoke, a sure sign someone had worked there until late. I cleaned the ash from the fireplace while assessing my surroundings, noting the bookshelf packed with books, some of which I recognized from my father's library. My uncle had assimilated them into his collection.

The most likely place to store important documents seemed to be the wooden casket on the desk. It was the right size and the scratches around the lock meant it was often used.

Outside in the corridor, I could hear the guards on duty exchanging quiet words. One asked the other if his child was feeling better, and the second responded that she was improving although his wife was exhausted from taking care of her, and that made her stroppy. The first man joked that his wife was always stroppy. They both chuckled.

A short while later I heard extra sets of footsteps along the corridor then the two guards greeted their colleagues arriving for the morning shift. They exchanged pleasantries and reported that the evening had been typically uneventful. They didn't mention how many cleaners were in each room. Moments later, retreating footsteps signaled the departure of the first set of guards. The two other cleaners with me soon left the office, but I remained behind. I slipped under the desk and waited for the door to close before peeking out from my hiding place. I was alone. The new guards didn't suspect one of the cleaners was still inside.

Using the slender tools I'd ironically picked from the pocket of a known thief a long time ago, I set to work on the casket lock. It was a complicated mechanism I'd not encountered before, and it took me longer than expected to open. But I managed it. I removed the governor's seal and lifted out the thick sheets of parchment underneath. The one I wanted was on top. A quick scan confirmed Rhys's concerns—the document declared that Tilting's governor had the power to make decisions concerning the city without the agreement of his council. It was signed with King Alain's flourishing signature. The imprint of the key and prancing deer, symbols of the royal family of Lockhart, were clearly visible in the wax seal.

Second only to the Glancian king himself, the governor was the ultimate authority in Tilting. Since King Alain was aging, he would be easy to manipulate by my ruthless, conniving uncle. The signature and seal on the document were proof of that.

I looked over the other documents before returning them to the casket, then relocked it. I slipped the lockpicking tools into the folds of cloth at my middle then considered my escape. The only exits from the office were the door to the corridor where fresh guards roamed, or the window. Although I'd climbed into and out of windows on higher levels several times, I decided to take the door. I didn't want to raise suspicions by having fewer cleaners leave the building than enter it.

I listened at the door but couldn't hear voices or footsteps.

With my brush and shovel in hand, I opened it and exited. The nearest guard, leaning against the wall, straightened.

I froze.

"You there! Halt!" He approached, hand on his sword hilt, but his fingers were relaxed so it was unlikely he intended to draw the weapon.

I started to breathe again and focused on maintaining my disguise.

"I didn't know you were in there," he said.

I blinked up at him and shrugged.

"I have to pat you down, make sure you didn't take anything."

I lifted my arms, confident the cloth wrapped around my torso kept my breasts flattened and thickened my waist enough that it diminished the appearance of my hips. Not for the first time, I was grateful I wasn't large-breasted. The guard didn't touch my chest anyway. He simply checked my pockets and found nothing but a smooth piece of flint and a broken tortoise-shell shoe buckle. They were the sorts of things boys collected when they came across them in the street. I kept them as part of my disguise.

The guard handed the items back to me. "Stay with the others, lad."

"Aye, sir." Dipping my head, I entered the next room where the cleaners were almost finished.

* * *

I DIDN'T WANT to wait for nightfall to report what I'd discovered to Rhys, but I couldn't call on him looking like a chimney sweep so I returned home. My room was tucked away in a dead-end court in a part of Tilting that was far enough from the filthy slum known as Merdu's Pit to make it attractive to working-class residents. Houses were small and often crammed with large families, but at least most residents were gainfully employed. There were few beggars in the streets and the prostitutes were discreet. My single room was only large enough for a bed, table and two chairs, but at least it had a fireplace.

I washed off the soot and changed clothes, then gave my laundry to my neighbor, Mistress Lowey, who also baked and sold delicious pies made from a blend of spices, the types and quantities of which she refused to share. When I'd guessed them all, she'd sworn me to secrecy and promised me a free pie once a week. I thought it an excellent bargain considering I had no interest in sharing the recipe anyway. With the taste of the buttery pastry still on my tongue, I made my way to the temple of Merdu's Guards. I passed through the center of Tilting, keeping one eye on the municipal buildings fronting the square. The day was overcast, the air chilly as it swept across the square. I crossed my arms over my chest and tucked my hands under my armpits as a boy would do to warm them. The sound of a carriage speeding over cobblestones had me turning toward it just in time to see it drive through a puddle and splash a group chatting beside the bronze statue of King Alain's ancestor.

One of the men shook his fist at the carriage and shouted abuse at the coachman as well as the occupant. A hand emerged through the window aperture and thumped the carriage door. The coachman pulled on the reins. Before the vehicle came to a complete stop, the guards dressed in the governor's livery of yellow, red and black jumped down from the footboard at the rear. One drew his sword and ordered the group to disperse while the other pushed the troublemaker to his knees.

"Apologize to the governor," the guard demanded.

"Why should I apologize? I'm the one who got wet!"

The guard kicked him in the stomach. The crowd gasped as the man doubled over, groaning. The guard kicked him again, this time in the side, sending the poor fellow rolling in the dirt in pain.

One of his companions stepped forward. "You can't do that!"

The first guard pointed his sword at the man's throat. "You'll find we can." He bared his teeth in a sneer. "Governor?"

"I'll forgive it this time." The honeyed voice of my uncle was at odds with the cruelty of his men and the tension pulsing from the group of bystanders. It seemed to calm them a little.

It chilled me to my core.

"Young man, mind your language," Uncle Roderic went on. "This is a public square. There are ladies present whose menfolk may object. Next time, I may not be here to protect you from them."

He signaled for the coachman to drive on. The guards jumped onto the footboards and sheathed their swords as the carriage drove off. I watched as it passed me.

The governor happened to be looking out.

I quickly flipped up my hood, but it was too late. With a hand on the door, he leaned out of the window aperture, and stared directly at me.

I ran.

I didn't wait to see if anyone followed. I couldn't hear footsteps chasing me, but my blood pounded ferociously in my ears so I couldn't trust my hearing. I darted into the marketplace where the crowds of shoppers made pursuit harder. Even so, I didn't stop until I reached the large tree outside the temple of Merdu's Guards. With my back to the trunk, I tucked my hand down my shirt and touched the talisman pendant, rising and falling against my chest in time with my heavy breaths. It was warm from my heated skin. It was safe, as was I.

I loitered in the shadow of the tree near the main gate of the temple, hoping Rhys would emerge sooner or later. He had never told me who in the order knew about me, aside from his three closest friends, so I didn't want to ask the priest guarding the gate to let me in. Although the order accepted visitors, women weren't allowed, and I was reluctant to break their rule, even if Rhys was the only one who knew I was female and I thought the rule was ludicrous.

I'd once considered scaling the temple's walls to see inside but dismissed the idea. They were too high to scale without being seen. Rhys assured me it was rather dull inside anyway, with nothing more than a training yard, garrison and outbuildings along with the temple itself.

The gate opened and a warrior priest emerged. It was Vizah, one of Rhys's closest friends. He spoke to the guard on duty, then both laughed heartily about an incident that had occurred at breakfast involving a young priest. After the guard closed the gate behind him, Vizah drew in a deep breath, rocking back on his heels as he did so. He seemed content, without a care in the world.

I moved out of the shadows and hailed him. "Vizah. Is Rhys inside?"

He didn't care that I hadn't addressed him as Brother Vizah. None of Rhys's three close friends cared that I dropped formalities. I didn't know if they knew I was a woman. Rhys had never told me if he'd mentioned it to them, and I'd never asked.

Of all of Rhys's friends, Vizah was my favorite. Despite the curved scar bracketing the corner of his mouth and his bear-like size, he wasn't at all intimidating. He was a mischievous rogue who liked to drink and fight, sometimes at the same time. His darker skin was a clue to his part-Zemayan heritage, but he had no idea who his parents were. The orphanage where he'd spent his childhood claimed he'd been left on their doorstep as a baby. At twelve, Vizah ran away after his constant misbehavior brought out the cruelty in the orphanage staff. At thirteen, the master of Merdu's Guards caught him stealing and took him in instead of turning him over to the sheriff. Like Rhys, Vizah formally joined the order when he came of age at eighteen.

"He is, but he's holed up with Master Tomaj and the high priest," Vizah said.

"The high priest? Sounds important."

"They elevated Rhys to second-in-command of the order. It's

an honor." If it was such an honor, why did Vizah sound a little apprehensive?

"Rhys must be pleased," I said.

"He should be."

Vizah looked at the gate, then turned back to me with a shrug. It was as though the action shrugged off whatever was bothering him, and he was once again his nonchalant self. He clapped me on the shoulder, hard, then chuckled when I stumbled forward. It was confirmation that Vizah didn't know I was a woman. I'd seen him in the presence of women, and he was always respectful. I doubted he would be so rough with me if he knew the truth.

"Did you need to speak to him, Jac?"

"I completed an errand for him and I didn't want to wait until tonight to report in."

Vizah nodded knowingly. I knew Rhys had told his friends that I occasionally spied for him. There didn't seem to be many secrets Rhys, Vizah, Rufus and Andreas kept from one another, my true gender being the exception. "I'll let him know you're here," Vizah said. "Do you need anything? There might be leftovers from last night's dinner in the kitchen."

"As delicious as day-old sludge sounds, I'll pass."

"We had a feast last night. Sludge is on the menu for tonight." He folded his arms over his chest and frowned down at me. "You're too skinny, Jac. When I was your age, I was the size of a horse."

Rufus and Andreas had come up behind him, and Rufus now clapped his hand on Vizah's shoulder as Vizah had done to me. The big man didn't move an inch. "More like a donkey," Rufus said with a straight face. I'd never seen him laugh in all the time I'd known him. Smirk, yes, and smile wryly, but never a grin or chuckle and certainly not a raucous laugh.

Vizah scratched his head. "Are you calling me an ass?"

Andreas clapped Vizah's other shoulder. "Ass, arse...both apply to you, Brother."

Vizah went to punch Andreas in the stomach, but Andreas anticipated it and deftly skipped aside. He winked at me, one of the few signs he'd ever given that made me think he did know I was female. Of all the friends, Andreas would be the most likely to see past the disguise. He was no stranger to the female form. I knew for certain he kept mistresses, sometimes visiting two or three on the same night. His womanizing was an open secret amongst the four men, but I doubted anyone else in their order knew. Their vow of celibacy was a sacred one and breaking it wouldn't be tolerated by the stricter members, or the master.

I wondered if Rhys would continue to tolerate it, now that he was second-in-command. Would he clean up his own act? Drinking in inns was off-limits, yet he and his friends openly frequented a tavern, something which the master overlooked, apparently. Would Rhys be forced to give that up? If he still kept mistresses, would he let them go?

Andreas's wink was a little unnerving, particularly when that shrewd gaze of his once again assessed me as if trying to identify feminine curves beneath my doublet and trousers. Fortunately, Vizah distracted him by withdrawing Andreas's sword from its scabbard.

He danced away, surprisingly fleet for a man of his size, and waved the sword above his head. "Come and get it."

With a growl of frustration, Andreas charged at him. Vizah ran off and dumped the sword in a pile of horse dung on the side of the street. Andreas swore as he extracted his sword carefully so as not to get any muck on himself. Vizah rocked back on his heels, laughing.

"Children," Rufus muttered with not a hint of a smile.

A bell clanged from inside the temple compound.

"Time for training," Rufus told me. "Wait here, Jac. I'll send Rhys out."

With stability across the three kingdoms and the one republic of the Fist Peninsula, the order of Merdu's Guards could have become lazy, yet they trained for hours every day, in heat or cold, rain or blazing sunshine. Despite the rigorous schedule, the horrible food, and many rules, I'd never heard so much as a mutter of complaint from Rhys or his friends. They loved the order. It was their home. It gave them shelter, sustenance, and respect. They were lauded across the entire peninsula, not just in the kingdom of Glancia. It was no wonder the brothers never left it for the secular world.

Rufus, Vizah and Andreas returned to the temple via the door beside the main gate. Moments later, Rhys emerged alone. He strode toward where I stood beneath the tree, his steps purposeful and his brow furrowed. Something bothered him.

"You don't look pleased," I said. At his blank look, I added, "I heard you've been promoted. Congratulations."

His lips flattened. "There was no one else."

"Aren't there fifty or so brothers in the order?"

"None of the right age and temperament who don't ruffle feathers of either faction and are liked by both Master Tomaj and the high priest. I'm just dull enough not to be offensive to anyone."

"No one would ever accuse you of being dull, Rhys."

One side of his mouth flicked up in one of his familiar roguish smiles before flattening again. He looked away and cleared his throat. "You have something to report?"

I made sure no one was close enough to hear and lowered my voice. "There was a document, just as you suspected. It was already signed by the king and carried his seal."

Rhys suddenly looked up, gaze sharp. It flicked over me from head to toe, assessing. "Did anyone suspect what you were doing?"

"No." I considered telling him about my uncle spotting me later but decided against it. Rhys had enough on his plate and there was nothing he could do about it. It was up to me to be more careful in future.

"Tell me what was written on it," he said.

I repeated every word, not missing a single one. My ability to memorize exactly what I'd seen was the reason Rhys paid me so well. "What will you do about it?" I asked when I finished.

The gate opened and a carriage slowly emerged, escorted on foot by a brawny man in his fifties dressed in a priest's tunic. If I didn't know it was Master Tomaj, I would have assumed he was just another brother. He was talking to a passenger inside the carriage. From where I stood, I couldn't see whether there was an escutcheon painted on the door, but I heard the master call the occupant "Your Eminence." It must be the high priest of Glancia.

"I must go," Rhys muttered before striding off to join them.

I slipped further behind the tree trunk, peering around it to watch. Amid the rumble of the wheels and clip-clop of hooves of a passing horse and cart, I heard Rhys tell the master and high priest he had news. The high priest stepped out of the carriage and the three men moved away so neither the coachman nor the guard at the gate could listen in. As the only one of the three who knew I was still in the vicinity, Rhys must trust me deeply to allow me to eavesdrop on the conversation.

Neither man asked Rhys how he'd come by the information. Both expressed concern over its existence, but not surprise.

"We need to speak to the king," Master Tomaj said. "Your Eminence, he listens to you. He'll retract the document if you advise him to."

"It's too late to retract it," Rhys said. "It already bears the royal seal."

"Brother Rhys is right," came the thinner voice of the high priest. "It's too late. The governor has the power he has coveted since gaining office. It's only a matter of time before he wields it."

"I suspect he'll target thieves first," Master Tomaj said. "He seems set on eradicating theft altogether without fixing the poverty at its root."

"I believe you are right, Tomaj. I have it on good authority that the governor wishes to push through a change to the sentencing of convicted thieves. He wants them put to death and all their belongings confiscated, as well as the property of their family members."

I was no longer a thief, but the thought chilled me to the bone. A death sentence for stealing a loaf of bread to feed a family was horrifically cruel.

"Even worse," the high priest went on, "the governor wants anyone who makes an accusation of rape to be held accountable if the rapist is found innocent. They'll be ordered to pay an exorbitant fine to the man they accused. Since the magistrate is the governor's puppet, and it's near impossible to prove rape anyway, no woman will dare come forward."

"Why?" Rhys exploded. "Why target the victims like that?"

"I believe it's in response to the rumors about his deputy. Apparently a woman accused him of rape. The governor is protecting his own."

Master Tomaj muttered something under his breath. In a louder voice, he added, "I thought he was a decent man when he first took office. I can't believe I read him so poorly."

"You weren't the only one," the high priest said wryly. "He was good at first. Then after he lost his niece in the fire...he changed."

I could have told them he hadn't changed. He'd simply begun to show his true self where before he'd hidden it behind a mask of civility.

"Something must be done to stop him," the high priest went on. "Do either of you have suggestions?"

"I defer to you both on that score," Rhys said.

"No, Brother. You are the second now. You must make the tough decisions alongside your master."

Rhys drew in a deep breath. "Very well. I propose we involve the dukes and lords. They don't want to see all the power of Tilting in the hands of one man any more than we do."

"They don't care about Tilting. Their interests lie in affairs of the kingdom, not its city."

"The affairs of Tilting *are* the affairs of Glancia," Rhys countered.

The high priest paused before saying, "You have good insights and instincts, Brother. This is why you were chosen. But I know the two dukes well, and they will not care if Tilting becomes the playground of a despot as long as he leaves matters of the kingdom to them. If they see the governor removing undesirables from the city then they won't care how he gets rid of them. You credit them with too much sense and feeling."

"His Eminence is right," Master Tomaj added. "With affairs of the kingdom so perilously close to boiling over, the only people who care about Tilting matters are its residents. If we want to save its people then we must be prepared to protect them with whatever means are at our disposal."

"You're proposing we go to war against the governor's men?" Rhys sounded incredulous.

"Let's hope it doesn't come to that," the high priest said.

"We need to exert our power, Your Eminence," Master Tomaj said. "The governor must be reminded that he cannot do as he pleases. Give me the word and I will flex our muscle and intimidate him into behaving."

"None of the religious orders can intervene in local matters, especially the warrior priests. We must remain impartial."

Frustration tightened the grizzled features on Master Tomaj's face. He seemed keen to resolve the matter quickly using the means at his disposal, namely an elite fighting force primed for battle.

"If we're not using brute force to stop him, diplomacy is what we have left," Rhys said.

Neither of the other two commented.

"Isn't it?" Rhys pressed.

"We'll think on it," the high priest said. He reentered the carriage and bade Rhys and Master Tomaj good day before instructing his driver to continue.

I continued to watch as Rhys and the master reentered the

temple complex via the gate. I should have been watching the carriage instead. I didn't pay it any attention until it stopped near me.

"You there," came the high priest's voice. "Don't move, lad. I want to speak to you."

I glanced at the gate, now firmly closed.

"Brother Rhys won't mind if I speak to you," the high priest said as he joined me at the tree. "I know he employs you as a spy. Master Tomaj knows, too. Who do you think approved the payment for your services?"

It was hardly a surprise to me that the master knew, although it was curious that the high priest did. Did he also know I was the governor's niece?

No, he mustn't. He called me lad just now, and it sounded like he believed the story of the governor's lost niece earlier. Rhys had kept both facts a secret.

The high priest studied me down his nose. "Your name is Jac, is it not?"

It was the first time I'd seen the high priest up close. He was older than the master, with white hair and a neatly trimmed white beard. His rotund middle strained his cloth of gold belt so much that I worried the clasp in the shape of a sun would pop off at any moment. Either he liked eating sludge or he dined on heartier fare up at the high temple. As Glancia's most senior priest who oversaw every order in the kingdom and answered only to the Supreme Holiness in the Vytill city of Fahl, he must need to host dignitaries from time to time. Still, if I were a priest or priestess, I'd be annoyed that he didn't suffer deprivation alongside me.

"It is. Your Eminence," I added, remembering my manners.

The high priest glanced back the way he'd come, as if judging the distance and whether I could have overheard their conversation or not. Then he turned back to me. His next words proved his thoughts went in a different direction altogether. "Brother Rhys speaks highly of you."

"He does?"

"He claims you have a memory like a trap, and a knack for discovering even the most intimate of secrets. To hear him, you'd think he was a proud older brother." The high priest showed no sign of humor or irony, so I was even more certain that he didn't know I was a woman. "I assume it was you who discovered a certain document that's of interest to Tilting." When I didn't respond, he smiled. "Discreet, too. I can see why Brother Rhys admires your capabilities. It's as if you were born for the role of spy."

Still, I said nothing. What did he want from me?

The high priest stepped closer. "I have a task for you, Jac."

"I only do as Rhys asks."

"I admire your loyalty, but as this involves Brother Rhys, I thought you would make an exception."

"Then I definitely don't want to be involved. Good day, Your Eminence." I walked off.

"He's in love with a woman who will ruin his life."

My breath caught in my chest. I hadn't realized I'd stopped until the high priest stood in front of me again.

"I see you want to protect Brother Rhys as much as I do. You are indeed a good friend."

"Why do you think he's in love?" I asked carefully.

"I know him well and I can tell. There has been a change in him these last years."

"Years?" I echoed numbly.

"It has been gradual and subtle, but I've noticed it. Lately, it has become more obvious. Ever since Master Tomaj marked Brother Rhys for promotion, I've kept a close eye on him and I can see the signs. Brother Rhys has matured, and he rightly deserves the promotion. He'll be master one day, when the time comes."

"As you say, that's maturity. It's not necessarily because he loves."

"He is in love. I'm quite sure of it. Whether he realizes or not..." The high priest shrugged. "The woman is no good for him."

"Why not? She might be exactly what he needs. Besides, shouldn't Rhys be allowed to decide who is good for him or not?"

My vehemence seemed to catch him by surprise. "I wasn't expecting such a fierce response, but I applaud it. It goes to prove you are precisely the person for this task. Once you discover how unsuitable this woman is for him—"

"I won't spy on him." I turned away.

He caught my elbow. His fingernails dug through my doublet into my arm. "I'm not asking you to. I want you to spy on *her*."

My pulse sounded loud as it pounded through my veins. "Who?" The word was a mere puff of breath, expelled before I could stop it.

"Her name is Giselle."

I swallowed. Breathed. *Giselle*. Not me.

"He has told you about her?" the high priest asked, frowning.

I shook my head.

"You look shocked, lad."

I hadn't expected to hear a name. I'd expected him to ask me to find the girl Rhys had fallen in love with, because the high priest didn't yet know who she was. I'd expected to learn that it was someone he met with occasionally in the house that once belonged to his father. I had hoped it was me.

The numbness faded away, replaced with a dull ache. Rhys wasn't in love with me. Why would he be?

"Giselle and Rhys used to be lovers." The high priest didn't seem at all shocked that a priest of Merdu's Guards had broken his vow of celibacy. It confirmed my thought that indiscretions were overlooked as long as the priests were discreet. "He was saddened when she left Tilting years ago. I heard a rumor that she has recently returned, which would explain Rhys's odd behavior lately, but I want to know if it's true. If she is back, I want to know her plans for Rhys." He removed a small coin pouch from the pocket of his robe. "Will you do that, Jac?"

"Rhys's relationships are none of my business, or yours."

He withdrew two ells and held them up for me to take. "I want to protect Rhys. Giselle isn't the type to settle down with one man. She'll break his heart again, I'm sure of it. He doesn't deserve that."

No. He did not. "I'll find out if she's back in Tilting," I said. "But that's all. What you do with the information is your business." And what I did with it was mine.

"Good lad. She may be difficult to find. Giselle is...elusive. She used to live above the Cat and Mouse tavern, so I suggest you start there." He held out the coins. "There'll be more when you report back."

I took the money. Not because I needed it, but because it would look less suspicious. I didn't want the high priest, or anyone, realizing I wanted to know more about Giselle for my own benefit.

CHAPTER 4

*W*hen I first settled into my disguise as a boy, I'd been surprised at how easy it was to move about the city. As long as I didn't attract attention through thieving, no one took much notice of me. Heads never turned as I passed. Gazes didn't fall to my chest when I spoke. Nobody whispered to their companion about my outfit or the way I'd arranged my hair or my unladylike snort in response to a stupid comment.

Being male was liberating and eye-opening. I could see the city as it was, not the way it was presented to me. The ugly side had shocked me into hiding when I first escaped my uncle's manor house. I was terrified of the brawls that broke out between drunks, and of the half-naked women inviting me to touch them. But slowly I began to see that even the ugliest parts of Tilting could be interesting. The prostitutes helped one another. Some drunks were surprisingly good company. As they got to know me, they shared their stories with me, and their laughter. Some fed or clothed me, if they had anything to spare, and some protected me. I'd made friends, of sorts, and it was one of those friends that I visited now.

I caught her on a bad day, however.

"They took her!" Minnow cried. "They swept her and the other women up like they were the dung left behind by their horses." Hands on hips, she paced the small kitchen of the tenement she shared with her partner, a prostitute who worked the area in which the Cat and Mouse tavern was located. "I have a mind to march down to the prison cells and…" She picked up a pot lid and threw it at the wall with surprising vigor for such a thin woman. The lid fell to the floor with a clatter. Minnow picked it up and pointed to a small chip. "Now look what they made me do!"

I'd never seen Minnow so upset. Her partner had a reputation as the fiery one. It was why she was such a popular prostitute with a regular clientele. Minnow had always been rather meek and sweet. In the year of my homelessness, she'd invite me inside on cold, rainy nights and feed me soup. She soon guessed that I wasn't a boy, but had kept my secret to herself. After Rhys's payments meant I could afford my own place, she sat me down and gave me sensible advice about keeping a man content while saving money on the side to one day gain my independence. After I explained that I wasn't being kept by a man for sexual favors, she'd been so relieved that she told me she had no idea what she was talking about anyway since she only knew how to keep another woman happy, not a man. We'd been friends ever since.

Aged about thirty, Minnow was striking if not beautiful with her square jaw and beaky nose. She kept house for her partner and the two lived quite contentedly on the proceeds of prostitution. They took care of young girls new to the profession and provided food and lodging for women in difficulty.

"Who took them?" I asked her. "The constables?"

She nodded as she set the lid back on the pot. Usually something bubbled away in one of Minnow's pots on the fireplace, but not today. She placed her face in her hands before gathering herself and sitting on a chair across the table from me. "The constables rounded them all up, every last one. If they were met with resistance, they used violence."

"I'm sure they'll be fined and released like every other time."

That was what always happened when the constables conducted a raid. This part of Tilting was notorious for prostitution. Men from all classes knew they could find a woman to suit their needs here. While Tilting's self-proclaimed upstanding residents either pretended the industry didn't exist or turned their faces away, the authorities tolerated the business as long as it didn't spill out to other parts of the city. The women were allowed to operate as long as they were discreet.

"This feels different," Minnow told me. "The women did nothing wrong, Jac. They were working their own patches, minding their own business. There have been no complaints as far as I'm aware."

"Have they been formally charged?"

"No. And if they don't charge them they can't fine them and release them."

"It's still early," I assured her.

She chewed her thumbnail. "Jac, I'm worried. Why did he have them removed?"

"He?"

"The governor. He's behind this. He must be."

I tried to think why Uncle Roderic would round up the city's prostitutes and imprison them without charge, but couldn't. The women provided a service. In this area, they were peaceful, unlike in Merdu's Pit where violence and crime were a disease that infected its desperate inhabitants.

Minnow got up and paced again. "It's because he's a sexless prude."

I stared at her. "Is he?"

"He doesn't have a wife or mistress, and he doesn't come here to use any of the women. He's not interested in men, either. I asked around after I met him. Folk who don't enjoy the pleasures of the flesh are always the worst, thinking those who do enjoy it are abominations. Some try to force their prudishness onto others. That's what I think he's doing now."

"When did you meet him?"

"A few years ago when he was searching for his niece. He personally came to the brothels around here, thinking one of us captured her and forced her into prostitution, or some nonsense." She was busy pacing and didn't look at me. She had no idea I was the niece in question. "Thank Hailia her body was found in that fire or he might have ripped these streets apart looking for her."

If the recent roundup of prostitutes had happened *after* my uncle saw me in the square, I would have worried there was a connection between the two incidents, and that perhaps he was hoping to flush me out, thinking I lived among the women. But according to Minnow, the women were arrested last night and he'd seen me just this morning. Their arrest wasn't my fault.

Minnow finally came to a stop in front of the fireplace. "I hope it is his overzealous prudery behind the arrests. The governor might be sexless but the men on his council aren't. I can name six who regularly partake of the services offered by the girls, and another three who are occasional clients. When they're made aware of the arrests, they'll vote to release them. The governor can't overrule them if they're the majority."

Even if I could tell her about the document I'd seen in my uncle's office, granting him power to bypass his council altogether, I wouldn't. Minnow needed hope, and knowing such a document existed would strip it away.

For the first time since my arrival, she looked at me properly. "Are you well, Jac? You're still thin. I have some bread, although it's a little stale. I haven't been to the market yet."

"I'm not hungry."

"So, what do you want?"

"Information. Do you know a woman named Giselle? She used to frequent the Cat and Mouse."

"Giselle? What do you want with her?"

"So you do know her?"

"As well as anyone could. She was mysterious, coming and going as she pleased. She belonged to no man."

That in itself was intriguing. How many women in Tilting could claim such freedom? "Was she nice?"

Minnow shrugged. "She was smart and witty, and quite the beauty. Generous with her money, too, although I can't say where it came from. Men adored her, and women admired her."

I sat back heavily in the chair with a sigh. "She sounds perfect."

Minnow chuckled. "Nobody's perfect, Jac. In Giselle's case, it was her elusiveness that made her intriguing. Why are you asking about her?"

"Is she back in Tilting?"

"I haven't heard, but I don't go to the Cat and Mouse much these days. Why do you want to know?"

I tilted my head to the side and arched my brows.

"All right, all right, I won't pry."

I sat forward. "You said you *can't* say where she got her money from. Does that mean you know and won't tell?"

She removed an onion from a sack and a knife from a wooden box full of utensils. "It means I can't say. I can only tell you she wasn't a whore."

"A seamstress?"

Minnow laughed. "Not her. If you're looking for her, you'd do best to ask around at the Cat and Mouse. If she's not there, you could follow her lover. He might lead you to her, if they're still together. He's a priest in Merdu's Guards." When I didn't respond, she added, "We shouldn't expect men as masculine as that to be celibate. It's unnatural. Some keep mistresses, but not whores, mind. *They* don't need to pay when women throw themselves at them."

"Are you certain Giselle's lover is a priest in Merdu's Guards?" Perhaps the high priest had been wrong.

"He was. I saw them together at the Cat and Mouse. Not the one with the good hair who all the girls pine for—Andreas I think his name is. It was one of his friends, a Glancian man with an easy, friendly nature. Always smiling and laughing, he was." She smiled to herself, remembering. "That was some time ago, though."

It was Rhys, without a doubt. Of Andreas's good friends, Vizah wasn't full-Glancian and Rufus didn't laugh.

I thanked Minnow and headed to the Cat and Mouse. Nobody paid me any attention as I sat in a corner of the tavern by the fire, hunched over like a lad asleep in the warmth. Through my lashes, I observed the patrons and listened to their conversations. They were all men, and most talked about the arrest of the whores. Some mentioned the governor's latest efforts to rid the city of thieves, or their concern for the kingdom's future without an heir, but others were in good spirits thanks to the free-flowing ale.

I was so engrossed in the conversations that I almost missed the figure coming down the stairs. If it hadn't been for the tavern keeper calling her name I would have missed her altogether. Giselle was dressed like a man beneath a black woolen cloak. With the hood up, her hair and face were obscured. The tavern keeper said he had a message for her then gave her the name of a street. From his accompanying shrug, I suspected he didn't know what the message meant. If he knew who gave it to him to pass on to her, he didn't say and she didn't ask. It was as if she were expecting it.

She left and I followed, keeping my distance. I worried my boots were too loud on the cobblestones. My concern forced me to ease back, but because of that, I almost lost her twice. Each time, I caught up again. It wouldn't have mattered if I did lose her anyway. She went directly to the address the innkeeper had given her.

She didn't knock on the door set in the stone wall. Instead, she did a very odd thing. She climbed a tree in the park opposite.

Her long, agile limbs easily took her to the upper branches where she could see over the wall. She'd scrambled to the top without hesitation and not a single leaf shook. Impressive.

We were in the better part of Tilting, where the lords kept their city residences. Houses were large, their owners wealthy. I climbed another tree, not quite as quickly as Giselle, but I didn't have the benefit of her height. I watched her as she watched the house. My tree was smaller so I couldn't see beyond the wall, but I presumed she was gathering information about the occupants' movements.

In the distance, the high temple's bell rang out, then an hour later, it rang again. As dusk began to settle and my legs began to cramp, Giselle finally climbed down. Instead of going to the house, she went around it. Her route was a little more difficult to follow this time, given the fading light, but I managed to keep up. She stopped at the river and pushed a small rowboat out from the bank. We were upstream from the factories and tanneries that used Upway River as a cesspit. Here, the river flowed pristinely past the private gardens of the houses, including the one she'd just been watching.

I slowly cursed as the cloaked figure of Giselle rowed the boat away. Following along the bank on foot wasn't easy. I had to scale fences and crawl through bushes. I got bitten by insects and my boots became caked in mud. While I came across more than one boat ready to launch, I decided against following Giselle that way. I would be too conspicuous on the river. I'd rather put up with bites and thorns than be exposed.

As I expected, Giselle rowed the boat to the bank at the bottom of the garden belonging to the house she'd been watching. After securing the boat to a tree trunk, she headed through the garden, using tree trunks, shrubs and the occasional statue to keep herself hidden. Dusk had given way to darkness, so she was difficult to spot in her hooded cloak. I was acutely aware that I'd still not seen her face, but also glad that she hadn't seen mine.

I'd scaled a vine on the wall to reach the balcony outside Rhys's room many times, yet I was surprised to see Giselle do the same. She pushed the cloak aside with a sweep of her arm, revealing those long slim legs clad in black leather trousers as she confidently found her footing.

I remained where I was. A woman's voice came from somewhere inside. I strained to hear, but she was simply instructing someone how to set the table for dinner. It wasn't Giselle's voice.

Mere moments after she entered via a window, Giselle re-emerged and descended the same way. She moved quickly, racing across the garden, not bothering to use trunks, bushes or statues to hide herself this time. She untied the rowboat and leapt into it. She rowed away, the faster flow downstream taking her well ahead of me. I couldn't keep up on the bank, and decided to abandon my pursuit.

Instead of going home, I headed to my usual meeting place with Rhys and lit a candle. I placed it on the windowsill. While I waited, I considered what I'd witnessed and what it meant. For one thing, Giselle had certainly returned to Tilting. That wasn't in doubt. The other thing not in doubt was that she was as good as me, if not better, at getting into and out of places. What was less certain was whether she was a burglar.

By the time Rhys arrived, I'd come to the conclusion that she must be. Her accomplice gave her the address of houses where small yet valuable objects could be stuffed in her pockets for quick removal. Perhaps her accomplice lived in that house and left the window open for Giselle to easily enter.

The question was, did Rhys know?

I was still considering whether I should tell him when he arrived. He blew out a relieved breath when he saw me. "You're all right."

"Is there a reason I shouldn't be?"

He threw his cloak over the back of the armchair. "You gave me your report earlier, so there was no reason for us to meet tonight."

"I didn't think I needed a reason. Neither of us do, usually."

"No. Of course not."

He picked up the fire poker and used it to move the burning log. His attention seemed caught by the rising sparks before he moved the log back. He returned the poker to the stand then rested a gloved hand on the mantelpiece. His fingers drummed the stone.

I extinguished the candle with my finger and thumb. "Rhys, what's wrong?"

His shoulders stiffened. "Why do you think something's wrong?" he asked without turning around.

"I can tell."

"Your mind can read others as well as remember everything?"

Why was he being so petulant? "I can tell because you can't be still. You always move when something's wrong. Nor will you look at me. Is it Giselle?"

He swung around to face me. "Giselle? What…? How do you know about her?"

"The high priest asked me to find out if she was back in Tilting."

He blinked slowly at me. "The high priest…why?"

"I suppose he's worried she'll distract you from your duties as the second-in-command of the order."

He rubbed his forehead. "I don't want to talk about Giselle."

I watched him carefully, until he turned to the fire again so I couldn't see his face. "She *is* back in Tilting, by the way. I saw her today."

He sighed. "This is not going well," he murmured.

"What's not going well? Rhys, what is it? Talk to me."

He didn't answer.

"Is it the promotion? Are you doubting yourself for the role?"

He grunted.

"You claimed you didn't want it, that there was no one else, but I know you'll be good at it, Rhys. Better than good."

"That's not it."

Then it had to be Giselle. She and the promotion were the only two changes in his life that could have brought on this melancholy. Perhaps it was both combined. I hardly dared ask, afraid of the answer. But I had to know. It was best to find out now rather than allow my feelings for him to grow.

"Are you worried because being the second-in-command makes it harder for you to leave the order?"

He raised his head. A beat passed. Two. "What would you say if I said I was considering it?"

My chest tightened. I couldn't breathe. He loved her so much he was considering leaving the order for her? Merdu's Guards was his family, his entire life. It wasn't merely a profession, like being a carpenter or constable, it was intertwined with his faith. A carpenter or constable could leave their work behind them when they went home, but a warrior priest's days and nights were consumed with prayer, contemplation and training. It was his *essence*. Not to mention Rhys's star in the order was rising. It was an awful lot to give up.

Particularly to marry a thief. I wanted to tell him Giselle wasn't worth it, but that wasn't my decision to make. Besides, it could harm our friendship and that was the last thing I wanted. I may never have Rhys as anything more than a friend, but I didn't want to lose even that.

Yet, as his friend, I still had to give him some advice since he clearly wanted it. "I think you're mad."

He lowered his head and resumed staring at the fire. I'd not given him the answer he hoped for.

I hated seeing him like this. I hated that Giselle was the reason for his sorrow, and I hated that I could make his choice easier by telling him what I knew about her. But I *had* to do it. Sometimes when you love someone, you have to risk losing them to help them. "Rhys, there's something you should know."

"I'm already aware. I heard that he saw you."

I frowned, trying to follow the shift in the conversation. "Are you talking about my uncle?"

He nodded.

"How did you find out?"

"One of my other spies informed me the governor spoke to the sheriff and asked him if it's possible you weren't killed in that fire. He told the sheriff he thinks he saw you today, passing yourself off as a boy."

"He did," I said heavily.

Rhys drummed his fingers on the mantelpiece again, only to stop when he realized he was doing it. He closed his fingers into a fist. "I'm worried about you, Jac."

I couldn't deny it felt good to know that Rhys thought about me at all, but I didn't want to be the cause of his worry. Rhys had always been so full of mischief and laughter, and I didn't want to be another burden on top of his new duties as second-in-command.

"Tilting is a large city," I assured him. "He won't find me."

"He already has once. Anyway, you can't be a boy forever," he said without taking his gaze off the flames. "Sooner or later, people will realize. They'll ask questions about the youth who never grows up. What if the governor conducts a search? If he offers a reward for the lad who looks like his niece, how long will it be before someone turns you in?"

I'd never wanted to put my arms around him more than I did in that moment. He needed comforting. We both did. To be embraced by his warmth, to feel his heart beat against my cheek, and the tension in his muscles ease as he relaxed against me... It was all I wanted.

I suddenly felt a little unsteady, so I sat in the armchair. From that angle I had a better view of his profile. Firelight softened the strong angles of his cheek and jaw, giving him a vulnerability I'd never noticed before. I tried to look away but couldn't. My gaze was drawn to him.

His was drawn to the flames. "You have two choices, Jac. You could leave Tilting."

"I'm not leaving. Where would I go?"

"I thought you'd say that." He cleared his throat and turned to face me. "Then you'd better get married."

It was so utterly unexpected that I burst out laughing.

Rhys didn't join in. His eyes shuttered. "Find it ridiculous, do you? Well, I don't. A married woman becomes the responsibility of her husband. Everything she owns belongs to her husband. The governor won't legally be able to get his hands on you or your pendant."

"I don't want to be a man's *responsibility*. I don't want to become his property, forced to do his bidding until the day one of us dies."

"A good husband won't force you to do anything."

I put up a finger as I thought of another thing. "A husband won't let me continue to spy for you."

"You won't need to spy. He'll support you. You'll have his children and keep house for him."

"*Ugh*. Sounds dull. Who would I marry, anyway? The only eligible man I know is my neighbor, the butcher's son, and he smells."

"He's the *only* one?" he scoffed.

"Getting married won't stop Uncle Roderic anyway. It will stop him from *legally* getting his hands on my pendant, but you forget about all the illegal methods he could employ. Marrying won't protect me. All it will do is expose me. I can't use my false name because that's for a man, so I'll have to give my real name, which will then be recorded in the city's marriage registers. Then it'll simply be a matter of time before news reaches Uncle Roderic that a woman going by the same name as his niece is getting married."

My logic seemed to annoy him. He strode past me, whipping his cloak off the back of the armchair as he did so. He stopped when he reached the door. "You're right," he bit off. "It was a stupid idea."

Why was he being so ill-tempered about this? It was so unlike him.

"Goodnight, Jac," he said, opening the door.

"Wait, Rhys. I almost forgot." I approached him, not wanting to speak too loudly with the door open. "I followed Giselle today and I need to tell you something. She's a thief."

"No, she isn't. She's an assassin."

CHAPTER 5

J spent a restless night wondering why Rhys would leave the priesthood for an assassin. I'd finally managed to fall asleep when the incessant peel of the high temple's bell woke me late in the morning. It only rang that many times when there was something to announce.

I scrambled out of bed and hurriedly dressed. I was still buttoning up my jerkin when I joined my neighbors in the court outside our homes. One woman had already sent her son to the market to see if the city's criers were spreading the news yet.

Mistress Lowey emerged from her kitchen, wiping her hands in her apron. Unlike the neighbors, she lacked enthusiasm. "We already heard about the deputy governor," she said with a shrug.

"What about the deputy governor?" I asked. Hopefully he'd been arrested on charges of rape after all, although I worried about the poor woman who'd accused him. She would have a difficult time convincing a judge to find her attacker guilty, and then she'd have to pay an exorbitant fine.

"It won't be about him," said Mistress Milkwood. "That's already old news. Anyway, he's not important enough for the high temple's bell to ring this long."

Several faces turned in the direction of the high temple, even though we couldn't see it from the courtyard.

Mine wasn't one of them. "What about the deputy governor?" I asked again.

"He's dead," Mistress Lowey said. "Murdered in his own home late yesterday. The news was all over the market this morning."

"Good riddance," Mistress Milkwood muttered. "The killer did this city a service getting rid of that flea." Nobody chided her for her heartlessness. The deputy governor had no supporters among ordinary Tilting folk. "Apparently, constables were crawling all over his house last night, looking for clues, but they didn't find the killer. Even the sheriff was there."

"I hope he got away," Mistress Lowey said.

"I reckon he escaped on the river. That part's quiet at this time of year. The toffs don't go boating much once the weather turns, and the factories and port are further downstream. If I were the killer, that's how I'd escape."

Mistress Lowey chuckled. "I'd like to see you climb up a vine and slip through a window."

Mistress Milkwood clasped her ample bosom in both hands. "I'd get stuck."

Both women laughed.

I did not. "Do you know for certain that the killer climbed a vine to get into the house?"

Mistress Lowey nodded. "I heard it from Ginny Styne, whose son-in-law is a constable. He didn't get home until dawn after he stayed outside the deputy governor's house all night, keeping watch in case the killer came back. Apparently, the murder happened in the master bedchamber when the deputy governor was napping before dinner. The valet went to wake him and discovered the body. The only way in without being seen by the staff was through the bedchamber window. A vine grows from the ground to the balcony."

"Don't be upset," Mistress Milkwood said to me. "He deserved it."

"I'm just shocked," I murmured.

"It is shocking to be murdered in your own bed, it's true."

I didn't tell her that wasn't the shocking part. The shocking part was that I'd been there when it happened. I could go to the sheriff and tell him what I'd seen. I could be pivotal in capturing Giselle and separating her from Rhys.

I dismissed the idea as quickly as it occurred to me. I'd never do that to him.

The son of our neighbor returned, his face flushed and eyes bright, eager to tell us the news. He pressed a hand to his side and drew in deep breaths. "It's the king," he finally managed to say.

"Is he dead, too?" the lad's mother asked.

He shook his head. "He found an heir."

We all stared at him. "How can he *find* an heir?" Mistress Lowey asked.

"*Where* did he find one?" asked Mistress Milkwood. "Under a rug?"

"Who cares?" said another woman. "It's an heir! We won't become Vytillian when King Alain dies!"

"We won't go to war," said the lad's mother, her eyes filling with tears of relief as she gazed upon her son.

Mistress Lowey grabbed my arm, her other hand fluttering at her chest as if to settle a rapidly beating heart. "Did you hear that, Jac? We're saved. We have a prince!"

The lad told us the marketplace had erupted with joy over the news.

I didn't feel joyous, but I was certainly relieved. The signed document in the governor's office no longer seemed so concerning. If King Alain was incapable of ruling, the new prince could become regent until such time as he became king and the document's validity would be questioned. All would be well, and Tilting wouldn't be at the mercy of my cruel uncle.

I headed into the heart of the city and saw that impromptu celebrations had broken out. The taverns were full, there was dancing in the streets, and minstrels played tunes on lutes and flutes. I learned a little more about the heir, including that he was King Alain's grandson, fathered by Alain's son to a commoner he'd secretly married before his own untimely death many years ago. It all sounded a little too convenient, but I wasn't going to question an outcome that benefited Glancia.

I decided to see if the revelries extended to the castle. Perhaps the newly found prince would make an appearance at the gate to speak to his people. The king's castle and the high priest's temple stood near one another, atop two adjacent hills. The bell housed in the slender tower of the latter had finally fallen silent. The tower and domes gave the high temple an elegance that was entirely lacking in its neighbor. The dark fortified walls of the ancient seat of Glancia's rulers were grim even in summer. Now, in late autumn, the castle looked as welcoming as a prison.

There was no sign of the new prince. The gate was guarded as usual, keeping the commoners out and the nobles in with their king and his counselors. It opened while I was there to let out a carriage pulled by two black horses. It didn't sport the governor's escutcheon, but I kept my hood pulled low to obscure my face just in case. Hopefully the murder of his deputy and the discovery of the new prince were preoccupying him enough that he no longer had time to look for me.

Some of the crowd who'd come to the castle with the same idea as me shouted out questions about the new prince, but with the curtains closed, the carriage's occupants weren't interested in responding.

I stayed awhile longer then traipsed back down the slope. I returned home, intending to stay in for the night, but I couldn't settle. My conversation with Rhys played on my mind, over and over. The downside of an excellent memory.

By the time darkness descended, I could stand it no longer. I needed to speak to him, although I had no idea what I'd say. The cold wind felt like tiny teeth nipping at the exposed skin on my face, but at least the soft leather of my gloves kept my hands warm.

Although I was sure no one was about outside the building where I usually met Rhys, I double-checked the vicinity before entering. If the high priest had anyone spying on it, I couldn't see them.

Inside, I went to collapse onto the chair, only to stop myself before I sat on the folded note there. Rhys's bold handwriting informed me to meet him at The Flying Goose if I happened to stop by. "Be careful," he'd added.

I kept my hood up, alert to my surroundings. There was no sign of guards wearing the governor's livery. Although a few constables patrolled, they weren't interested in me.

The Flying Goose wasn't the closest inn or tavern to the temple of Merdu's Guards, but that was precisely why it was the favorite haunt of Rhys, Vizah, Andreas and Rufus. Although drinking in public taverns and inns was tolerated by their order, it was frowned upon by some who believed the priests should have no pleasures whatsoever. Rhys said they simply preferred to drink where others from their order did not. At The Flying Goose, they could indulge in vices without worrying about censure, as long as they were discreet. Vizah would gamble with what little money he'd managed to save from the meager monthly allowance the order doled out to each priest, while Andreas would meet his mistresses in one of the bedchambers. Rufus simply drank, becoming more and more glum with every tankard.

If Rhys kept mistresses there, he was discreet. He didn't gamble and he drank in moderation. At least, he usually did. This time, he was drunk when I arrived. The signs were subtle, however. It was only because I knew him very well that I spotted them. His cheeks were a little flushed and he held himself a little less rigidly than usual. If there was to be an attack now, he'd be slow to react.

"Jac!" He signaled for me to join them. "Have a drink with us. We're celebrating."

I asked one of the serving women to bring me an ale then sat between Rhys and Rufus. Rhys smiled at me. It was unnerving. I didn't know what to expect.

"Have you met him?" I asked. "The new prince?"

Rhys shook his head. "He's not in Tilting yet. Master Tomaj and I were summoned to the castle, along with the high priest and a few nobles who happened to be in the city. We were informed that King Alain's grandson was found and that he was of age."

"Everyone simply believed it?"

"There was proof." He studied me. "You don't want there to be an heir?"

"Of course I do, but... I suppose it doesn't matter." I leaned closer and kept my voice low. "At least now there'll be someone to petition about the governor's overreaching powers."

The serving woman brought me a tankard of ale and placed another in front of Rhys. Then she slid onto his lap and looped her arms around his neck.

He stood quickly, dislodging her. Despite his inebriation, he caught her before she fell on the floor. He cleared his throat. "Sorry."

The serving woman thrust a hand onto one hip. "You're no fun anymore. Thank the goddess for Andreas."

Rhys indicated the tankard. "I didn't order that."

"It's from your admirer." She jutted her chin at a woman two tables away.

Even seated as she was, I could tell the woman was tall, even for a Glancian. But where Glancians were usually fair-haired, she had the glossy black locks and flat features of a native to Dreen, the kingdom to the west. She was also strikingly beautiful.

Giselle, I presumed.

Rhys showed no surprise. He must have already known she

was here. He picked up the tankard. I expected him to send it back, but instead, he saluted her with it. Then he drained it.

She watched him, openly admiring. When he finished, she crooked her finger, beckoning him. He crossed his arms over his chest and remained seated.

She laughed and turned back to her companion.

Vizah, who'd come up behind Rhys, clapped him on both shoulders. "Giselle's back."

"Nothing gets past you," Rufus said.

"What's she doing here?"

"What do you think?"

Vizah considered it a moment then glanced at Rhys. "Ohhhhh."

"She's probably here for work," Rhys growled.

"So you haven't seen her since her return?" Rufus asked.

Rhys sank in his seat and concentrated on the inside of his tankard.

"Is she the reason you've been acting strangely lately?" Vizah asked him.

Rhys shot him a flinty glare.

Rufus rolled his eyes. "Idiot," he muttered.

"Who's an idiot?" Andreas asked. He pulled up another chair, turned it around, and straddled it. "Let me guess. Is it Vizah?"

Vizah stiffened. "Why would you think it's me?"

"Experience." Andreas clinked his tankard against Rufus's.

Vizah scowled. "I just wanted to know if Rhys is acting strangely lately because his former lover is back in Tilting."

"Giselle?" Andreas looked around until he spotted her, chatting to her companion. "Ah. Now it makes sense."

"The reason why Rhys is acting strangely?"

"How the deputy governor was killed." Andreas said it quietly enough that only we could hear. To me, he added, "She's an assassin for hire. She usually only takes jobs where she eliminates what she calls undesirables."

"Who decides if they're undesirable?" I asked.

He had no answer to that.

"I already knew she did it," I told them. "I saw her go into the house then leave via the river."

Rufus, Andreas and Vizah cast me admiring looks. Rhys continued to stare into his tankard.

"Merdu's blood, you're good, Jac," Vizah said. He leaned forward. "Since you've clearly been following her, can you tell us?"

"Tell you what?"

"If Rhys has slept with her."

Rhys slammed his tankard down on the table, drawing the attention of several patrons seated at neighboring tables, including Giselle. His nostrils flared. I'd never seen him look so angry at one of his friends. Indeed, I'd never seen him look angrily at anyone.

Vizah swallowed heavily. "I get the hint. You're keeping that vow nowadays. Probably just as well. The high priest wouldn't like it, especially now you're the second."

Rhys's anger extinguished as quickly as it flared. "Can we talk about something else?"

"Speaking of breaking vows," Vizah said with an arched look at Andreas. "When are you going to give the whores a rest from your prick?"

"Vizah!" Rhys snapped.

"What? Why are you giving Jac the side-eye? He's old enough to know about women."

"First of all," Andreas said, "*my* women are not whores. I don't need to pay for it. Secondly, that's not why Rhys is telling you to shut your mouth."

Vizah frowned. "Then why?"

Rufus rolled his eyes again. "Idiot."

"Why?"

"You really don't know, do you?"

Vizah shook his head. "Don't know what? Rhys?"

"It's not my place to say," Rhys said.

"What isn't? Jac's old enough. Isn't he?"

"You're the idiot for not—" Rufus hissed in pain and leaned down to rub his shin. Rhys had kicked him under the table. "For not getting me another drink."

"Get your own drinks," Vizah grumbled. "I'm not your servant. Anyway, I haven't got any money."

Andreas removed his hat and dragged his hand through his thick golden hair. The entire cohort of serving women sighed in unison. "You lost at dice again, didn't you? You should give up and do what I do instead, and the drinks will flow all night, for free."

"I am not going to sleep with the serving women to get free ale. That's asking for trouble."

"They won't get into trouble. The innkeeper loves me after I stopped his son getting into a fight once. He won't dismiss them for keeping me happy."

"Not that kind of trouble. The women kind. I'd say more," Vizah added, shooting a glare at Rufus, "but I don't want to be called an idiot again for speaking about sex in front of Jac."

Rhys cleared his throat. "Change of subject. The new prince...who wants to have a wager on whether he'll make a good ruler?"

"Shhh." Rufus glanced around. "Merdu, keep your voice down, Rhys. It's treason to talk about the heir like that."

"Why?"

"I don't know but there must be some law about that kind of talk. It sounds seditious to me."

Vizah watched as a serving woman delivered a tankard to Andreas then brushed his cheek with her knuckles before walking away, hips swinging seductively. "You're suspicious of everything, Rufus," he said.

"I said seditious, not suspicious. And stop staring at the women."

"Why? Andreas does it."

"I don't *stare*," Andreas said. "I *admire*."

"And Jac's been doing it. He can't stop staring at Giselle."

My face flamed. I thought I'd been discreet, watching her from beneath my lashes, but if Vizah had noticed then I'd failed miserably.

Vizah laughed, the sound a low rumble in his barrel chest. "She's a little old for you, Jac, but I don't think she'd mind. As long as Rhys—" He grunted as he winced. "Why did you kick me?"

Rufus and Andreas both chuckled. I was certain they both knew I was a woman now, although before tonight I hadn't been sure if Rufus knew. It seemed Vizah was the only one who hadn't guessed, and the others were having too much fun to enlighten him. All except Rhys, that is.

Rhys swiped up his tankard. "Leave Jac alone. He's too young."

Vizah frowned at me. "How old *are* you?"

"Twenty," I said.

"Definitely old enough." Vizah's frown deepened. "You're very small for a man of twenty years. Rhys, you should pay him more. He needs a good feed."

"He's not twenty," Rhys said. "Fifteen or sixteen. Seventeen at the most. Too young."

"I *am* twenty," I said through a clenched jaw. "As Rhys well knows. He just can't accept it, for some reason."

"I understand now," Vizah said with a knowing nod. "It's got nothing to do with Jac, does it? You just don't want to talk about sex."

Rhys lowered his tankard. "You're right. Let's not."

Vizah wasn't at all worried, despite the icy glare Rhys shot him. "You should talk about your feelings. It'll help you release any lingering doubts you may have about giving up sex for good now that you're the second."

Andreas snickered while Rufus leaned forward. "This will be interesting," he said.

"I don't have lingering doubts," Rhys growled at Vizah.

"Isn't that why you're acting strangely lately? Now that you've been promoted, you've decided to keep all your vows, even that one."

Rhys craned his neck to peer past the other patrons toward the bar area. "I need another drink."

"Don't replace women with ale," Vizah bumbled on.

"Or gambling," Andreas added with a pointed look at Vizah.

Rufus lifted his tankard to Andreas. Andreas clinked his against it then both drank deeply.

It seemed Rhys hadn't told his friends he was considering leaving the order for Giselle. "How long were you with Giselle last time?" I asked him.

Andreas grinned. "Yes, Rhys, tell Jac *all* about your relationship with Giselle."

Rhys ignored him. "There is no *last* time. That implies there is a *this* time. There isn't."

Was he lying because he didn't want his friends to know he was considering leaving the order for her?

Rufus cradled his tankard in both hands. "Rhys takes his oaths more seriously nowadays." He lifted the tankard to his lips. "Fortunately drinking isn't forbidden."

"Nor gambling," Vizah added. Both men looked to Andreas.

Andreas looked smug. "What the master doesn't know about my private affairs can't hurt him or the order."

"Women are a distraction," Vizah intoned, as if he were repeating something he'd heard thousands of times. "Staying celibate keeps us focused."

Andreas barked a laugh. "Women are a distraction yet drinking and gambling aren't? Right now, you three are as focused as a sleeping baby."

"Enough," Rhys growled. He sounded tired, as if this were an argument he'd arbitrated many times.

Rufus thumped Andreas on the shoulder. "You're right. What the master doesn't know can't hurt him. But what happens when Master Tomaj is no longer with us, and the next master takes over?" He arched his brows at Rhys. "*He* knows what you get up to in the rooms back there."

Rhys's jaw firmed as he lowered his gaze to the table.

Andreas shifted uncomfortably in the chair. "Master Tomaj has years left in him. He's as strong as the castle's walls and healthier than men half his age. By the time Rhys takes over, I might have given women up, too."

Rufus snorted in derision.

I waited for Rhys to tell them he was considering leaving the order so he could be with his assassin lover, but he said nothing. He asked a passing serving woman for another ale.

Andreas and Rufus exchanged looks of concern whereas Vizah seemed more interested in the game of dice being played at a nearby table.

Rufus rested a hand on Rhys's forearm. "You'll make a great master, my friend," he said in quiet earnest. "Do not doubt it."

"Tomaj will be with us for years," Rhys said. "Other candidates will come to the fore in the meantime."

Again, Rufus and Andreas looked at one another. "You don't believe that any more than we do," Andreas said.

Rufus shook Rhys's arm. "There's no one else who has the respect of every brother within the order as well as the high priest and king."

"If you don't do it, the order will fall apart," Vizah said, proving he was listening. "Anyway, why wouldn't you do it? It's an honor."

Rhys's ale arrived. He thanked the serving woman then promptly drank half.

Although Vizah seemed to have asked his question quite innocently, Rufus and Andreas appeared to be waiting for Rhys to comment. Indeed, from the way they stared at him it was as if they were *willing* him to give a reason why he didn't want to become the master. They knew he'd reluctantly taken on the role of second-in-command, so they must suspect he had no interest in becoming the master one day. Perhaps they suspected he was considering leaving the order for Giselle.

Rhys remained silent, and eventually Rufus and Andreas gave up. They stood and announced they were departing. Vizah left, but only to join the dice game. I should have left, too. The silence between Rhys and I threatened to become smothering and I didn't want it to douse the bright flame that was our friendship, even for a moment. We'd always been able to talk easily, or simply to sit comfortably in one another's company without awkwardness.

Giselle's return had changed everything.

She sat with her friends, but I was very aware of the glances she cast our way from time to time. She wore men's clothing, but I doubted she had to shorten the pants like I did. They made her legs look shapely whereas mine looked like sticks.

"Why are you drunk?" I suddenly asked him.

He released his tankard. "I'm not."

"Is something troubling you?"

"I'm not troubled because I'm not drunk. I mean, I'm not drunk because I'm not troubled." He rubbed his forehead.

I shifted my chair closer. Our knees touched under the table. We both jerked away. "Talk to me, Rhys. You've always been able to discuss everything with me."

"Not everything." He sighed, then added, "He's not going to die soon, Jac. Master Tomaj. He can do a hundred one-armed push-ups in the time it takes to sing the order's hymn."

Not only was he definitely drunk, but his unprovoked denial meant he was worried about Master Tomaj. And that must make him concerned about his own future in the order, and whether leaving was a good idea.

He suddenly grinned. "I can beat him. I do one hundred and fourteen. Want to see?"

I smiled, too, relieved to see he was back to being the carefree Rhys I loved. His dimples were two of my favorite things.

He got up, pushing his chair back so hard that it fell. He went to stop it but stumbled, only to right himself before falling completely. "I'm fine," he called out. "I think I should go home. Jac, help me. You can be my crotch."

"I think you mean crutch."

He tried to click his fingers but couldn't manage it. "I knew it wasn't crotch." He threw an arm around my shoulders and leaned a little of his weight on me. "Where's my sword?"

"Where it always is, in its scabbard at your left hip." Merdu and Hailia, he'd become very drunk very quickly.

"Need help, Jac?" Vizah asked.

"He's fine," Rhys answered before I could. He ruffled my hair. "He's a good lad. Come on, Jac. I'll take you home."

"I'll take *you* home," I said, circling my arm around his waist and steering him toward the door.

"He looks too heavy for you," one of the serving women said as we passed her. "Take him to my room." She winked. "You can stay, too, if you like."

I felt Rhys tense. "Absolutely *not*. Jac is—"

"Too young," I said before he could say something that might expose my disguise. "Come on, you big oaf. Let's go before anyone else propositions you." I glanced at Giselle as we passed her table.

She was even more alluring up close. Her long, fine fingers lightly stroked her tankard. The languid, mesmerizing movement was in contrast to the humor shining in her dark eyes as she watched us.

No, not us. Me. She watched *me*.

She rose to her feet and picked up the black hat she'd placed on the table. She approached me, her painted red lips curved with her smile. It was a nice smile, and I found myself smiling back.

She leaned down. The scent of orange blossoms enveloped me as she whispered in my ear. "Never trust a man who denies his natural urges. He'll break your heart." She slipped away through the crowd of patrons near the door before I'd had a chance to respond.

I stared in the direction she'd gone. Did she see through my disguise and know I was a woman? Could she tell I had feelings for Rhys? Was she jealous?

"What did she say?" Rhys growled, proving he wasn't so drunk that he hadn't noticed his beautiful lover. Or was she his *former* lover?

"Nothing."

We followed Giselle out of the tavern, but there was no sign of her. Not even the faint scent of orange blossoms lingered in the air.

"She's very beautiful," I said. "Mysterious, too, and brave. It's no wonder you love her."

For a moment, I thought I'd overstepped, perhaps offended him by alluding to his broken vow. Instead, he laughed. "Hailia and Merdu...you're jealous, Jac."

I went to pull away from him but the arm around my shoulder tightened. "I, uh..."

"You are. *You're* jealous of *Giselle*. Now I understand."

"Understand what?" I felt his gaze on me and dared a sideways glance at him.

He was watching me. He wasn't even trying to hide it. "You thought I was doing it for her. I wasn't, Jac. I wasn't going to leave the order for her. That was for you."

The ground beneath me seemed to shift violently.

I replayed the previous night's conversation with Rhys in my head. By the end, I needed his support as much as he needed mine. I'd been so consumed by jealousy of Giselle, that I'd not listened properly. He hadn't said he was leaving the order for her. Not once.

He was tempted to leave the order for *me*, to protect me from my uncle by marrying me. I'd dismissed his idea without quite realizing what his idea was. Indeed, I'd shot it down rather spectacularly. He'd been upset by my dismissal, and now I knew why. He had feelings for me.

How deep did those feelings go?

I steered him around the corner, my steps slow as I reluctantly directed him to the temple of Merdu's Guards. It was also the same direction as his secret room. The temptation to go there instead made my breath quicken.

"Don't be jealous of her," Rhys murmured.

I stopped suddenly and forced myself to laugh to cover my embarrassment.

Light from the torch in the recessed doorway of a cobbler's shop gave his gaze an intensity as he studied my features. Slowly, slowly, his lips curved, turning his smile from playful to wicked. My heart responded with a resounding thud, echoed by the blood in my veins. Was it a warning? Or a declaration?

Rhys's hands rested on my shoulders, comfortingly heavy. I only came up to the middle of his chest, but I didn't feel overwhelmed or dominated. I felt cherished. The pads of his thumbs skimmed the underside of my jaw. He didn't wear gloves—perhaps he'd left them in the tavern—but his skin was nevertheless warm, his touch achingly soft.

I felt reckless. I wanted to kiss him. I wanted to take his face in my hands and draw him down to me or push him into the shadows and do more than kiss.

But I did not. I liked to think I resisted because I was trying to do the right thing, to not force him to make a decision that went against his sworn oath, but I wasn't that selfless. The reason I didn't act on my feelings was because I didn't want to lose him altogether. A single kiss would put our friendship in jeopardy. It would be one rash, wild moment we might not recover from. I only wanted him if I could have him to myself. I didn't want to share him with the order—I didn't believe he wanted to leave, just that he felt obliged to do so, to protect me from my uncle through marriage.

Despite every part of me craving him, I managed to not succumb to my baser instincts. I stepped away.

Rhys wasn't as clearheaded. He closed the gap between us and kissed me.

CHAPTER 6

*S*omehow, through the dense fog of my desire, I managed to think. I pulled away. "Rhys," I gasped out between ragged breaths. "Are you sure? Will you regret this in the morning?"

"I don't care," he rasped.

It wasn't the answer I wanted, but I didn't press him further because he was kissing me again, and all common sense vanished. Impulse took over. I flung my arms around his neck and buried my fingers in his hair. This time there was no tenderness in the kiss. It was a surging tide of desperate need, three years of pent-up desire finally breaking free. His arms circled around me and held me against his body, leaving me in no doubt that he wanted me as much as I wanted him.

When we finally stopped for air, I touched my forehead to his. "I didn't know… You're very good at hiding your feelings."

He lightly touched his lips to mine, so I felt his smile. "I'm very good at a lot of things, Jac. At least I *was*. I'm probably rusty now." He took my hand in his and pressed it against his chest. His heart beat madly beneath my palm. "I want you, Jac, and I'm tired of pretending I don't. Come with me." He led me away, heading in Hailia knew which direction.

I became aware of the sting of cold air on my cheeks, the smell of smoke in the air from the many fires trying valiantly to keep the chilly autumn night at bay. And I became aware again of how drunk Rhys was when he stumbled as he turned to look at me over his shoulder.

I tugged on his hand, forcing him to stop. "Rhys...are you sure? You should think—"

"I don't want to think." It came out as a growling groan, part frustration and part regret.

That regret would grow as he sobered. It would fester and infect, until it consumed everything that was good between us. It would destroy the most precious thing we had—our friendship.

I released his hand.

He didn't reach for me. His response, or lack of it, confirmed that I'd made the right decision. Last night, he'd been prepared to leave the order for me, but that was when he thought marriage would protect me from my uncle. After pointing out that it wouldn't, he'd changed his mind. Before our kiss, he'd said he wasn't talking about leaving the order for Giselle, that was for me.

Was. Past tense.

He cared about me and desired me, but when the factor of saving my life was removed from the equation, caring and desiring weren't enough for him to leave the order.

Two men walking past stopped a few paces away. "Is that a priest of Merdu's Guards?" one said to the other.

"Not every man wearing a brown tunic is a warrior priest," his friend pointed out. They walked on.

Rhys tilted his head back and blinked up at the ink-black sky. "I'm sorry, Jac." The heaviness in his voice almost undid me.

I managed to keep the tears welling in my eyes from spilling, but only just. "Don't be. We can still be friends, can't we?"

"Of course. Come on. I'll walk you home."

"You never have before and you don't need to now. Besides, I probably should walk *you* home. You can't go ten paces without tripping."

My attempt to lighten the mood fell flat. He merely sighed. "Goodnight then."

"Goodnight, Rhys."

I walked away and did not look back. Whether he watched me leave or whether he immediately left, too, I didn't know. I didn't *want* to know, nor did I want him to see me crying.

* * *

I TRIED WALKING off my listlessness the following morning. With my hood up to obscure my face, I maintained a brisk pace through the market where hawkers sold fresh produce from their stalls and carts. The permanent shops in the surrounding streets seemed to buzz as shopkeepers and their customers discussed the two important events affecting the city. Few mourned the passing of the deputy governor, although not everyone voiced a negative opinion of him. Some thought he was a good support for the governor. Uncle Roderic wasn't particularly liked, but many respected his aim to clean up the city's crime. Others were not so enthusiastic, having seen first-hand how brutal his methods could be.

I avoided the square housing the municipal buildings so as not to accidentally run into him again, and instead headed past the castle gate. There was no word on when the newly found prince would arrive, or where he was now. I stopped at the fore-court in front of the high temple. Should I report to the high priest? If so, how much about Giselle's activities should I tell him? Would he even be prepared to receive me?

Some things are best to get over and done with. It might ease the knots in my insides.

The high temple's guards didn't look as intimidating as those manning the castle gates. For one thing, they were dressed as priests, albeit in black like the high priest instead of brown. For another, they didn't simply stand there looking stern. They welcomed me and asked me how they could assist me.

I stated that I'd been tasked by the high priest himself to run an errand and needed to report back. One of the guards directed me to an antechamber to wait. I expected the high priest to send one of his staff, so was surprised to see the high priest himself enter the room. I remembered to bow.

Apparently, it was the right thing to do because he seemed pleased to see me. "I would have called on you, Jac, but it's good of you to come here."

"You don't know where I live," I pointed out.

He smiled and invited me to sit on one of the four chairs pushed against the wall. The rest of the room was empty, and entirely devoid of comfort. No rugs covered the cold stone floor, and the chairs were hard. A single painting took up one entire wall. It depicted the handsome, strong Merdu pointing sternly at a swirling black pit in the ground. Ugly figures tried to escape from the pit, their claw-like hands scrabbling at the earth and each other. Partly obscured by Merdu, the beautiful goddess Hailia gathered two children to her side. It encapsulated the religion of the Fist Peninsula, with the divine fatherly figure banishing evildoers into Merdu's Pit, while the matronly goddess comforted the innocent. I used to think it unfair that the poorest part of Tilting was called Merdu's Pit by the rest of the city, until I'd accidentally stumbled into it soon after I ran away from my uncle's house. As a stranger in their midst, some of the slum's dwellers had chased me for sport until I'd managed to escape, a little bloody and bruised, but alive. Yet unlike the figures in the painting, its evil went unpunished. It seemed to thrive, much like mold under the right conditions.

If my uncle wanted to clean up the city, he should start there. Yet he was targeting the whores and petty thieves of other slums, good folk who were forced to be whores and thieves out of necessity rather than desire. No doubt it was easier to tackle crime where ruthless gangs weren't in control.

"Have you discovered if Giselle has returned to Tilting?" the high priest asked.

"She has," I said.

"And has Brother Rhys seen her?"

"Only from afar."

"They haven't had a liaison?"

"No."

"Did she attempt to meet him?" he asked.

"No."

He regarded me with a frown. "How can you be sure?"

I simply smiled as he had done when I pointed out that he didn't know where I lived.

"She's an interesting one," he went on, his tone matter-of-fact. "She's not typical for a woman. Some men find that tempting. I'm glad to see Rhys isn't one of them. Thank you, Jac." He rose. "You've been most helpful."

"Before you ask, I won't do any more spying on Giselle or Rhys."

"I wasn't going to ask that of you. My questions have been answered." He walked with me out of the antechamber. "It's good to see that Brother Rhys is taking his new position as second-in-command seriously."

I wasn't sure if he expected a response, so I remained silent.

"He's maturing," the high priest went on. "Master Tomaj has noticed it, but others in their order were worried about Rhys's future and therefore the future of Merdu's Guards since he will lead the order one day. They lay blame at Giselle's feet for tempting him to break his vows, but you have reassured me, Jac. Thank you. Now I will reassure them. Rhys will make a fine leader. Perhaps the strongest the order has had in over a century."

"Your Eminence," I said, bowing.

We were once again in the large entrance hall with its high vaulted ceiling. Like the antechamber, it was sparsely furnished, in keeping with the vow of poverty taken by all priests, no matter which order they belonged to. The only exception was the head of the religion in Glancia, standing before me, with his cloth of gold belt.

"Good lad," he said. "May Merdu walk beside you." He laid a hand on my shoulder.

A flurry of activity at the temple's main entrance drew our attention. The high priest strode toward it. The priest who'd just arrived bowed and greeted him. I recognized him as one of the warriors in Merdu's Guards.

The high priest invited the newcomer in. "What is it, Brother Milo?"

"Master Tomaj sent me," the priest said. "He wants you to know that the governor's men are tearing through the slums, demanding the surrender of the deputy's murderer. They're threatening violence if no one comes forward with information by this time tomorrow."

The high priest rubbed his bearded chin. "That is worrying news."

"Brother Rhys doubts anyone in the slums knows anything. He spoke to the sheriff whose investigation suggests the killer was quick, clever and experienced. He left no trace behind."

"An assassin?"

Brother Milo swallowed. "Your Eminence, Master Tomaj wants to know if he can send some brothers with the governor's men tomorrow to keep them in check. He thinks our presence will stop them using violence to get their answers."

The high priest hesitated then nodded. "Tell Master Tomaj that Brother Rhys and his closest friends in the order should be among the number. They know that area well and will be a calming influence." The high priest dismissed him.

Once Brother Milo was gone, the high priest turned. He seemed surprised to see me. He must have thought I was out of earshot. "You're still here, Jac."

"I didn't want to interrupt." I indicated the main entrance

through which Brother Milo had just left. To get to it, I would have had to pass them.

"There's a side door." The high priest pointed to it. "Next time, use that."

"I doubt there'll be a next time, Your Eminence." That sounded somewhat rude, so I bumbled through an explanation. "You said your questions have been answered."

"So I did. Brother Rhys was right. Your memory is faultless. Good day, lad."

"Good day, Your Eminence."

I exited through the unmanned side door. It seemed the guards on the main entrance weren't really guards after all, just staff to welcome guests.

Although I was tempted to go past the temple of Merdu's Guards, I avoided it. I wasn't sure what to say to Rhys.

Later that day, I changed my mind. The sooner we moved past the first awkward encounter after that kiss the better. It had to be done if our friendship was to continue.

I wasn't at all surprised to see the candle burning in the window of Rhys's secret room. We always thought alike. Just as I suspected, our meeting *was* awkward.

"We need to talk," he announced the moment I set foot in the room. "Last night shouldn't have happened. I don't want to talk about it."

"But you just said you did want to talk. Is there something else on your mind?"

"Right. I mean no, there isn't." He started to pace the room, arms crossed over his chest. "I meant we can't do that again. Not if we want to stay friends." He suddenly stopped. His gaze locked with mine. "I really want to stay friends, Jac."

"So do I."

"Good. Then we're in agreement. It can't happen again, and we won't discuss it anymore."

I should have agreed, but I wasn't ready to dismiss our kiss so easily and with such finality. "And if we can't go back to the way we were?"

He stared at me, mouth ajar, as if he couldn't believe I hadn't agreed in a heartbeat. "We have to." He dragged his hand through his hair. "We have to, Jac. Your friendship means...a lot to me."

It took all my willpower not to throw my arms around him and tell him all would be well. I may not be able to touch him ever again for fear of succumbing to my baser instincts, but I could try to reassure him with words. "Your friendship means a lot to me too, Rhys. I agree. Last night won't happen again."

He blew out a breath and sat. His body may have finally been still, but his fingers continued to drum on his thigh. He hadn't lit the fire, which probably meant he didn't intend to stay long. Sitting down would imply he'd changed his mind. "The governor sent his men into the slums to hunt down his deputy's killer."

"I know. I went to the high temple to hand in my report about Giselle, and a warrior priest arrived."

"Brother Milo," he said, nodding.

I crouched by the fireplace but was unsure whether to start a fire or not. How long would he stay? How long would I? Studying him was no help. All it did was fray my nerves even more as his fingers continued to beat an erratic rhythm on his thigh.

"I only told the high priest that Giselle is here in Tilting and that you saw her but haven't...had a liaison. Does he know she's an assassin and that she killed the deputy governor?"

"No, and nor will he. He doesn't condone violence. If he knew what she was, he'd probably hand her over to the sheriff. Thanks for keeping her secret, Jac. She owes you."

"Don't tell her," I said quickly.

He lifted his hands in surrender. "I have no intention of seeing her." It was as if he felt compelled to reassure me, much as a husband would reassure his wife.

I shook off the notion and added kindling to the fireplace.

"Did the high priest say anything else?" he asked. "Anything about the order?"

"He said you'd make an excellent leader one day, now that you're maturing."

"Maturing?" He scoffed. "Last night would prove I'm not."

I swung around to face him.

"I meant getting drunk, not the kiss," he said.

"I thought we agreed not to mention it."

His mouth kicked up with his wisp of a smile. "I should have let him see me like that, and Master Tomaj, too. Then they might change their mind and groom someone else to take over."

"You still don't want to do it, even though you've decided to stay in the order?"

He huffed a humorless laugh. "Maybe I don't want to be called mature."

"And I'm the one everybody calls a boy."

He flashed a grin. "Are you making that fire or just piling up sticks?"

I used the flint on the mantelpiece to light the kindling then blew gently on the flame until the fire took hold. "I overheard the high priest directing Brother Milo to tell Master Tomaj to send you, Vizah, Rufus and Andreas into the slum alongside the governor's men tomorrow." When he didn't respond, I looked over my shoulder at him. "Be careful, Rhys."

"It'll be fine," he said, not taking his gaze off the fire. "They know us there."

"It's not the residents I'm worried about. The governor is frustrated, and his men are always spoiling for a fight. They'll outnumber you."

"They wouldn't dare test Merdu's Guards."

He spoke with such confidence that I was immediately reassured. I placed a larger log on top of the kindling and watched it catch alight. I didn't turn around until I heard Rhys move.

He sat forward. At first I thought it was merely the flames

dancing in his eyes that gave him an air of mischief, then I realized he was fighting back a wicked smile. "What do you say to a little nocturnal mission with me?"

Knowing Rhys, it would be reckless and mad. If it were anyone else, I'd refuse on the spot without hearing it. But I could never say no to his schemes. Someone needed to join him to make sure he didn't get into too much trouble. "Go on."

"I have a plan that will thwart the governor and render it unnecessary to search the slums for his deputy's killer."

Anything that would keep Rhys out of a highly combustible situation was a good idea in my book. "All right, I'll join you."

"Good because you gave me the idea so it's only fair that you're involved."

"What's the plan?"

"Extinguish the fire and grab your cloak. You'll need to cover your hair, so the moonlight doesn't shine off it. Do you have your lockpicking tools on you?"

"Always."

"And a cloth to cover your nose and mouth?"

I removed a cloth from my pocket that I sometimes wrapped around my neck for warmth. "Why this?"

"I suspect it will smell where we're going."

"You suspect? Rhys, where are we going?"

He grinned, flashing his dimples.

He was still grinning as we set off along the street. His step was light and quick as he strode ahead of me. When he realized I'd fallen behind, he turned and walked back, still smiling. "I'll race you, Jac."

"That's not fair. My legs are shorter than yours." Just in case he decided that wasn't a compelling enough reason not to race, I added, "I don't even know where we're going."

"Good points, but I know the real reason you won't race me is because you're slow."

"I am not!"

"You run like a girl."

"That's not the insult you think it is."

"Who says I intended it as an insult?" He chuckled and I couldn't help laughing as I shook my head.

"You're incorrigible, Rhys." It felt good to be teasing him again, and to be teased by him.

But it wasn't quite the same this time. It felt a little forced, like we were both desperate to regain the relationship we'd shared before the kiss. We were trying to return to the normality of the last three years, not to the shifting sands of today's reality.

I had doubts that we could go back, no matter how hard we tried. Too much had changed. It wasn't just our relationship that had changed. Rhys had, too. It seemed the people around him had also noticed it. Had he suggested this mission in response to the high priest's comments about him maturing? Was Rhys trying to prove to me that he hadn't changed?

Or was he trying to prove it to himself?

CHAPTER 7

*T*he evening was still young when we arrived at the temple of Merdu's Rest, the priestly order of doctors and apothecaries who took care of infirm and dying priests. Although the goddess Hailia was associated with healing, priests took care of their own. I supposed it would be undignified for dying men to be cared for by women when their bodies hadn't been seen by the opposite sex in decades, in some cases. Priestesses had their equivalent order, Hailia's Rest. Their smaller temple was located in the same street as the priests'. We had no interest in it. We needed a dead *man*.

Rhys had explained on the way that he'd gotten the idea from my own faked death. Although mine hadn't been deliberately faked, it had served my purpose and stopped my uncle from searching for me, at least until he saw me recently. Rhys hoped he'd be convinced a second time, if we could find a suitable body.

"Why not a woman's body?" I asked as we passed the temple of Hailia's Rest.

"Do you think the governor will believe a woman capable of cold-blooded murder? Or that she could climb a vine?"

He had a point.

We stopped opposite Merdu's Rest, an elegant temple with rounded domes of the same style as the high temple, only smaller. Unlike the temple of Merdu's Guards, there were no walls surrounding it. It barely even had a forecourt, just a narrow path in front of four stone steps leading to the entrance.

"We'll wait for the high temple bell to signal evening prayers, then we'll go in through the side door," Rhys said. "There are no torches there. Can you pick the lock in the dark?"

"Of course. Rhys, are you sure you want to use the fresh corpse of one of your fellow brothers? It could deny him a proper burial in sacred ground."

"The order isn't just for ill and dying priests. The city's unclaimed deceased men are brought here. Vagrants and those with no family or who can't be identified. The priests prepare the bodies for burial and pray for their souls. They're kept for a week, sometimes less in the heat of summer, in case someone comes forward and claims them. It's always better to bury someone with a name in sacred ground than without. We're not taking the body of someone with friends and family, Jac. Also, I'll pray for him."

For a religious person, that was enough to justify what we were about to do. I still had my reservations.

"The priests will notice a missing corpse." I indicated the temple. "They'll realize something is going on when that same body finds its way back here tomorrow."

"Their master will take their concerns to the high priest. The high priest will deem it wiser to say nothing, since finding the deputy governor's killer will put an end to the governor's threat of violence. The high priest likes peaceful solutions." He leaned back against the wall of the building behind us, ankles crossed, arms loosely by his sides. He was as calm as could be. "Any more questions?"

"Just one," I said. "What if this goes wrong? What if my uncle doesn't believe the ruse a second time?"

"That's two questions. Have faith, Jac."

"That's not an answer."

His jaw firmed and he stared at the temple with grim determination.

The high temple's bell rang out in the distance. Time for evening prayer.

"Let's get this over with," I said.

Rhys bowed his head. His lips moved in silent prayer. After a moment, he looked up. "Ready." It seemed he had to follow the religion's rules of prayer time even when he was on a mission.

We entered the narrow lane where the temple's side door was located. It wasn't as dark as I thought it would be, thanks to a sliver of moonlight slicing across the cobblestones. I crouched at the door and set to work. Moments later, the click of the lock opening sounded loud in the empty lane.

Rhys entered first, then signaled for me to follow. Light from torches positioned in wall sconces helped guide our way through the warren of the corridors and back rooms. Rhys grabbed one and led the way down a set of stone steps to the basement. The air was even colder, making it the ideal room to prepare bodies for burial, particularly the unclaimed ones that needed to be kept for a week.

I caught a glimpse of four lying on tables before Rhys blocked my vision.

"Don't look," he said. "They're naked."

"I've seen naked men before."

"When? Who?"

"None of your business."

The only naked men I'd seen were at the river, frolicking in the shallows on hot days. Sometimes they invited me to join them, but I always declined, for obvious reasons. I stayed to enjoy the view, however. It was quite an education for a sheltered young lady.

"Stop being a prude, Rhys, and step aside. I assure you I won't faint from the sight."

"Me, a prude? Ha!"

"Oh, that's right," I teased. "You haven't kept *that* particular vow."

"Low blow, Jac." He stepped aside. "We need a relatively fit looking body, one capable of climbing a vine and rowing a boat."

It didn't take us long to settle on a man aged about thirty with a stubbled jawline and in need of a haircut. Old scars marred his torso and hands, but there were no obvious signs of foul play.

"He drowned." Rhys indicated the bluish tinge of the skin and the wrinkly palms and souls of the feet. He tilted the head to the side and held the torch close for better light. "No sign he was held underwater, so my guess is he was so drunk he fell unconscious and stumbled into the river. A relatively peaceful way to die."

A chill rippled down my spine. "How can you speak so calmly about death?"

He held the torch up to see my face. "Because death isn't the end. All believers know that." The heat from the torch and his intense gaze chased the chill from my bones.

I cleared my throat. "We can't present a naked body to the sheriff. To make the story of a drunken drowning feasible, he needs to be dressed."

"That trunk probably has their clothes. See what you can find while I pray for him." He stood by the body and closed his eyes.

His prayer was said out loud this time, although he kept his voice low. It was melodic, the words soothing, as he prayed to the god and goddess to embrace the poor soul who'd become lost and lonely. "If he was without faith…" Rhys paused. "If his faith wavered, show him the path back. He needs your guidance and love."

I opened the trunk only to step back from the power of the smell coming from the pile of rags inside. I turned away, coughing, then gulped in some fresher air before holding my breath as I rifled through the clothes. Thankfully it was easy to determine which ones belonged to our body.

Rhys came up alongside me with the torch. "Do you need light?"

"You'll need it to look for his boots. I'm not going back in there." I held a pair of trousers, shirt and jerkin at arm's length. "He wore these when he died. They smell of the river, and not the nice part either. He died not far from the factories, if I'm not mistaken. There's even some mud still on them." I deposited the clothes and boots beside the body. "Shouldn't there be mud on him, too? And if he was a vagrant, why isn't he dirtier?"

"The priests have cleaned him. It's part of the burial ritual. You dress his top half. I'll look for the boots."

He wasn't a large man, but carrying a dead body out of the temple unseen wouldn't be easy once we'd dressed him. I was considering the best way to do it when Rhys simply picked him up and slung him over his shoulder. The body draped there like a shawl, torso and arms dangling at Rhys's back.

"I'll go first and check if the coast is clear," I said, torch in hand.

I was about to climb the stairs when I heard footsteps walking above. I waited, a finger to my lips in warning.

Rhys tilted his head to the side, listening.

Once the footsteps receded, I led the way up. I peered around the corner, and seeing no one about, signaled for him to follow. I placed the torch back in the wall sconce and pushed open the same door through which we'd entered. I raced on my toes down the lane, but stopped when I realized Rhys wasn't with me.

He'd stopped further back but was now heading toward me. The body was no longer across his shoulder, but at his side, propped up by Rhys's strong arm. The toes of the boots skimmed the ground, no doubt making even larger holes in the worn leather than was already there. The head lolled forward. He looked like a man helping his drunken companion home.

"The factories are that way," I said to Rhys when he turned left instead of right.

"We have a stop to make first. You're going to earn your wages."

"This is a paid job? But it's not officially sanctioned. How will you get the money from Master Tomaj?"

He flashed me a grin. "Let me worry about that."

"I hate it when you're mysterious. It's no wonder people stop believing when the priests are so secretive."

"People?"

"People who like answers."

"There isn't an answer to every question in life, Jac."

It was a typical response from him whenever the topic of religion arose. Thankfully, it arose very rarely. Despite his life revolving around it, he didn't mention it much.

"There's no secret about our order," he went on. "We train to fight. We fight when needed."

"And yet there is a high wall around your temple complex and women aren't allowed inside."

He stopped and hitched the body higher. A passerby gave Rhys an odd look before noticing his priest's tunic. "Need help, Brother?"

"No, thanks. My friend had a little too much tonight."

The man chuckled. "We all have a friend like that. Good night and good luck."

Once the man had turned the corner, Rhys picked up our conversation as if there'd been no interruption. "Women aren't allowed because we train semi-naked a lot of the time. There are high walls because it was once a fort. Like the castle, it was built to withstand a siege. There are no mysteries or secrets, Jac."

"Oh really? Are you telling me everyone knows I spy for you?"

"That's different," he mumbled.

"Ha! Tripped over by your own logic."

He trudged on, half-dragging, half-carrying the corpse beside him. I could tell without looking at him that he was annoyed. *This* was why we rarely spoke about religion.

"Are you still talking to me?" I hedged.

"No." After a few more steps, he said, "You like picking holes in my faith. Why?"

He'd never asked me such a direct question about my beliefs, or lack of, before. "I don't *like* to pick holes, Rhys. I just..." I sighed. "I don't believe the same things as you do, that's all."

"Fine. I don't care."

"Don't you?" I asked archly.

He stopped again and looked at me. "No, Jac, I don't. We can still be *friends*." He walked off again, leaving me staring at his back. By emphasizing the 'friends', it made the absence of any other kind of relationship more obvious. As if I weren't very aware of the absence already.

Usually when we touched on religion, the subject was quickly changed. Not this time. To my surprise, Rhys didn't try to change it. "Sorry, Jac," he said when I caught up to him. "I know I sound defensive, but... The thing is, I can see the holes in the logic, too."

"You don't have to justify yourself, Rhys."

"Thanks." He hefted the body higher, lifting the feet off the ground, before settling the weight again. He might not find the body heavy, but he was finding it awkward.

I set aside my repulsion and slipped the dead man's other arm around my shoulders, helping Rhys carry him. We shared grim smiles over the top of the lolling head.

"The thing is," Rhys went on, "the order got me through some very difficult times after my father died. I never knew my mother, so he was my entire world, and I was at that age when a boy becomes a man. He was good friends with Master Tomaj, so it was natural for him to take me in when I had no one else. I wasn't the easiest youth." He huffed a laugh. "I got drunk a lot. I was arrested more times than I can count. I did a lot of other things I should have been arrested for but was never caught. Master Tomaj persisted with me when everyone told him I was a lost cause. He was more patient with me than my own father would have been." He adjusted the weight of the body again. "At some point, I joined the brothers in their training. It taught me discipline and restraint, and gave me a purpose, a reason to stop drinking and doing stupid things."

"You don't call this stupid?"

He laughed softly. "My purpose is noble this time."

"Rhys, I understand why you joined the order."

"But you don't know why I stay, not when I see the same holes that you do or disagree with some of the rules." When I didn't respond, he continued. "I don't think priests and priestesses should be celibate. Nor do I agree with the rigid hours of prayer. It should be done when the time feels right, not when a bell tolls. Sometimes, I used to question myself as to whether I'd done the right thing in joining. I'd ask myself should I stay or go? I decided to stay, and the reason why is always the same."

I'd never realized he'd questioned his devotion to the order. By always avoiding discussions of religion for fear it would divide us, it had kept a very important part of Rhys from me. "Why?"

"Because I want to. I feel as though I'm in the right place."

It was a response that provoked no counter-response. As someone who preferred to deal in facts, not unproven beliefs, I couldn't argue with him. It was an indisputable fact that a person couldn't decide to feel a particular way. They just did.

"Does that make sense?" he asked.

"It does. I understand now."

If he noticed my voice sounded strained as I held back my tears, he didn't say anything. The small spark of hope I'd held that he would one day leave the order for me, despite what he'd said after the kiss, extinguished. My heart shattered. It wasn't until that moment that I even realized I'd held some hope that he'd change his mind, that the feelings we both felt were strong enough to convince him to leave the order to be with me.

Without hope...what was left?

I plodded on, the body getting heavier with every step. It was a relief when Rhys announced we'd arrived.

I blinked, looking around. "The deputy governor's house is down there."

"We're not going that way. I'm going to wait here while you go around the back and pick off a piece of the vine that grows up to the balcony. Make sure to include leaves or flowers, something that easily identifies it as having come from that particular vine."

I shucked off my cloak but didn't want to place it around the smelly clothing on the corpse, so I folded it up and placed it near Rhys's feet. I left him and raced around to the rear of the properties, following the same route I'd used when I followed Giselle on the night of the murder. It was darker tonight, the moon offering very little light to help me find my way. The leaves from a low-hanging branch struck me across the face, stinging my cheek, and I stepped in a large puddle that hadn't been there last time.

The poor light meant I didn't feel so exposed as I raced across the lawn and twisted off a section of the vine. I made sure to include some russet-colored leaves and a small berry that had shriveled in the cold. In a strong wind, both would fall off, so I was careful to protect them as I returned to Rhys.

I tucked the vine, leaves and berry into the corpse's boot, twisting one end around the boot laces so that it wouldn't easily fall out. Now all we had to do was take the body to the river. Going by the smell on the clothes, it had to be returned to the industrial part of the city. In the morning, a worker would find it and alert the constables. Hopefully they were smart enough to check it thoroughly and find the evidence we'd planted.

It was a long walk from the exclusive residential area where the deputy governor had lived. We'd only traveled a few streets when Rhys offered to take the full weight of the body. I hesitated before slipping free. "I saw a barrow earlier. We can put him in that." I handed Rhys my cloak, which I still hadn't put back on, then retreated the way we'd come.

I turned the corner just as a carriage passed, its lamps swinging, providing enough light for me to see the governor's escutcheon on the door.

"Merdu," I muttered as I crouched behind a bush.

But it was too late. I'd been seen. The occupant of the carriage ordered the driver to stop.

As it slowed, two guards jumped off the footboards and ran toward me.

"Come out!" The shout wasn't from the guards. It came from my uncle as he stepped down from the carriage.

Without my cloak, I had no hood to cover my fair hair. The color was common among Glancians, so I doubted Uncle Roderic could be certain it was me, and the light was too poor for him to have seen my face properly. "Show yourself!" he demanded as he hurried after his men.

Crouching where I was, I was a sitting duck. I sprang up and ran. I had a head start, and was quick, but it wouldn't be long before I tired. Stamina wasn't one of my strengths.

I took a circuitous route, intending to find somewhere to hide, only to realize I was back where I started. Rhys stood with the corpse in the shadows of a large tree on the side of the street.

"Jac, what's wrong?"

I bent double, gasping in air. "My uncle. Must hide."

He hurriedly placed the corpse on the ground then linked his hands to form a cradle.

I placed a foot in his hands and he pushed me up into the branches. I scrambled higher and settled in position, just as the carriage appeared.

It came to a stop as Rhys picked up the body, my cloak wrapped around it with the hood up. I touched the pendant hanging around my neck, and did my best to calm my breathing, but it wasn't easy when my nerves trembled.

Uncle Roderic stepped out of the carriage. "You! Who are you hiding under there?"

The guards fell into step alongside him and drew their

swords. "It's a priest, sir," one of them said as he re-sheathed his sword.

The governor squinted. "I know you. You're Master Tomaj's deputy, from Merdu's Guards."

"I am," Rhys said.

"Are you drunk?"

"I'm not but my friend is." Rhys moved the hood aside just enough to show the corpse's hair. It was darker than mine.

Uncle Roderic made a sucking noise between his teeth. "Did you see anyone run past? A small lad, short fair hair."

"No. Is he a thief? Vandal? We should alert the constables."

Uncle Roderic ordered his men back to the carriage. Before climbing in himself, he cast a sneering look at Rhys. "What a disgrace," he muttered.

Rhys didn't move until the carriage was out of sight. "Need help getting down, Jac?"

I dropped from the lower branches onto the ground then dusted off my hands. "That was almost like old times. I thought we'd have to escape across the roofs again."

"Thank Merdu we didn't. This fellow is getting heavy." He looked along the street in the direction the carriage had gone. "That was close. Jac, I'm worried about you."

The last time he'd told me he was worried about me, he'd offered to marry me. That had led to awkwardness and then a retraction of the offer and more awkwardness. I didn't want to go through that again.

"I'll be fine." What else could I say?

I fetched the barrow, and we bundled our corpse into it. The rest of the journey went a little faster. Downstream from the factories, we positioned the body so that it looked as though it had washed up onto the riverbank, leaving the boot with the evidence tucked inside in the water to soak the vine, leaves and berry.

"Thank you, friend," Rhys said, patting the corpse's shoulder. He picked up my cloak from the barrow and held it out to me.

"I'm not putting that on," I said. "It stinks."

"It's too good to throw out and I can't take it back to the garrison with me."

I took the cloak but didn't put it on.

"We have to return the barrow," he said. "Get in. I'll push."

Being pushed around in the barrow by Rhys could be fun, and we both needed a good laugh. "All right."

I climbed in, only to overbalance the unstable barrow. It began to tip, but I was saved from falling out by Rhys. He scooped me up into his arms and held me. Firmly. I felt his chest rise and fall and heard the hitch in each breath as he struggled to steady it. He watched me closely from beneath lowered lashes.

He must see me, and the depth of my feelings for him. How could he miss it?

"Jac." He winced, as if saying my name hurt. "I can't."

"I know."

"I want to," he whispered. "So very much."

"So do I."

"I'm sorry." He set me gently down.

I touched his jaw, allowing myself a moment of indulgence before withdrawing. "Don't be sorry. It's all right, Rhys. I understand."

He closed his eyes and turned away.

I swallowed but the lump in my throat remained. "On second thought, I'm tired. You return the barrow. I'm going home."

He picked up the barrow's handles and pushed. He did not look back.

I headed in the opposite direction, not bothering to wipe the tears from my cheeks.

CHAPTER 8

I awoke to the feeling that I was being watched. "Rhys?"

"Not Rhys. But he did ask me to give you this." Rufus held up a pouch bulging with coins. He tossed it to me when I sat up.

I stifled a yawn and blinked sleepily at the figure standing by the shuttered window. "Why did he send you?"

"Because Vizah doesn't know you're a woman and therefore can't be trusted to be alone with you. Who knows what he might say. And Andreas *does* know you're a woman and therefore can't be trusted to be alone with you. Who knows what he might say."

Despite my glum mood, I smiled. "You're wittier than everyone thinks."

"Just wait until I start correcting your grammar. Everyone thinks that's hilarious."

When I'd asked why Rhys sent Rufus, I'd meant why hadn't Rhys come himself, but I didn't ask again. I knew why. Rhys was putting distance between us.

I pushed off the blankets, only to stop and arch a brow.

Rufus turned around while I dressed. "Your trick worked," he said. "The sheriff believes the corpse is the killer."

"Rhys told you what we did? Who else knows?"

"Just me, Vizah and Andreas."

"He tells you three everything."

"Not always. But the things he keeps from us are easy to guess, if you know him well enough to see the signs."

I eyed the back of his head as I pulled on my trousers. "You can turn around now."

"I should go." He didn't move, however. "Jac, can I ask what your plan is?"

"Plan?" I shrugged. "I don't have one."

He still didn't head for the door. In fact, he perched on the edge of my table. "You can't be a lad forever."

"I'm aware of that." I wasn't sure if Rhys had told him I was the niece of the governor, and why I'd run away, so I didn't elaborate. The fewer people who knew the better.

"Have you heard of Lord Zeally?"

I blinked at the odd question. "No."

"He's a minor lord with an estate to the east. He's my brother."

"You're noble born? That explains a lot."

He humphed. "He's my younger brother."

I frowned. "Then shouldn't you have inherited the title?"

"I gave up my inheritance to join the order."

"Why?"

"There." He pointed at me. "That question proves you don't really understand what it means to be called by a greater power to serve a greater good. I gave it up because I wanted to join Merdu's Guards. Being a warrior priest is more important to me than being a nobleman. My purpose is as clear to me as you standing there. Merdu's Guards is where I belong. I know it in here." He tapped his chest.

Rhys had said something similar, that he felt as though being a warrior priest was right for him.

"Your point, Rufus?"

99

"I simply want to know what your intentions are." He rolled his eyes. "I sound like an overbearing father. I don't want to be overbearing, but Rhys is my friend and I don't want to see him... torn."

It was the first time any of Rhys's friends had acknowledged that there was something between he and I, something that went beyond friendship. It wasn't surprising that the clever and observant Rufus was the one to notice, or that he was prepared to tackle it head-on.

"If you're asking whether I will try to tempt Rhys away from the order, then you can rest assured that I won't. We came to an understanding last night. I know what the order means to him. If I have a plan for the future, I can assure you it doesn't involve being with Rhys."

I thought that might satisfy him, but it didn't. Not quite. "You have plans to leave Tilting?"

"No. This is my home. I know no other place."

His lips flattened. He didn't like my answer. "I won't ask you to leave—"

"Then don't."

"I think you want what's best for Rhys, as do I." He stood and headed for the door. "Good day, Jac."

I watched him leave as I reeled from the strange conversation.

I was still replaying it in my mind when there was a knock on my door. I opened it and stifled a gasp. "Giselle! What are you doing here?"

"I wanted to meet you properly. You intrigue me and I want to get to know you better."

"How did you find me?"

"I followed Rufus. Don't blame him. He didn't know. I'm too good for that."

I smiled to myself. She may be good, but I was better.

"After I heard a body had been found with convincing

evidence that pointed to him being guilty of murdering the deputy governor, I went to the temple to speak to Rhys about it. It wasn't hard to guess it was his idea. He knows everything that goes on in this city, thanks to his spies, and he must have heard the governor was going to tear through the slums until the murderer was found. Ever the savior, Rhys would go to great lengths to protect them. You're one of his spies, aren't you? I could see he trusts you, so it wasn't a great leap to realize you helped him last night. I wanted to meet you. Your name's Jac, isn't it?"

I didn't like that she knew so much about me. It was time to prove she wasn't the only one in possession of information. "Why did you need to speak to Rhys about the body? What business is it of yours?"

She looked oddly pleased that I'd answered her question with one of my own. She leaned forward. Her sleek black hair, chopped short at her shoulders, fell forward, enveloping us both in the scent of orange blossom. "To thank him, and you. You see, it was me who killed the deputy governor."

I stepped aside. "You'd better come in."

She reminded me of a cat when she moved. Her lithe limbs seemed to effortlessly glide rather than walk, yet every bone, muscle and sinew was poised to pounce at a moment's notice. "I see from your lack of reaction that you knew," she said. "I suspected Rhys guessed it was me, so I assume he confided in you."

I closed the door. "I was the one who told him."

It was rather satisfying seeing her surprise. It quickly vanished, however, replaced by admiration as her gaze took me in anew. "You followed me?"

"I saw you use the vine to climb into and out of the house. I didn't know whose house it was until later."

"I had no idea you were even there. Well then, I'm even more glad I followed Rufus now. You, Jac, are someone I want to know better."

It was my turn to be surprised. No one had taken this much interest in me since I met Rhys, three years ago.

She smiled at my reaction then looked around my room. "Cozy." She fingered the blanket on my bed. "Soft, feminine."

I self-consciously touched my short hair but dropped my hand when she smiled at me. I invited her to sit on the chair. "I'll light the fire."

"No need. I won't be here long, and neither will you, if you agree to come with me." She stood by the fireplace and crossed her legs at the ankles as she leaned against the mantelpiece. Clad in trousers with high leather boots, and oozing the confidence and swagger of a man, she ought to seem masculine. But she was too beautiful, her figure too feminine, to be mistaken for anything but a woman.

"Agree to go where?" I asked.

"The temple of Merdu's Guards. I thought we could watch the priests train."

"Women aren't allowed."

"That's a stupid rule, so I broke it long ago. Come on. I'll show you a way in."

"Why do you want to watch them train?"

"Because I like watching muscular men who are capable in a fight get hot and sweaty." She shrugged. "Also, I have nothing better to do."

It was such an honest answer that I laughed.

She smiled. "You don't have many female friends, do you?"

"None who'll watch Merdu's Guards training with me."

She threw her arm around my shoulders. "Then I'll be your first."

* * *

GETTING into the temple was much easier than I expected. Giselle had a key to one of the side doors. Since it was always locked, it was only ever guarded during times of attack. According to

Giselle, the last direct attack on the temple had been over a hundred years ago. She led me up a tight, circular stone stairwell in the corner tower. It was cold and smelled musty, with moss growing on the walls.

"Where did you get a key?" I whispered as I followed her.

"Andreas."

"He gave it to you?"

"I stole it from him when he was asleep after we'd made love."

"You were with Andreas *and* Rhys?"

"Not at the same time." She looked at me over her shoulder. "I gave up Andreas for Rhys. When Rhys takes an interest, it's hard to say no."

If I'd doubted that she and Rhys had once been lovers, she'd just confirmed it. It seemed he was happy to break his vow of celibacy for her, but not for me. My bruised heart took another blow.

"And Andreas just accepted it?" I asked her.

"Andreas had his hands full, quite literally. He had another two mistresses." She continued up. "He was probably happy to hand me off to someone else. I can be…time-consuming."

I could well imagine Andreas preferring his women to be undemanding.

Giselle opened a small door at the very top of the tower. "Keep low. No one will stumble upon us up here, but if one of the men down below happens to look up, they'll see us if we're not careful."

We approached the crenellated parapet and peered through the embrasure. On the opposite side of the open yard, the onion-shaped dome identified the building as the temple where the priests prayed and conducted services. The building was small, so couldn't be seen from the street behind the complex's high external wall.

In front of it was the gravel training yard where the warrior priests sparred. Giselle pointed out the garrison where the men ate and slept. It was a rather utilitarian structure with a stone foundation and red-brick walls. The part of the complex where we crouched was the oldest building, the original fort, that now housed the administrative offices.

"There's Vizah," Giselle said, pointing to Rhys's friend.

"He's not sparring."

"He's a trainer. All the best warriors are. They train the younger and less skilled. There's Rufus and Andreas, too." The three men guided their students, occasionally correcting their stance or a maneuver. "They'll join in the drills soon. The much older men you see at the edges are the keepers of the weapons, administrative staff, that sort of thing. Mostly former warriors no longer able to fight. I can't see Rhys yet."

"He's in the gallery with Master Tomaj," I told her. Like us, Rhys was watching the sparring from a higher level. He stood on the covered walkway on the first floor, his hands resting on the balcony as he peered down. He and Master Tomaj seemed to be talking intently.

After a while, Rufus, Vizah and Andreas shed their shirts and joined in the sparring. They formed groups, each group practicing with a different weapon, and one group used no weapons at all, just fists, feet and bodies. There was no laughter or chatter. The only sounds were grunts, the clash of steel and iron, and the slap of flesh against flesh. If I hadn't known it was a practice session, I would have thought they intended to kill each other, except that the priest with the upper hand never followed through with the final, winning blow. He'd help his partner up then they'd resume fighting.

"Enjoying yourself?" Giselle asked, winking at me. "Wait until they've worked up a sweat."

It was impossible to deny that the men were an impressive sight with their broad chests and shoulders on display. "You could charge the women of Tilting an entry fee and make a fortune."

Giselle laughed.

My gaze drifted back up to Rhys on the gallery. Master Tomaj suddenly grasped Rhys's arm. He seemed in earnest as he said something. Whatever it was, Rhys didn't like hearing it. He wouldn't meet the master's gaze until Tomaj shook Rhys's arm. Finally, Rhys lifted his chin in agreement. Master Tomaj embraced him, and Rhys returned it. Despite the height difference, the two men looked like father and son from a distance.

They parted and Rhys walked along the gallery before disappearing inside. Moments later he reappeared in the courtyard. He removed his shirt and collected a sword from one of the weapons keepers. Rhys adjusted his grip, testing the sword's weight in his hand, before settling into a fighting stance.

It was as if it were an invitation for the others to attack him. The group with swords went first, sometimes singly, other times teaming up to attack from different sides. Rhys dispatched them all with minimal effort. Swords were his preferred weapon, so Giselle told me. When I thought he was cornered by four priests wielding halberds, he still escaped by running at a wall then using it to jump off and flip over his opponents. I'd seen him use walls to his advantage before, but I didn't know he could flip as well as a gymnast.

I couldn't tear my gaze away. I'd felt Rhys's strength before, but seeing his muscles flex beneath smooth skin and the ridges of his stomach tense, was new. The youths who swam in the river looked nothing like him. Their bodies had been nice to look at, but Rhys's was fascinating. Tempting.

"Don't forget to breathe, Jac."

My face flushed, which made Giselle chuckle.

The priests not involved in the fight had stopped to watch, until Master Tomaj clapped his hands. He ordered the remaining priests from the other groups to take up swords then attack Rhys, Andreas, Rufus and Vizah.

It took some time for the four friends to prevail against almost thirty men, but they managed it by working together, using the confined space to their advantage against a larger number of opponents.

Through it all, Giselle and I remained silent. Once they'd finished, and the men were shaking hands as they caught their breath, Giselle sat with her back to the parapet, and stretched out her legs.

"Now you see why watching them spar is one of my favorite things to do when in Tilting," she said.

"I've never seen them fight before," I said. "Not like that. They're incredible."

"That's why they're allowed to do as they please, with no repercussions from the master. They can break all the vows they want and he'll overlook it."

"Others in the order don't, so I hear."

"True. But the master protects them, especially Rhys."

"Does Rhys need protecting?"

Giselle shrugged. "Not so much anymore, apparently. I hear he's quite the good priest these days. He's changed."

If only I had an ell for everyone who said that.

I continued to watch the men, not yet ready to stop even though they were dispersing now that training had ended. At one point I thought Rhys must know we were there, as he suddenly looked around. But then Andreas distracted him with a slap on the shoulder while Vizah threw a bucket of water at him. Rhys chased him, grabbing a fresh bucket of water, but Vizah had a head start so Rhys dumped the water onto Andreas's head instead.

Andreas threw his arms up as water streamed down his bare torso. "Why me?"

"You were his co-conspirator," Rhys said.

Vizah bent over, laughing. Rhys and Andreas exchanged glances, then picked up a bucket each and worked together to corner Vizah and throw the water over him.

The other men laughed, even the master, still standing in the gallery above. Rufus was the only one who shook his head. "Children."

Rhys, Vizah and Andreas turned to him, grinning.

Rufus quickly ducked into the garrison.

"Should we go?" I asked.

"Soon." Giselle crossed her ankles. "The men will wash up and retreat to the dining room to eat. When they're sitting down, the place will be almost empty. We'll go then."

"You know their routine."

"It's always the same." She patted the stone floor beside her. "Sit, Jac. I have a question for you."

I sat. "Go on."

"Ever since you told me you followed me to that scum's house, I've been wondering how I didn't see or hear you."

"I followed at a distance."

She frowned. "Even so..."

"It's why Rhys hires me. I'm quiet, discreet. Also, I have an excellent memory and can pick locks."

Her frown deepened. "I didn't take a direct route, and you must have been well back or I would have seen or heard you. How did you not lose me altogether?"

"I did lose you a few times, but I should admit that I overheard the tavern keeper give you the address."

She narrowed her gaze. "You did?"

"I suppose since I knew where you were going, I instinctively knew which route you'd take and was able to pick up your trail again."

"You 'suppose?'"

I shrugged, not sure how to explain it.

"Huh. Well done. Tell me about this excellent memory of yours."

"I can't forget anything. Not a single word that I've heard or read, or any sights I've seen. As long as I'm concentrating at the time, that is. Distract me and I'm useless."

Giselle continued to stare at me.

I cleared my throat. "Why did you kill the deputy governor? Is it because you heard he was a rapist?"

"And because someone paid me to kill him."

"Who?"

She gave me an arch look. "Someone who also heard what he'd done and couldn't see any other way to make him pay. The governor protects his own, the turd." I was still mulling that over when she said, "Jac, I don't know why you need to dress as a boy and I don't care."

For a moment I thought she knew my uncle was the governor and that I'd run away from him four years ago. But then she continued, and I realized the comments about him being a turd and the way I dressed weren't connected.

"That's your business. We all have our secrets. But I do question how long you can keep it up."

I crossed my arms over my chest, a little affronted at her gall in asking. We hardly knew each other. "You're right. It isn't your business why I dress like this." I shrugged. "Why do *you*?"

"I'm not passing myself off as a boy, or man, or..." She waved her hand in the general direction of my chest. "Whatever this is. Everyone knows I'm a woman. I prefer to dress like a man because it makes it easier to do what they're doing." She jerked her thumb over her shoulder.

"Fighting?"

She smiled.

"Like the men?"

"You seem skeptical."

"You think you can match them?"

"I'm not sure. I've never fought a warrior priest." She watched me grapple with the notion before adding, "Physical strength isn't everything in a fight, Jac. Did you notice Brother Aemon?"

"The wiry one?"

She nodded. "He's smaller than all the other warrior priests, but he bested most of his opponents. He's quick and agile, and he used their size against them. He's also smart and observant."

I recalled each move Brother Aemon had made while I watched his group practice with daggers. She was right. He had defeated almost everyone. Only Rufus stopped him when he joined in.

Giselle got to her feet but stayed low. "They'll be eating now. We should go."

I followed her back down the stairs then out through the side door into the street. She locked the door behind her and we walked together to the main road.

"You dress like that because you're hiding from someone, aren't you?" Giselle asked. "You want everyone to see just a boy, not the pretty girl. Or are you a woman? I admit it's very hard to tell how old you are."

"Old enough," I said, wincing at how stupid it sounded. But I'd had to say something or she might guess from my silence that she was right.

"How do you see this playing out?" She indicated my body again, the padded middle and flattened breasts.

For the second time that day, someone was asking me my plans. Whereas Rufus was asking because he was concerned about me being a distraction for Rhys, I suspected Giselle's intentions were different. "I don't know," I admitted.

When we reached the intersection, she held out her hand. I shook it, like a man's. When she firmed her grip, I firmed mine. She smiled. "Goodbye, Jac. Good luck."

Although I wanted to stay and watch her leave, she didn't move, so I walked away first. When I reached the corner, I turned to see if she was still there, but she'd gone.

* * *

MISTRESS LOWEY WATCHED me taste her latest creation with all the patience of a child presented with a gift box. "Well? How is it? Too much spice?"

I savored the mouthful of eel and pastry mixed with a blend of spices that exploded on my tongue like fireworks. I'd never tasted anything like it. "The borrodi and amani are just right, but you need to decrease the tumini. It overwhelms the others. Just by a little," I reassured her when her face fell. "It's almost perfect."

"You're right. I knew it before I gave it to you, so I don't know why I expected you to say anything else." She picked up the rest of the pie. "I'll give this to the Finnigan boy. He eats anything."

"Don't waste it on him. I'll finish it. It's one of your best, Mistress Lowey," I said gently. "After the minor change to the tumini, it'll become your customers' new favorite flavor."

She clucked her tongue at me. "You're a charmer, Jac. Now, you be sure to eat it all. You're too skinny."

"I think I'll enjoy it down by the river."

"It's getting dark. Be careful."

She wrapped the pie in a cloth and tied the ends together to make it easy to carry.

I pecked her cheek and headed out, but not toward the river. One slice of pie had been enough to fill me. I decided to give the remainder to Minnow, who would in turn feed it to a hungry soul who'd fallen on hard times. With the whores still not released, some of their loved ones would be struggling without a regular income.

I hadn't got very far when I heard a set of light footsteps. It wasn't late and the road was quite busy, so it could simply be someone walking in the same direction as me. I tested it by making a turn then another and another.

The footsteps continued.

I ran, but only as far as the next corner. After I slipped around it, I sank into a recessed doorway. A figure passed by, clad in black with the hood up to obscure his face and hair.

No, not *his* face. Hers. The scent of orange blossom lingered in her wake.

I stepped out. "Why are you following me, Giselle?"

She whipped around, one leg out in a move smoother than any dancer could manage and hooked my leg with her foot. I couldn't keep my balance on the slippery cobblestones, and fell onto my hands and knees in a bone-jarring crunch. Before I had a chance to recover, she grabbed my arm and shoved me onto my back. She loomed above me, knife blade at my throat and a slick grin on her lips.

"Got you," she sneered.

CHAPTER 9

*T*he cold steel of Giselle's blade pressed against my throat. She straddled me, her weight pinning me to the cobblestones. I wasn't strong enough to dislodge her, and that blade would draw blood the moment I moved. I didn't dare try.

"Why...?" My voice was barely louder than a whisper.

"How did you know I was there?" she asked.

"Wh-what?"

"How did you know I was there?"

"I heard your footsteps."

"But you knew it was me. You said my name. I was behind you and you didn't once turn around, so how did you know?" Her questions were strange considering they were said with curiosity rather than anger.

"I didn't know until you passed. You wear an orange blossom scent."

"Lots of women wear orange blossom."

I was quite sure she had no intention of killing me, so I felt confident enough to push her in the chest. "Why did you trip me up?"

Giselle stood. "Sorry about that." She put out a hand to help me to my feet. "It was a test."

I hesitated then accepted her hand. "I assume I failed. Although in my defense, when I realized it was you, I relaxed."

"Never relax, not around anyone." She sheathed her dagger. "That's lesson number one."

"You're my self-appointed teacher now? Lucky me."

"Don't you want to learn from the best?"

"Learn what? How to get caught following someone?"

"How to fight off an attacker, and use a knife and other weapons."

"Are you suggesting you want to teach me to be an assassin?" I whispered the last part, just in case someone was in earshot.

"You can be my apprentice."

An assassin's apprentice? It sounded ridiculous, yet she looked quite serious. "Why me?"

"You have potential. You need some intense physical training to build up muscle and fighting skills, but you have some good natural qualities that can't be taught. With training, I can make you better."

"You're mad. What makes you think I want to be an assassin? I abhor violence."

"Then why haven't you walked off yet?"

I walked off. "Thanks, but no thanks."

"What's here for you in Tilting, Jac?" she called after me. "Do you have family? Commitments?"

I kept walking.

"If you're staying for Rhys, then you're the mad one. He'll never leave the order, not for anyone. It's in his blood." When I didn't turn around, she added, "If you decide to take control of your own future instead of mooning after him, give your name to the publican at the Cat and Mouse. He'll tell you where to find me."

I took long strides, eager to get as far away from her as fast as I could. So much for having made a new friend today. Giselle had simply been testing me all along, trying to determine if I had the qualities she was looking for in an apprentice. Perhaps she thought I was desperate enough to accept, but I'd told the truth when I said I abhorred violence. I couldn't imagine killing anyone. She didn't understand me at all.

She was right about one thing, though. Rhys would never leave the order. I'd thought we could be friends, but watching him today as he trained, and the fact he'd avoided me this morning…perhaps friendship wasn't enough.

Without his friendship, what was left for me in Tilting?

* * *

WINTER WAS my least favorite season. I'd never liked the cold and always tried to spend as much time as possible indoors. This winter, I avoided going outside more than ever. When I did, it was only to see if the candle burned in the window of Rhys's secret room. It did, twice. Both times, he gave me brief instructions for the task he wanted me to do before leaving. The tasks were simple, mere errands rather than spying. I knew he was simply giving them to me to keep me busy and have a reason to pay me. I appreciated his thoughtfulness, but I felt a little guilty for taking money for such easy tasks.

Mistress Lowey's kitchen was my favorite place in winter, with its delicious smells and warmth. It became a hub, of sorts, as our neighbors had the same idea as me. I enjoyed the company. I *needed* the company. They also brought news.

King Alain's heir arrived in the city. Prince Leon made some public appearances, but otherwise kept to the castle. He probably felt overwhelmed at being thrust onto the stage with no prior education in the art of royal performance. The cynical side of me thought it served him right for forging paperwork, but Rhys informed me it was impossible to forge the required documents since they were unearthed here in Tilting and Leon was miles away at the time. It would seem he was legitimate. The house of Lockhart would survive.

He'd been found just in time. An heir for King Alain kept the Vytill king on his side of the border, and stopped the dukes and minor lords of Glancia from trying to maneuver their way onto the throne.

The machinations of the kingdom weren't as important to me as the city's. The lives and livelihoods of Tilting's residents depended on the governor's whims. He already controlled the magistrate and sheriff, and with the document signed by King Alain in his possession, he could overrule his council, too, giving him full power. The threat of that document hung over me like an axe poised to strike. If my uncle had control of every council decision, large and small, he could assign more constables to find me.

But Uncle Roderic's council wouldn't agree to such a wasteful allocation of resources. While he kept that document out of play, I was safe. He must be biding his time, waiting to see what the new prince was like before showing his hand.

The rest of the winter wore on with only two events breaking up the monotony. Firstly, the whores were released. Minnow came to tell me the news in person. She invited me to join the party they had planned to celebrate, but I thought it best to decline. Some of the clients might mistake me for fresh meat.

The second event was even more monumental. King Alain died. The kingdom plunged into mourning. He'd been admired, but more importantly, he'd been a constant presence, sitting on his throne in his castle for over fifty years. Even I, who barely spared a thought for royalty, felt somewhat bereft in the days after his death. He was Glancia's father, in a way, and his grandson was so young in comparison. How would Leon live up to the towering reputation of Alain?

It would seem the folk of Tilting wouldn't find out up close. King Leon decided to move his court to a new palace in the east of the kingdom, not far from the harbor town of Mull. I'd never heard of it. Mull. Even the name sounded inconsequential.

Mull quickly became a place of consequence, however. Soon after he made it his home, King Leon invited all the lords and ladies to join him there, with particular emphasis on those with eligible daughters. He was looking for a bride. The noble families soon moved into the glamorous new palace, leaving entire streets of Tilting empty. The castle was also empty, except for a skeleton staff, the rest being let go since King Leon had his own staff at the new palace.

Tilting's wealthy streets weren't the only part of the city to change. The river's docks swelled with workers looking for employment after a violent earthquake severed the eastern-most headland of the Fist Peninsula from the mainland. Even they soon left Tilting, however, after realizing Mull's harbor was growing in importance and work could be found there.

After a few months, Tilting became a different city. Its most powerful leaders were gone, taking their influence with them and leaving a void behind. Although the heart and soul of Tilting lived on in its people, that void was ripe to be filled.

And Uncle Roderic filled it. He finally produced the document.

With the former king's seal on it giving the governor the power to overrule his council, my uncle was able to do as he pleased. And what pleased him was to find me.

Rhys came to warn me on a bright summer morning. It was an unexpected sight to see him standing on my doorstep during the day, away from our secret meeting room. It was a worrying change to the pattern that had come to dominate my life.

I invited him into my room, but he declined. "I don't intend to stay. I just came to warn you." He removed a flyer from his pocket and unfolded it. "The governor has offered a substantial reward to anyone with information that leads to the arrest of this youth."

The face in the sketch was mine.

I took the flyer and stared at the eyes that were my own yet devoid of color and life. "No one I know will think this is me."

"It states that you're a girl disguising yourself as a male youth. Many people who know you have already guessed what you truly are. That reward will tempt them to betray you."

"They won't do that to me."

Mistress Milkwood waved at me as she crossed the courtyard. She would be heading to the market where these flyers circulated. The one in my hand stated I was a criminal and needed to be brought to justice. Would Mistress Milkwood believe it? Even if she didn't, would she act to collect the reward?

"Why does my uncle still have that document?" I asked. "Didn't King Leon revoke it before he moved to Mull?"

"Apparently not. The Tilting council have appealed to his majesty, but there has been no response from the palace. The new king is too busy finding himself a wife," Rhys bit off. "Gather your things, Jac. I'll take you to our secret room. You'll be safe there."

"For how long?"

"As long as necessary."

I squeezed the bridge of my nose. I'd known I'd have to give up my disguise one day, but I thought it would be when I was ready, after my uncle died or became too old to be a threat anymore. My hand was being forced too soon.

Rhys grasped my shoulders and dipped his head to peer at me. "Get your things now, Jac, and come with me."

"No. Not there."

"Why not?"

"Mistress Blundle and the other neighbors have seen my face, and it's connected to you and the order. I won't endanger you, too, Rhys."

"I can look after myself."

I handed back the flyer, well aware that my hand shook. I turned to go inside.

"There's another option," Rhys said, following me in.

I got down on my knees beside the bed and pulled out an old bag from under it. All I needed to take was some clothes. Everything else could be left behind. I stood and found myself toe-to-toe with a seething Rhys.

He grabbed the bag's handle. "Give up the pendant. He wants it, not you."

I wrenched the bag free. "It's the only thing I have of my mother's."

"When your uncle passes away, you can make a claim for it. There must be an inheritance law that says you have a claim on sentimental items."

I didn't know if that were true, but I did know there was a good chance I'd never see it again if I gave it up. I didn't *want* to give it up, and certainly not to Uncle Roderic. My mother had pressed upon me the need to keep it safe and with me at all times. I wouldn't fail her.

"You believe in the legend, don't you?" Rhys asked, incredulous. "Is that it?"

Perhaps I did believe it. Or perhaps I simply *wanted* it to be true, so that I could wield the power myself, and defeat my uncle once and for all. I hated being weak and reliant on men, including the fierce tower of muscle before me. While it was reassuring to know he would protect me, what would happen if he was no longer around? Besides, I meant what I said. I wouldn't endanger him if I could help it. Which I could.

I opened my trunk and removed two folded shirts and shoved them into the bag.

"For Merdu's sake, Jac! It's not real. It's just a story." When I didn't respond, he snatched the bag away. "I won't let you risk your life for an object that can be replaced."

I removed more clothing from the trunk and rounded on him. Fury darkened his face and turned his features stony. I knew his anger wasn't directed at me, that he was worried, but I couldn't help thinking that part of his anger was because I didn't believe as strongly as him in the religion. I was open to other possibilities, including the existence of the sorcerer and their power locked within a pendant. Rhys's faith wouldn't let him consider an alternative to Merdu, Hailia, and the minor gods and goddesses. Our differing beliefs had always been lurking between us, threatening to cause a rift.

It was a rift that could either be bridged or it would push us further apart. The outcome was up to us, and I'd hoped to tackle the subject at a later time that felt right. It was another thing my uncle's actions had forced upon me before I was ready.

"Are you threatening to take the pendant off me?" I opened my arms wide. "Go ahead, Rhys. You're stronger than me. I can't stop you."

"Don't, Jac," he growled. "Don't do this."

"Afraid of touching me, Rhys? Is that what's holding you back?"

His gaze shuttered, his ferocity not quite extinguished, merely smoldering. He crossed his arms over his chest. "Tell me where you're going. I'll come tonight and we can talk about this like reasonable people."

"I *am* being reasonable, Rhys. It's you who isn't reasonable. It's one thing to have faith in something you can't see or touch—"

"Says the woman who believes a pendant holds power!"

"—but it's another altogether to base your entire life around that faith, especially when you don't even agree with all its rules! You eat tasteless food because you're *told* to eat it. You can't keep nice things because you're not *allowed*. You won't even satisfy your most basic need because at some point long ago, a sexless person decided everyone should be like him and forbade his followers from experiencing the pleasures of the flesh because he believed it would help them serve the god and goddess better." I slammed the trunk lid down and rounded on him again. "Oh, no, wait. You *do* satisfy your urges, just not with *me*." I grabbed the bag and shoved the rest of my clothes inside. "Point taken, Rhys."

I'd never seen him look so stunned. He stared at me, unblinking, his lips parted. He scanned my face, as if searching for the woman he used to know, the one who may not have been meek, but was certainly mild-mannered. I'd never shown any anger toward him before, never told him what I thought of his life as a priest.

That was because I'd never really had a strong opinion on the matter. It had simply been a fact about Rhys that I accepted. Yet that acceptance had begun to wane over the last little while. I wasn't even sure when it began. It had crept up slowly, then accelerated after that kiss. Meeting Giselle and hearing about Rhys's other women certainly hadn't helped. Discovering that he'd been willing to break his vow of celibacy for others but not for me had been the final straw. Years of pent-up frustration had spilled out of me under the pressure.

It was an enormous relief to release that frustration. As much as I hated being the cause of his hurt feelings, I knew deep down it would have come out sooner or later.

Rhys's throat moved with his hard swallow. "I can't tell whether you're saying that to push me away to protect me from your uncle, but if that is the case, it won't work. I won't be pushed away when you need me the most. I will always protect you, Jac, even if it means jeopardizing my position in the order."

I put the bag down, took a step toward him, and shoved him in the chest with both hands. He hardly budged, but I felt a little better for it. "You're not listening to me, Rhys!"

There was nothing more to say to him that wouldn't be repeating myself, so I picked up the bag and marched outside. Rhys's horse was tethered in the courtyard. Some of the younger children patted him while others kept a cautious distance. The delicious smells from Mistress Lowey's kitchen filled the small space, as it always did at this time of day. It was a familiar, comfortable scene.

Yet something was amiss. Mistress Milkwood hurried to her home, her head bowed and gaze averted. She slammed her door closed, just as I heard the sound of horses' hooves approaching quickly.

"Someone's coming," I said.

Rhys took the bag from my grip and threw it back inside my room, then picked me up by the waist and lifted me high. "The roof. Go!"

I grabbed the edge of the tiles and with Rhys pushing on the soles of my boots, I managed to gain purchase and haul myself the rest of the way. I scrambled up the slope to the ridge and rolled over to the other side. Still gripping the ridge, I lay low and peered down to the courtyard.

Several constables streamed through the entrance on foot. Behind them, on horseback, came the sheriff, Uncle Roderic and four of his guards. Although the constables were the sheriff's men, it was my uncle who gave them orders.

"Search every room! Don't let anyone leave."

My neighbors emerged from their homes and demanded to know what was happening.

"You've been harboring a fugitive," Uncle Roderic announced. "She has been hiding under your noses as a boy."

Their gazes turned in the direction of my room. Mistress Lowey gasped only to cover her mouth with her hand.

My uncle pointed. "Whose horse is this?"

"Mine," Rhys said. I couldn't see him from my position on the roof, but his voice was loud and clear. I felt sick. Why couldn't he keep his mouth shut and leave quietly?

Uncle Roderic moved his horse forward. "You look familiar."

"I'm Brother Rhys from Merdu's Guards. I've been looking for the fugitive, too. Information led me here. It seems she left in a hurry."

I breathed a sigh of relief. Rhys had lied to save himself. Thank the goddess his masculine pride hadn't got in the way of common sense.

The sheriff gave one of the constables an order. Moments later, I saw the constable hand my bag to the sheriff.

"When did she leave?" the sheriff demanded of my neighbors.

Most shook their heads or shrugged, but Mistress Lowey stepped forward. "Some time ago. There was a disturbance and she panicked and ran off."

Hailia bless you, Mistress Lowey.

Uncle Roderic ordered the constables to fan out and search the other residences, beginning with Mistress Lowey's. She stepped aside, chin up and chest out, then followed the two constables who entered her home.

It was time for me to go. I would stay on the roofs until night-fall then drop down to the street and make my way to Minnow's house. She would give me shelter until I could decide what to do next.

"You! Priest!"

My uncle's bark halted me. Panic constricted my chest. Had he seen through Rhys's lie?

But it was worse than that.

"I remember you now," Uncle Roderic snarled.

"He's Master Tomaj's second," the sheriff said.

"He is. But I also know him because I saw him the night I saw her." He pointed at Rhys. "You were protecting her then, weren't you? Just as you're protecting her now."

My heart surged into my throat. I couldn't leave. I had to see what unfolded next, in case Rhys needed me.

I peered over the roof's ridge and down into the courtyard. Rhys came into view, leading his horse. He stopped near my uncle. I closed my eyes, willing him to keep moving, but when I opened them, he was still there, standing alongside his horse.

"It's true," Rhys told him. "You stopped and asked me about a youth with short hair. Something like that. I don't recall. But I wasn't hiding anyone. Not then and not now." He sounded calm. Too calm, given the circumstances. My uncle would know it was an act.

"What were you doing out that night?" Uncle Roderic demanded.

"That's none of your business." Rhys gathered up the reins and prepared to mount.

Uncle Roderic withdrew his sword and pointed it at Rhys. "I have a right to know everything that happens in my city."

Rhys removed his foot from the stirrup and turned to face my uncle. "This isn't your city. It belongs to the people. And my business is Merdu's business. You dare to challenge Merdu's warrior?" At my uncle's hesitation, Rhys put a hand to the sword blade and moved it aside. "I don't want to hurt you, or your men."

Uncle's Roderic's face distorted with his sneer.

"Sir," the sheriff said, his voice pitched high. "Sir, we cannot detain a warrior priest. Master Tomaj and the rest of the order will descend upon us."

Uncle Roderic watched as Rhys mounted. He didn't sheath his sword, but he didn't stop Rhys either. "You are a plague on your order, Brother. Liars and oath-breakers have no place in Merdu's Guards. I will be watching you and when you make a mistake, I will expose you for the unworthy scum you are. Not even your fellow brothers will want to save you then."

Rhys rode out of the courtyard.

I sank down and lay on my back. My breaths came in rapid bursts and my pulse pounded loudly. Tears slipped out of the corners of my eyes, down the sides of my face to dampen the tiles. My argument with Rhys had been bruising, but I wanted nothing more than to throw my arms around him and thank him for protecting me.

But meeting him again would be dangerous. My uncle had him in his sights now. I didn't doubt that he'd follow through on his promise to expose Rhys's broken oaths. While he broke none by seeing me, I wouldn't put it past Uncle Roderic to falsify evidence then present it to the high priest. While Master Tomaj and the other brothers would protect Rhys, the high priest wasn't so sentimental or forgiving.

While I lay there with the sun drying my tears, I knew I had to leave Tilting. I had to leave Rhys. It was the only answer.

I would hide away for now and bide my time until I was ready, and I would avoid Rhys in the meantime. I wouldn't go anywhere near the order's temple or the secret room he kept.

Drawing in a deep breath to steady my frayed nerves, I set off across the roofs of Tilting, heading toward the slums. Minnow would take me in, just as she took in other young women in need of help.

* * *

I WAS DETERMINED NOT to go near Rhys, but I broke my vow a few months later. Mysterious events in Mull affected the entire kingdom, including Tilting, and distracted my uncle from his task of finding me. It gave me a reprieve. I could breathe again and I slept through the night for the first time since he'd come for me in my home.

I did not continue my work for Rhys, however. My uncle wouldn't be distracted for long and I didn't want to draw attention to Rhys's connection with me. Despite the candle flame flickering in the secret room's window, I stayed away.

Until tragedy struck Merdu's Guards. Master Tomaj died, and I knew Rhys would be reeling from the loss. Tomaj had been Rhys's anchor when his world had collapsed upon his father's death. Rhys could have given up on himself and spiraled out of control, but Tomaj had guided him and loved him as any father should. Their bond had been special.

Although Rhys had his priest brothers for support, he would need *all* his friends to gather around him now. He had always been there for me when I needed him, now it was my turn to be there for him.

I climbed the vine to the secret room's balcony and lit the candle in the window. Then I waited for him to come.

CHAPTER 10

$\mathcal{R}$hys did not come to me.

  He was announced as the new master of the order of Merdu's Guards the day after Master Tomaj died. He wasn't even given time to mourn.

I placed a candle in the window of our secret room the following night, but he still didn't come. Nor did he come the next night. I fell asleep waiting and awoke at dawn and returned to the home Minnow kept with her partner.

On the third night, on the day Master Tomaj's body was buried, I didn't light the candle. Instead, I entered the temple complex using the door Giselle had showed me. I picked the lock and headed up the steps to the tower parapet. I watched the priests perform a ceremony in the yard as dusk fell. Rhys stood at the front of the entire order and each priest knelt before him, one by one, and said something I couldn't hear. They appeared to be officially making Rhys their new master. It was thanks to Vizah's booming voice that I realized they were swearing an oath to serve Rhys and be loyal to him.

Rhys accepted each brother's oath with a nod. Then, as the sun gave its final gasp, the dinner gong sounded, and the priests entered the garrison. Rhys remained behind until he was the last one left. He drew in a deep breath.

As he did so, he tipped his head back and looked directly at me.

I doubted I could have escaped via the tower steps in time, but I didn't try anyway. I sat down, out of sight from anyone down below, and waited.

He joined me moments later, his chest heaving, a pulse in his throat throbbing. His jaw was set hard, his nostrils flared, every muscle of his face straining for control. To some, he might look his most furious. But I knew he was trying hard to master his emotions.

I opened my arms and he came to me. He sat and tucked his arms around me, gathering me onto his lap, then buried his face in my neck. I cradled him, stroking his hair, as he wept silently.

Some time later, he pulled away. He wiped his cheeks with the back of his hand. "Sorry," he muttered.

"Don't be. Not with me."

He looked down at our linked hands, but I doubted he saw them. "He shouldn't have died. Not yet. He wasn't old. He was healthy, strong. He wasn't supposed to die for years. And now… he's gone and I…"

"You're the master of the order."

"I shouldn't be. I'm not ready."

I cupped his face and looked him in the eye, still brimming with vulnerability and sorrow. "He chose you to be his second because you are incredible, Rhys. You are strong and capable, and your heart is good."

"But I'm not ready."

"No one is ever ready for leadership."

He closed his eyes. "I don't want it."

"The best leaders never do. It's others who see the potential in them." I stroked my thumb along his cheek, and he opened his eyes. They were still haunted, his gaze more intense than ever.

"Jac," he murmured, his voice a purr that whispered across my skin. "I'm sorry."

I quickly released him and got up.

He stood, too. "Jac—"

"It'll be all right, Rhys."

I entered the tower and raced down the steps, my feet moving so fast it was lucky I didn't trip. I pushed open the door at the bottom and didn't bother to relock it behind me.

I thought he might follow—part of me hoped he would—but he did not.

I raced up the street and returned to Minnow's home where I finally allowed myself to sob, too.

* * *

A THUNDERSTORM SIGNALED a dramatic end to summer and the beginning of autumn. As the weather cooled, I remained holed up in Minnow's spare room during the day, only going out at night. I didn't mind. The crisp, quiet evenings were perfect for a city stroll. Only Minnow and her partner knew I was there. I made sure my face wasn't seen by anyone when I went out. With its likeness still nailed to every noticeboard and bollard around Tilting, I'd not dared leave the house without my face covered.

I hadn't contacted Rhys since that night on the temple's tower, a week ago, and I'd avoided going anywhere near him.

Giselle returned to Tilting at the end of that week. I saw her speaking to a man in the semi-dark outside the Cat and Mouse. The blunt cut of her hair and the lithe, feline figure were unmistakably her. I waited until her companion left, then I stepped out of the shadows.

She saw me and smiled. Then it suddenly vanished. "Jac, look out!"

I turned and came face to face with the pointed end of a constable's sword. "You're under arrest."

I slowly put my hands in the air. "Why?"

"Governor's orders."

"What have I done wrong?"

"I don't know and I don't care."

Out of the corner of my eye I saw a broken crate on the ground, a rotting lettuce leaf still inside. If I could subtly maneuver my way over to it, I could use it as a shield.

The moment my feet moved, the constable's blade bit into the skin at my throat. "If you resist arrest, my orders are to kill you, *girl*." His top lip curled with his sneer as his gaze traveled my length. He licked his lips.

I stilled. I didn't dare move a muscle, or look away.

At the edges of my vision, I spotted Giselle bob low and creep around. Then she leapt out and tackled the constable side-on. They fell to the ground in a tumble of limbs and flash of metal. The breath left the constable in an "oof" as Giselle sat on his chest, her hands pressing down on his wrists so he couldn't use his sword. He tried to buck her off, but she didn't budge.

"Run, Jac!" she shouted.

"I can't leave you."

The constable tried to buck her off again. She kneed him in the groin, rendering him momentarily immobile. "I can take care of him. Go!"

I ran off along the street, only to stop as four more constables approached, swords drawn. I turned and ran the other way. Another four constables blocked my exit.

Behind me, Giselle swore. When I turned to see why, she'd almost disappeared into a building. A back door would give her the means of escape.

I, however, was trapped.

My arrest was pathetically swift. I did manage to throw one punch, but it hurt my knuckles and didn't seem to affect my target's jaw. It didn't even break his skin. He simply snorted and made sure to wrench my arm hard behind my back as another fished inside my shirt. He squeezed my chest, only to pout in disappointment at the bandage covering my breasts. He pulled out the pendant, broke the chain then pocketed it.

He replaced the chain with a leash and tied a length of rope around my wrists behind me. He tugged on the rope end and ordered me to move.

The other constables weren't required but they flanked me as if I were the city's most dangerous criminal. Minnow stood in the doorway of her house, a hand at her throat, her brow furrowed. I gave my head a slight shake. I didn't want anyone to know she'd been protecting me.

It soon became clear that I'd been betrayed by one of the young whores who came and went from Minnow's house. She must have seen me there. She watched our procession pass by, a hand on her hip, the other hand out to collect her reward. The constable who'd arrived first directed her to go to the council office the following day to collect. She didn't meet my gaze.

There was no sight of Giselle. I didn't expect there to be. She had her own skin to save. She wouldn't want the burden of saving mine, too.

"Where are you taking me?" I tried to sound defiant and brave but the tremble in my voice betrayed me.

"Holding cell," said the one pulling on the leash.

"Governor's orders," added another.

I wouldn't be in the holding cell for long. My uncle wanted the pendant, not me. Once he verified it was the right one, he had no further use for me. It would be an acceptable explanation to claim I'd died in custody after attempting to escape. No one would question it except Rhys, and he had no authority to do anything about it.

Rhys. Losing a friend so soon after the loss of Tomaj would be a heavy blow.

The walk to the sheriff's holding cells was quite a distance. We passed through more slums, skirted the market area, and approached the park from the west. The vast expanse was a beautiful spot for picnics and walks in the light of day, where lovers met in the dim evening, and the homeless slept on dark nights.

It was that darkness that made it an excellent place for Rhys and his men to hide until the moment was right.

As our procession passed, three warrior priests emerged from the shadowy depths with no warning, as if magic had conjured them. Led by Rhys in all his ferocious glory, sword in hand, who blocked the road ahead, with Rufus and Andreas flanking him. A horse in the park snuffled and a bridle clanked. Vizah must be with their mounts, ready to leave at a moment's notice.

"Let him go and no one will be harmed," Rhys ordered.

The constables drew their swords. The one holding me audibly gulped, but he was also the only one to respond. "Step aside, Priest. This is not your affair."

"Let. Him. Go."

One of the constables snickered. "Him? You mean *her*."

"Is she *your* woman?" asked another. "I knew you priests weren't as righteous as you pretended to be. No man is."

Andreas broke rank and charged at the constables. Rhys ordered Rufus to back him up, then he plunged into the fray himself. He came for the constable holding me with a wildness in his eyes and a snarl on his lips.

I'd seen them practicing, but this was different. Lives were at stake. The constables intended to kill. They knew they were within their rights to defend themselves. There would be no retreat when they beat their opponent, no shaking of hands and starting over.

But the constables didn't gain an advantage. Not even for a moment. Rhys's blade nicked the hand of one of the constables, causing him to drop his sword with a cry of pain. Rhys forged a path to me, using his body to push aside any constable who got too close, sending them into the path of Rufus or Andreas where they were swiftly disarmed. Twice more, Rhys cut a constable's sword hand. He kicked another in the stomach, winding him. Rhys dispatched them all, with Rufus and Andreas cleaning up behind him, gathering dropped swords and forcing the constables onto their knees.

The one holding the leash around my neck pulled on it, hard. The cord burned, biting into my skin, my windpipe. I couldn't breathe. My body slammed against the constable's and his arm wrapped around me, pinning me. I couldn't even move my hands to crush his balls in my fist.

"Come any closer and she dies," he snarled.

Rhys adjusted his grip on the sword. He lowered himself into a fighting stance.

"No, Rhys!" Rufus shouted. "Don't!"

Don't kill him, he meant.

If he did, the sheriff could arrest him. Not even Merdu's Guards were immune from a murder charge if there was enough evidence. And there were seven witnesses lined up on the side of the road who would testify.

I tried to gasp in air, but the rope was too tight. The edges of my vision blurred and I felt my body weaken.

Rhys attacked. Not with his sword, but with a knife. I wasn't sure where he'd pulled it from. His boot, perhaps. By the time that thought registered, Rhys had plunged the knife blade into the constable's thigh.

He roared in pain and clutched his thigh, releasing me. He hadn't seen it coming either.

Rhys caught me as I fell. I sucked in air, my body filling up in desperate need, but my sore throat protested. I choked and coughed as pain raked at my throat. It felt like I was swallowing nails.

Rhys untied my hands and removed the cord from around my neck, then he scooped me up. He cradled me against his chest, as I had cradled him a week ago on the temple's tower. His heart beat erratically, his breaths came short and fast.

"Jac," he whispered in my hair.

I clung to him, my fingers scrunching the tunic at his back. I wanted to stay there all night, enveloped in his arms, feeling the muscles twitch as they slowly unwound.

But I knew I could not. "You can't be seen here." My voice came out as a rasp, but Rhys would have heard it. Even so, he didn't release me. His arms tightened again.

"Rhys," Andreas said sharply. "We have to go."

Vizah emerged from the shadows, leading four horses, but it was Giselle who filled my vision as I pulled away from Rhys.

She inspected the wound on my neck. "I have a salve for that."

Vizah brought Andreas and Rufus their mounts. "Next time, one of *you* hold the horses."

"You didn't miss much," Andreas said. "Rhys did it all."

Vizah gave the reins of a horse to Rhys. The big man laid a hand on Rhys's shoulder as he studied him. "You don't have to do it alone."

Rhys acknowledged him with a curt nod, but he watched me. His gaze suddenly narrowed. "I think someone's coming."

I heard it too. A horse. No, not one. Dozens, as well as the unmistakable rumble of wheels rolling over cobblestones.

Rhys released me, pushing me toward Giselle. "Take her to the Cat and Mouse. I'll come when I can."

Giselle grabbed my hand and pulled me away into the park while Rhys mounted but didn't ride off. He turned to face the newcomers. Pain flared in my throat again as I gasped in more deep breaths. I stumbled, but Giselle helped me to maintain my balance. She tucked me into her side and half-carried me further into the park where she pressed me back against a large tree trunk to rest.

Uncle Roderic's voice demanded the release of the constables. It must have been his carriage I'd heard, with his usual retinue of guards accompanying him on horseback. "What is the meaning of this? I was told there was a prisoner! Where is she?"

"This brother attacked us, sir!" one of the constables cried. "The girl escaped."

"I know it hurts," Giselle hissed in my ear, "but we have to run."

"I can't," I managed. "No breath."

"Master," I heard another familiar voice say. "That is *Master* Rhys, of Merdu's Guards." It was the high priest, and he sounded furious.

I leaned back against the tree trunk and closed my eyes in relief. The high priest would protect Rhys and the others. He wouldn't allow my uncle to arrest servants of the god.

"I don't care who he is!" Uncle Roderic shouted. "He interfered in city affairs! Arrest him!"

"No!" the high priest said. "He does the god's work."

"I said arrest him!"

"Take your men and leave, Governor. If you do not, then every warrior priest will come for you, and when they have finished with their vengeance, Merdu will banish your souls to the pit. Not even the merciful goddess will want to save you and your men."

I suspected it was the constables who backed down before my uncle. He'd never had much time for religion, and I doubted he believed in an afterlife. He wanted to win in this life and win at any cost.

"Search the vicinity," he ordered.

God's blood. I pushed off from the trunk, ready to run, but the words of one of the constables made me stop.

"Sir, I have her necklace."

A wave of nausea rose within me. In the turmoil, I'd forgotten about the pendant.

Uncle Roderic ordered his guards and the constables to retreat.

After they'd left, I heard the high priest's angry snap. "That was a poor use of the order's men, Master."

"I disagree," Rhys said.

"We weren't here on the order's business," Rufus added. "This was personal."

"There is no *personal*." The high priest's tone remained ice-cold. "Everything you do is the order's business. Every act you perform, every word you utter, and every breath you take is on behalf of Merdu's Guards, no more so than now you are its master, Rhys. Go back to the temple and compose yourselves. There's a problem in Mull that requires your attention. I was on my way to tell you about it when I saw the governor's carriage heading this way at speed with all his men."

Giselle tugged on my hand. "I don't think they're coming after us. Can you breathe now?"

I nodded and squeezed her hand. We slunk off through the park together.

Although it was easier to breathe, my chest still felt tight. Despair constricted it. My mother's pendant was gone, my only link to her and the women of my ancestry with it. If the story of the talisman was true, then Uncle Roderic was in possession of enormous power.

Although I could break into his home or office and steal it back, he was too clever to simply leave it lying around or in a locked box. He would hide it, or keep it on his person. My uncle was always well guarded. Could I even manage to get close to him without Rhys's help?

The answer was irrelevant because he would refuse to help. He'd already made it clear he didn't believe in the legend and didn't care enough about an object to risk his life, or mine, for it.

The high priest had also made it clear that, as master, Rhys had a responsibility to his order. The fact that Rhys didn't counter him proved that he agreed. In my heart, I knew it was the way of things now. The days of escapades across the rooftops were over, as were our meetings in the secret room. Rhys couldn't spend his evenings chatting idly with me anymore, or drinking in the tavern with his friends, or kissing women. He was the master of the most powerful religious order on the Fist Peninsula, and he had a great responsibility. He needed to use diplomacy and sound judgment in the future. He had to keep the respect of all his priests, not just his friends, and he must be seen to be on the side of justice. He would make a fine master, as long as he wasn't subjected to distraction or temptation.

I was both.

I'd made up my mind a week ago to leave Tilting, but I'd been putting it off. Now it was time to follow through on that decision before I ruined Rhys's life.

But I couldn't simply slip out of Tilting without telling him. He'd worry that I'd succumbed to my injury. After everything he'd done for me, I owed him a goodbye.

As I sat on the bed in Giselle's room at the Cat and Mouse with the cooling salve tingling the cord burn at my neck, I penned a woefully inadequate note to Rhys. It didn't say all the things I wanted to say. For one thing, I didn't tell him I loved him or that I was leaving so he could fulfil his duties as master of Merdu's Guards. It simply said it was best if I left as soon as possible. Then I thanked him for 'everything'.

I reread it—it was definitely inadequate—then gave it to Giselle to deliver. "Before you go," I said, "can I ask you another favor?"

"Of course. Anything."

"Is the offer to be your apprentice still open?"

Her smile started slowly then quickly spread. "It is. Are you sure, Jac? It means leaving Tilting."

I indicated the folded note in her hand. "That's why I'm saying goodbye to Rhys."

She studied it. "Ah. You don't want to say it in person? He said he'll come as soon as he can. For one thing, he'll want to see for himself that you're all right."

"Tell him not to come. Tell him I don't want to see him. Say anything to put him off. I can't face him, not to say goodbye. It's too hard. If he wants to write me a message, then he can do so."

Giselle slapped the note against her hand. "I'll deliver it

now." She paused at the door. "For what it's worth, I think you're doing the right thing. He won't leave the order for anyone. You need to move on with your life. Once you start presenting yourself as a woman, the men will all start noticing you, and you'll realize there are many more fish in the sea. You'll forget about him."

I shook my head. No man could compete with Rhys.

She must have mistaken my head shake for modesty. She approached and sat on the bed. "You're very pretty, Jac." She touched my chin. "You have the most striking eyes." She released me and stood. "When I'm finished with you, you will be the most alluring woman in Glancia."

* * *

I FELL asleep but awoke when I heard the door open and close. "Well?"

She sat on the edge of the bed. "He asked how you were. I told him you were recovering and would be fine. Then I handed him the note."

"And?"

"He ranted for a bit, but when I explained that you were in an impossible situation, he calmed down. He understands, Jac." She tapped her chest. "Deep down, in here, he knows it's the right thing for you to do."

I blinked back hot tears. "Did he give you a note for me?"

"Not a written one. He just wanted me to tell you goodbye and that he'll always be fond of the time you spent together."

"Fond?"

She lifted a shoulder in a shrug. "I think he felt awkward talking to me about you."

"Did he say anything else?"

"Not about you. He told me he has to leave tomorrow for Mull."

I settled back against the pillow. "Can we leave tomorrow, too?"

She smiled as she stood. "We can, and it's fortunate we'll be heading west since they're heading east."

"Where are we going?"

"My home. It's in Dreen."

PART II

CHAPTER 11

I discovered that I liked Dreen. The kingdom on Glancia's western border had known peace for a long time, and that peace reflected in the residents' welcoming nature. Although it was the largest of all the countries on the Fist Peninsula, it had the smallest population. Farmhouses dotted its rolling green hills, while its two cities could barely be described as such. Logios, the center of learning for all students on the peninsula, not just those from Dreen, was nestled into the side of a hill to the north of the capital, Upway.

It was to Upway that we traveled. It was Giselle's home, and not all that far from Tilting, even though both cities were in different kingdoms. It was something of a melting pot of different folk, so a fair-haired Glancian wasn't an uncommon sight. Most of its residents were Dreenian, however. Giselle fit in, with her dark, straight hair and flatter face, but she was exceptionally tall for a Dreen woman. Even I felt tall for the first time in my life.

Giselle's home was much like her, sleek and practical. The chairs lacked cushions, there were no rugs covering the floors or ornamentation on the walls. Kitchen utensils were mostly made of tin and there was only two of everything—plates, bowls, cups, spoons. I wondered if the second one got used much before my arrival.

"This is your room," she said, opening a door. It smelled musty, but nothing that a little airing out wouldn't fix. "Sorry it's so small."

"All I need is a bed." I put my bag down. Having left Tilting in a hurry, it was woefully light.

"Fortunately, you're not used to fancy."

Not in the last few years, but my bedchamber in my childhood home had been a palace compared to what I'd lived in after escaping from my uncle.

"What's through there?" I pointed at a door opposite my room.

She hesitated. "My office." She removed a key hanging on a leather strip around her neck. I hadn't noticed it tucked under her shirt all this time. "I keep it locked, even when I'm home. It houses my most valuable possessions."

"Client information?"

"Amongst other things." She unlocked the door and let me walk in first.

It wasn't what I expected. The room was barely large enough for the desk positioned in the center and the cabinet of drawers. A low bookshelf drew my attention first. Books were expensive. Usually only the wealthy could afford them, and some academics who spent all they earned to accumulate them. My parents had owned some, as did my uncle, but I'd not had the opportunity to read one in years. Perhaps I'd have time in between training.

I trailed my fingers across their spines. Some were bound with leather covers, others in soft animal hide, and even a few in just hard board. Some of the titles were familiar, although I'd never read them. "What are they about?"

"All manner of topics. Geography, medicine, history of the peninsula and beyond. Culture and beliefs, magic and sorcery." Giselle pointed them out as she spoke. She removed one with a red cover, elegantly decorated with a gold border, a sun and moon motif in the center. "I need to reread this for a job I'm considering." She tucked it under her arm and pulled out another. "This one might interest you. It's mostly about prophecies, but it might mention the legend your mother told you."

I'd told her the governor stole the pendant from me because he believed the legend that the sorcerer had placed power within it. I hadn't told her the governor was my uncle. It wasn't a relationship I wanted anyone to know.

"Thank you," I said, flipping open the book. "I'll start now."

"No. Now, you are beginning your training. You can read tonight." She ushered me out of the office.

"But it's late and we've been traveling all day."

She simply smiled as she locked the door of the office behind her. Then she began my training.

I trained all day and some nights. The sessions were a mix of physical activity that ranged from lifting weights to increase my strength, to long runs around the city to improve my stamina. She taught me to use a sword, knife, stick, spear, and rocks as weapons, as well as how to fight without any weapons at all. We trained in the cold and wet, we trained in the pitch black of night. She'd wake me early, sometimes even in the middle of the night, so that I'd learn to fight instinctively, even when a lack of sleep meant I was too tired to think properly.

"You have very good instincts," she'd said to me, "but they need to be better. That's where your excellent memory will help."

"I don't understand."

"Your body remembers. Even when your mind is distracted or tired, your body will recall its training and will move in a way that saves you without you even thinking. Trust me, it will be important."

She said that phrase a lot.

It was the beginning of a grueling autumn, but it wasn't all terrible. Giselle had new clothes made for me. The trousers were snug compared to my old ones, and by dispensing with the waist padding and the cloth wrapped around my breasts, I almost didn't recognize my own figure when I saw it in the mirror for the first time. I had feminine curves.

"See?" Giselle said as she teased my hair off my face. "You're beautiful."

"All Glancian women are pretty, so they say."

She clasped my shoulders from behind and peered at our reflection over my shoulder. "But you have a quality that other Glancian women don't have, and that makes you an intriguing puzzle that people will want to solve, particularly men. Beauty is merely the packaging around the puzzle, and as you say yourself, pretty packaging is common. The puzzle is unique."

I made a scoffing sound. "But I don't *feel* beautiful."

"You will." She tugged on the ends of my short hair. "Perhaps if you grow it a little, you'll feel more feminine."

"Can I use the same tonic you use on your hair? It's so sleek and shiny."

She laughed. "We'll buy you a different bottle tomorrow from the market. The tonic I use is for thinner, naturally flat hair. You need something for thick Glancian hair."

The following night, she took me to a tavern. The pomade in my hair kept it off my forehead and without the curtain obscuring my eyes, I was a little self-conscious. Before we entered, Giselle touched my chin. "It's all about confidence, Jac. Behave as if you belong and no one will question you."

"But I don't feel confident."

"You will eventually. For now, simply pretend. It's what I did for the first year after I left my family." It was one of the few times she'd mentioned having a family. When I'd asked her about her parents in the early days of our journey from Tilting to Upway, she'd brushed me off then changed the subject.

That first time going to a tavern opened my eyes to how men treated women without an escort. My bottom was pinched a half dozen times before I managed to find a stool to sit on. I was leered at, propositioned, and had my breast squeezed. Giselle punched that fellow in the nose. It was as good as an announcement that I was under her protection.

"Next time, you'll do the punching yourself," she told me.

And I had. It was both satisfying and amusing to see the man stumble back onto a table. It was a little less amusing when the other man whose ale had been spilled wanted revenge. A brawl soon broke out among the drunkards.

Giselle and I fled the tavern. "Knowing when to retreat is just as important as fighting," she said as we ran.

"Can we drink in a nicer part of the city?"

"That's not much fun. Besides, you need to learn to look after yourself, and that won't happen if you're sipping good wine beside a fireplace. You need a rough port tavern where good manners means not burping in someone's face."

We jogged all the way home in the frosty night, and I was pleased to reach Giselle's house and find I wasn't breathing heavily, thanks to the regular training. Instead of having an early night, however, she decided to go out again. We headed to the docks.

"I want you to tell me everything you notice," she said. "I want to know every flag flying on the ship masts, every conversation you overhear, how many mice scurry past your feet."

"Why?"

"I'm testing you."

"On what? My knowledge of flags?"

"That, and your memory and observational skills."

"My memory is faultless. You know that."

She clapped my shoulder and flashed a smile. "Then I expect you to pass with flying colors."

There were numerous small tests like that as autumn rolled into winter. Events in Glancia seemed a world away as the days blurred together. My training gave me little time for anything else, which was a blessing. It meant there was less time to think about Rhys. I still thought about him every day, however, usually as I stared up at the night sky as we walked through the city. Was he looking up at the same sky, wondering how my life was going without him? Did he think of me at all?

Giselle always seemed to have a knack for knowing when I was thinking about him. She also had a knack for distracting me from those thoughts, either by making me do more training, or taking me to a tavern. After I punched that fellow who'd squeezed my breast, the men became a little more respectful. When one desired me, he would ask to take me to one of the bedchambers instead of demanding or trying to grope me. Although I was often propositioned, I didn't take a lover, despite Giselle's encouragement.

She had several lovers, mostly men but sometimes women, too. No one seemed shocked so I pretended that I knew that sort of thing happened all the time. Then after a little while, I no longer raised an eyebrow. It seemed perfectly natural for Giselle to bed whomever she pleased.

One evening, when she said she was slipping off for a while with one of her regular lovers, I told her I was leaving and going to bed early. After hearing some news from Glancia earlier, I felt a little homesick. How long would it be before I saw Tilting again? I wanted to go back. The question was, should I?

The house was quiet, but I couldn't sleep. I decided to read until I drifted off. Giselle wouldn't mind if I borrowed one of her books. Although I hadn't been in her office since the day I arrived, she'd never actually banned me from entering. She simply kept the door locked to keep the collection safe from burglars.

The lock presented a little more difficulty than I expected, but I got it open with my picking tools after remembering a very old lesson from my father on a similar mechanism. I studied the spines of the books, but the one about Zemayan beliefs caught my attention. It was the one with the red leather cover that Giselle had been reading soon after my arrival. I removed it from the shelf and sat on the chair at the desk, making space by pushing some correspondence aside.

A letter in the middle of the pile caught my attention. It bore the Tilting governor's seal. The seal was still intact, so Giselle hadn't read the letter yet.

The front door opened, and cool air brushed my cheeks. I waited for Giselle to find me. I intended to confront her about the letter, but she spoke first.

"What are you doing in here? Does a lock mean nothing to you?"

"I thought you'd be proud. That lock is complex." I held up the letter. "Why are you corresponding with the Tilting governor?"

She approached the desk and accepted the letter with a frown. "I've been dumping the correspondence there all week. I haven't got to any of it yet." She broke the seal and unfolded the single sheet. "That's interesting. It's about you."

"Me?" She handed it to me, and I read. "He wants to hire you to find the girl disguising herself as a boy called Jac."

"Apparently."

"He's offering a nice sum."

"Not nice enough." She took back the letter and tossed it onto the desk. "What aren't you telling me, Jac?"

I looked down at the book.

She picked it up and closed it. "You told me he wanted you because you had the pendant. He has the pendant now, so why does he want me to find you?"

I blew out a breath and met her gaze. "He's my uncle."

"Ohhhh. So you're the niece who died." She sat on the edge of the desk, frowning. "Except clearly you didn't die. I think you need to tell me everything."

And I did. She listened, riveted, and when I finished, she clutched the book to her chest and stared at me. "That explains the nice accent, your...bearing, I suppose you'd call it. I could tell you weren't born in a gutter. Why didn't you tell me before now?"

I shrugged. "I didn't want anyone knowing the connection."

"You didn't trust me?" She sounded hurt.

"I felt ashamed having that man as my relative."

She nodded. "That makes sense. I'd hate being related to him, too." She tapped the letter. "Don't worry, Jac. I won't turn you over to him."

"I never doubted it." I stood. "I was going to read for a while in bed. Why are you home so early? Did your lover lack the stamina?"

"Quite the opposite. He wanted to invite another woman to join us. I do not share."

"Remind me never to take a potato off your plate."

She chuckled then stood and, remembering the book in her hands, tapped the cover. "Why were you looking through this?"

"I'm researching the old family legend about the sorcerer placing power into my pendant. The sorcerer is a Zemayan belief, so I thought a book on that subject might teach me something."

"I read this not long ago and there was nothing about that in here, but you could try another." She scanned the bookshelf then pulled out a thick book with black lettering on the spine. "Try this one. It's about the history of the peninsula."

"How will that help?"

"Never discount history. Knowing the past is always helpful. The legend is old, and the Zemayan culture and belief system is old…the book might mention the sorcerer."

I accepted the book, but something else had just occurred to me. "The pendant hasn't given Uncle Roderic the power he sought, so he thinks I can unlock that power for him." I pointed at his letter. "*That's* why he wants to find me. It's not because I'm family. It's because the pendant isn't working."

"You're probably right. He certainly hasn't taken over the city yet, let alone the entire world." She gave a rueful laugh. "He probably thinks your mother told you a secret to unleash the power. Perhaps a spell."

I looked down at the history book in my hands. "I'll look through this."

She held up the book on Zemayan beliefs. "And I'll read this one again, just in case I missed something last time."

* * *

Spring brought warmer weather and an announcement from Giselle that I was ready for my first mission.

I didn't feel ready.

"I've only been training six months," I said after we completed a light session in the park. "Shouldn't it be longer?"

"For most people, I would agree. But you *are* ready, Jac. Your excellent memory accelerated your learning, just as I thought it would. The client has sent me a sketch of the target and a potential place to carry out the job. It shouldn't be too hard for your first."

Job. Target. It was all so clinical. "Who's the victim?"

She grabbed my arm and turned me to face her. "He's not a victim. He's a cruel, sadistic man who preys on women right here in Upway. One of the brothel madams is the client. She sent me enough information to satisfy me that he deserves to die. I'll say it again. *He* is not the victim. Those women are. You must understand that, Jac, or this life will destroy you. Before you go any further along this path, tell me you understand."

"I do."

She squeezed my arm. "Good. It is difficult the first time, but you'll get used to it."

I followed her out of the park, feeling somewhat numb about the evening ahead, still not believing that I was ready to go on my first mission, or that I was going to end a man's life. Perhaps being numb was the only way to get through it.

Several hours later, as clouds came in and obscured the crescent moon, I set off alone. The target, as Giselle called him, was a sailor from Freedland whose ship was moored in the deeper part of the river. Every night he rowed ashore with some fellow sailors, and while they visited taverns and brothels, he picked out his victims from the whores who worked the streets, the ones with no brothel madam to protect them. I'd studied the sketch of his face but added my own knowledge to the identity. As a Freedlandian, he would be short and stocky with tanned skin, and powerfully strong. The sand people of the republic on the southern point of the Fist Peninsula were known to be rough and lawless, so he would likely fight without honor. He would be armed, but probably just with a knife, not a sword.

With weapons secreted about my body, I prowled through the streets in search of him.

I never found the Freedlandian sailor. In fact, I'd never expected to. I was ambushed by three men on the very street where I should have seen him. They'd been waiting for me behind barrels and crates, stacked on both sides of the narrow street. I quickly dispatched the first with my knife, which I was already holding. He fell to the ground and did not get up. As the two others came at me, I ducked under the sword blade of one and swept out with my foot at the other, tripping him. Springing up to my full height, I parried a strike then another and another.

The third fellow came at me again, this time from behind. I managed to dance out of the way of the second man's blade just in time to also avoid the sword of the third. A swift kick to the knee had him shouting in pain and falling to the ground beside the first attacker. With two men removed, I concentrated all my effort on the third, who proved more resilient. He was an excellent swordsman.

But Giselle was right. My memory served me well. My body recalled all of the training and instinctively reacted to each strike and parry with a countermove. The most difficult part was ensuring my reactions were unpredictable. I beat him by cutting his sword hand across the knuckles, slicing open his glove. He dropped the sword, but he wouldn't be permanently injured.

"You can come out now, Giselle," I said, not yet sheathing my sword.

Giselle emerged from the shadows further along the street. "Well done, Jac. Not only did you defeat them, but you also realized it was a test."

I waited until the men had retrieved their swords and sheathed them before I thrust mine into the scabbard. "I didn't know at first. I hope you're not too hurt," I said to the first man I'd cut in the side.

He winced as he drew his hands away from the bleeding wound. "I'll recover."

Giselle paid them and put her arm around my shoulders, steering me back the way I'd come. "How did you know?"

"I went to the port this afternoon after you told me about the target. There were no Freedlandian ships docked. It's possible one could have arrived after I left, but the port master said none were expected. So I assumed you were testing me, but I wasn't completely sure until I saw you. Those three were determined. They didn't hold back. Did they know it was just a test and not to hurt me?"

"Of course. You did very well, Jac. Very well indeed." She patted my shoulders before releasing me. "I suspected you'd gone to the port this afternoon, but what I meant was, how did you know I was there? I no longer use the orange blossom soap."

I laughed lightly. "It's a pity. I liked the orange blossom."

"Then how did you know?"

"Your silhouette is distinctive. I could just make it out in the shadows." I touched her straight hair, the ends just skimming her shoulders. "I know no other women with a feminine figure who wears their hair like you wear yours."

She touched the ends of her hair, skimming her shoulders. "Very good. Excellent, in fact. If you doubted before that you were ready, I hope tonight sets your mind at ease. You are most definitely ready."

"But against men who are prepared to kill me?" I shook my head. "Or if all three were as good with the blade as that third one? Or if there were more? I'm not sure, Giselle."

"Trust me, Jac. You're ready." She almost sounded a little annoyed that I continued to doubt her judgment. "Now, get some sleep. Tomorrow, we'll discuss your first mission. A real one, this time."

I continued walking. "What if I can't do it? Those men who attacked me...I didn't want to kill them."

"That's because you knew they weren't a real threat after your reconnaissance at the port. When someone truly wants to kill you, you'll have no qualms killing them first. Look at Rhys."

I stopped. "What?"

She stopped, too, frowning. "That's quite a severe reaction to the mere mention of his name. All I meant was, Rhys and the other brothers are willing to kill to defend innocent lives. If they can do it, so can you."

"I suppose."

My answer didn't interest her. She was still focused on my reaction to the mention of Rhys's name. "Are you still infatuated with him?"

"I'm not infatuated. He was my friend for a long time. I miss his friendship, that's all."

"He rescued you when you were at your lowest, so it makes sense."

I continued walking. I didn't want her to see my face.

"You were young and impressionable, too." Giselle's soft voice was full of emotion that had me once again wondering about her own past. "Rhys was the first person to show you any kindness and respect since your mother's death. It was no wonder you invested all your emotional needs in him."

She wasn't altogether correct. Minnow had shown me kindness, as had some of the other whores who came and went from her house, and Mistress Lowey, too. But I didn't correct her. She was right in that I had focused a lot of my attention on Rhys. Perhaps my immaturity was to blame, and my desperate need to love another and be loved in return.

"You will love again, Jac, and next time, it will be better because it will be real, not an infatuation with a man you can never have. But only if you let the ideal of Rhys go. Stop seeing him through the eyes of the girl you were, and see him through the eyes of the independent, incredible woman you've become."

"I'll try, if I ever see him again."

She flashed me a smile. "Hopefully, that's some time away. I have no plans to return to Tilting soon."

* * *

PLANS CHANGED RAPIDLY, however. A week later, just before we were due to set off for the kingdom of Vytill to undertake my first mission, Giselle informed me we were going to Tilting instead. She'd received a letter from the publican at the Cat and Mouse. From the look on her face, I could tell it brought troubling news.

"What's the matter?" I asked.

She folded the letter in half. "A friend is dying."

"Rhys?"

"No. She's a dear friend, and I need to be there for her at the end. You could stay here, but I think you should come with me. You should steal back your pendant from your uncle. It belongs to you, and is your only connection to the women who came before you."

I nodded slowly, warming to the idea. The pendant may not hold any of the sorcerer's magic, but I still wanted it back. "When do we leave?"

"First thing. But promise me something, Jac. Be careful. Steal it when your uncle is not there. You need to stay out of his way now that he's looking for you. And stay away from Rhys, too."

"I plan to, on both counts."

Despite my intentions, however, it proved impossible to avoid either man.

CHAPTER 12

$\mathcal{T}$ilting had changed in the months we'd been away. The lords and ladies had returned and now went about their business as if they'd never been visiting the palace in Mull. They drove in their carriages with the curtains open or rode on their high-stepping horses through the park, keen to be seen in their finery. They were very visible and seemingly happy to be back in the city.

The constables were less visible, however. Talk at the Cat and Mouse centered around the stripping back of the governor's powers, although no one seemed to know how this had come about. The rumored changes to sentencing had never gone ahead, so thieves were no longer in danger of being hanged if they were caught, and the victims of rape once again had a voice in court and wouldn't suffer repercussions.

The governor also no longer had the power to pass decisions without the approval of the council. I was safe. I couldn't be arrested without just cause. Even if he did capture me, he wouldn't harm me while he thought I could unlock the power within the pendant.

It was a relief to be able to walk through the city without fear, and to know that I was right and that Uncle Roderic's plan to use the magic in the pendant hadn't worked. It was likely it held no magic, after all. The myth of the sorcerer was probably just that, a myth. Rhys would be pleased that his religious beliefs remained unchallenged.

Rhys. Although every street, every corner, and every rooftop reminded me of him, I avoided going near the temple of Merdu's Guards and the room where we used to meet. Instead, I focused on getting my pendant back.

I was familiar with the routine of the governor's office. There was no reason to believe anything had changed. If I wanted to get in, I could use the same method I'd used when I memorized the document that gave him extra power. I'd have to tuck my hair away, now that it was longer, but I could pass as a boy again if necessary. I decided to watch his home instead. While Giselle called on her dying friend, I studied the comings and goings from Uncle Roderic's house from the roof of his neighbor's manor.

Once it became too dark to see, I climbed down, using water pipes and vines as my ladders, and set off, intending to return to the Cat and Mouse. The sight of Andreas talking to a woman beneath a lamppost stopped me in my tracks. My breath caught in a gasp of surprise.

The woman noticed me and thrust her hand on her hip. "Get going! This is my turf and he's with me."

Andreas turned. "I am not with— Jac? Is that you?"

I spun on my heel and walked quickly away. I should have run.

Andreas jogged up to me. "It is you!" He threw his arms around me and hugged me tightly. "Thank the merciful goddess. Vizah! Rufus! Look who it is." I tried to leave before they arrived, but Andreas was still holding my shoulders. His gaze swept over me. "Well, well. You grew up."

It wasn't until then that I spotted Vizah and Rufus lounging by a door to a nearby tavern. They'd been keeping watch on the area. They now joined us.

"Merdu and Hailia," Rufus muttered, shaking his head. "Jac. There had better be a good explanation for this."

I opened my mouth to speak, but Vizah got in first. "That's not Jac." He squinted and peered closer at me. "Merdu's blood. It *is* Jac!" He pointed at my breasts, drawing little circles in the air. "Good disguise. They look real. How do you get your hips to look so natural? Why are you pretending to be a woman anyway?"

Andreas snickered into his hand.

Rufus rolled his eyes as he shook his head. "Jac *is* a woman. She always has been, you dolt. She used to disguise herself as a boy. Seems she's no longer bothering."

Every sentence deepened the frown scoring Vizah's brow. He gently gripped my chin and angled my face to the light. He grunted. "Who's going to tell Rhys?"

"Rhys knows," I said. "He has always known."

Andreas put up a hand. "As have I. Women are my specialty. Speaking of which, I wasn't *with* that whore. She collects information for us, and I— Looks like she's gone." He shrugged. "Her news must not have been that important after all."

"You don't have to explain anything to me," I said.

He puffed out his chest. "True. You already know I don't need to pay my lovers."

Rufus smacked Andreas's shoulder with the back of his hand. "Don't flirt with her."

"I wasn't. I can't help it if I'm naturally charming." He tossed his head, making his golden hair ripple.

Rufus rolled his eyes again.

Vizah hugged me. "Rhys will be so relieved."

"Don't tell him I'm back in Tilting," I said.

He pulled away, frowning. "Why not?"

"He's been looking for you everywhere these last months," Andreas added.

It was my turn to frown. "Why?"

Rufus huffed a humorless laugh. "What did you think he was going to do? Just accept your disappearance?"

"Disappearance?"

"I don't like the thought of you disrupting his life again," Rufus went on. "Especially now that you look like..." He flapped a hand at my body and face. "But it's cruel to let him go on thinking you're dead or were abducted. *You* may not care about him enough to be kind, but *we* do."

"Dead?" It was so absurd that I started to laugh, only to stop again when none of them joined in. "No. He knew I left Tilting. I wrote him a note to tell him."

"He didn't receive it. Who did you give it to?"

Giselle. She'd *told* me he'd read it and even what he'd said in response.

She'd lied.

I didn't tell them, however. I felt too sick to speak. Rhys thought I'd died, and so soon after losing his beloved Master Tomaj, too. Thank Hailia he'd had these three at his side.

Rufus crossed his arms over his chest and glared icily at me. "He lights the candle every night in your meeting place, hoping you'll see it and know he's searching for you. Every night, Jac."

I felt like I'd been punched in the gut. My breath came in rapid bursts and my legs buckled. I needed to sit down. I searched the vicinity for a crate or barrel, but gave up without really taking in my surroundings. "You know about that place?"

"We do. No one else does."

"He'll be there now," Vizah said.

Rufus pointed a finger at me. "No, Jac. Don't go."

Andreas pushed him aside. "Ignore him, Jac. You should go. Rhys needs to see you."

"No," Rufus said again. "Look at her!" Vizah and Andreas both looked. "It's a terrible idea. He'll... They'll... It's just a very bad idea."

"Bollocks," Vizah said. "You know what he's been like. Seeing her will be good for him."

Rufus gave up on them and appealed to me. "You understand why it's a bad idea, don't you? *We'll* tell him you're alive. That will make him feel better—"

Andreas interrupted with a snort.

"—and he can move on, knowing you left him of your own accord," Rufus continued. "There's no need for you to see him, Jac."

I'd returned to Tilting determined not to see Rhys. Hearing that he thought I'd died or been abducted had made that conviction waver, but Rufus was right. I should stay away for Rhys's own good. For mine, too. Besides, I had another person I very much wanted to see that night, and she had a lot of explaining to do.

"Tell him I'm alive," I told Rufus. "Then tell him I don't want to see him."

Rufus released a breath. "Thank you for understanding."

"Rufus!" Vizah cried.

Andreas threw his hands in the air. "I think it's a mistake. Jac, if you change your mind—"

"I won't."

Rufus grasped Andreas's tunic at the shoulder and pulled him away. "Let her go. She has her business, and we have ours, or have you forgotten why we're here."

"Zelda has gone," Andreas pointed out. "Whatever she wanted to tell us obviously wasn't that important."

Rufus checked over his shoulder to see if Vizah followed.

Vizah took a few steps in their direction, then glanced back at me. He smiled. "You're pretty, Jac. I can't believe I never noticed before. It's probably just as well you're not going to see Rhys. He's not looking his best. He really let himself go after you disappeared." He trotted after the others.

I turned and headed for the Cat and Mouse, more furious than I'd ever been in my life.

* * *

GISELLE CUT a lonely figure nursing a tankard of ale. Seeing her dying friend had taken a toll. But not even sympathy could dampen my anger.

I stood beside the table, arms crossed, and glared down at her. "Why didn't you deliver my note to Rhys?"

She sat back with a heavy sigh. "You've seen him?"

"His friends. He thought I'd died or been abducted, because he never received my note. You told me you'd delivered it. Why did you lie?"

She put up her hands in surrender. "I'm sorry. I truly am. I know it hurt him, but it's kinder in the long run to let him think you were dead."

"How is it a kindness?"

"Because death is an ending. He needed closure or he'd never move on."

"That's bollocks. You did it for selfish reasons. You knew he'd try to talk me out of going with you, so you wanted to avoid us meeting before I left."

She stood and reached for my shoulders, but I stepped back. "That's not true, Jac. I've known Rhys a long time, and I could see that he cared enough about you to not be able to stay away, but not enough to leave the order for you. If he knew you were still alive, he'd always be doubting his choice to stay in the order, always wondering if he made the right decision. By letting him think you'd died or didn't care enough to tell you were going, I removed that choice and self-doubt. I know you feel as though I betrayed you, but if you set aside your hurt feelings for a moment and think about it, you'll agree it was in his best interests. Yours, too."

"He's about to find out I'm alive and well."

"They're going to tell him? Fools. I suppose it's too late to stop them."

"Probably."

She pulled out the chair beside hers. "Have a drink with me. I don't feel up to arguing with you, but I could do with some company."

She did look rather miserable. I signaled to the serving woman, then sat. "How is your friend?"

Giselle gave me a sad smile. "It was hard to see her. Knowing death is coming made every moment together feel important, special."

I accepted the tankard from the server. "I remember when my mother was dying. The fever took her quickly, but not so fast that we didn't have time for final goodbyes. I was grateful for that."

"Was she sad to die?"

"She was worried about leaving me, but not sad for herself. She believed she would be reunited with my father in the afterlife."

"You don't believe in religion, do you?"

I shrugged. "I don't know. It's a comfort to think there's something more after death, but I find it hard to believe that gods and goddesses have any influence over our lives."

"That's why I don't believe at all. It's too fanciful for me. I'm a pragmatic person."

"So I noticed," I said wryly.

"You and Rhys could never have had a future together, even if he left the order for you. He believes every word they teach in the temples." She saluted me with her tankard. "But you're more like me, Jac. We don't have a spiritual bone in our bodies."

I raised my tankard, too, but the bitter taste her words left in my mouth affected my enjoyment of the ale. Giselle didn't know me as well as she thought she did.

I drank quickly then said goodnight before heading upstairs to my room. I threw on my cloak, raising the hood, and opened the window. The cool spring breeze caressed my cheek and ruffled the ends of my hair poking out from beneath the hood. I drew in a deep breath, filling my lungs with the faint scent of blossoms, then searched the shadows. It came as no surprise to see a familiar figure lounging against the wall opposite.

I rested my palms on the windowsill and drew in another deep breath. Then, mind made up, I climbed out and used the pipe to slide to the ground. There was just enough light coming from the torches flickering on either side of the tavern door for Rhys to see me.

He didn't move, however. He didn't greet me. He made no sound.

"Rhys..." I began.

"Don't," he growled. "Don't try to justify giving your message to someone else to deliver. You should have told me in person, Jac. Didn't I deserve that?"

There was enough light that I could see his face. I'd expected a little happiness and relief at seeing me, but clearly his anger overrode any tender feelings. His features were all hard planes, his eyes ice-cold. I'd thought his stance relaxed when viewed from my room, but it was rigid when seen up close.

I wanted to take him in my arms and smooth the tense muscles and melt the ice, but I didn't trust myself. Giselle was right about one thing. Being apart from Rhys was best for both of us. That hadn't changed. I closed my hands into fists at my sides and kept my distance.

"You grew your hair," he said gruffly.

I touched the ends of my hair, peeking out of my hood near my shoulders. "You grew a beard." Apparently this was Vizah's definition of Rhys letting himself go. I certainly couldn't see any other difference. Rhys looked as athletic and strong as ever, and his warm scent was still pleasant.

He scratched the beard, as if he'd forgotten it was there. "I've been told it suits me."

"By a blind man?"

He huffed, not quite a laugh, but I was relieved to hear it.

"I'm sorry, Rhys. You're right. I should have told you in

person. I just...couldn't." He turned his face into profile. "How have you been?"

He pushed off from the wall and walked away. "How do you think." It would seem I wasn't going to be easily forgiven.

I followed him, even though I wasn't sure if that was what he wanted, or whether it was a wise thing to do. "Wait, Rhys."

"I can't. I'm busy."

"Then why did you come? The others told you I was fine, and they'd never lie to you. You didn't need to see me in person."

"It was a mistake to come here," he said over his shoulder.

His long legs made it difficult for me to keep up. "Rhys, stop!"

He rounded on me. The ice in his eyes had completely melted, replaced with a burning fury I'd never thought him capable of feeling with me. The affable man wasn't in evidence. Not in the least. "Why should I stop to talk to you now, when you didn't talk to me before you left? Nor did you call on me once you came back. Not even after learning I thought you'd died or were abducted."

"I told you—I couldn't do it. I couldn't face you."

My words might as well have been swept away by the wind before they reached his ears. "I left a candle in our window in the faint hope you were alive so that you'd know I was thinking about you and was searching for you. I even confronted the governor, demanding he release you!"

"Oh. I'd wager that didn't go down well."

"Is that meant to be a joke, Jac?"

"I'm trying to lighten the mood, Rhys."

"Don't bother. I haven't been in a light mood for six months. I doubt I will be again soon."

Seeing him lash out because he was in pain was like a knife to my heart; knowing I was the cause felt like the knife was being twisted. This time I did reach for him.

He jerked away. "Don't."

"Fine," I said through clenched jaw. "You're right. We should go our separate ways. It's for the best."

"I'm so glad *you* know what's best for me since apparently everyone thinks I can't be trusted to make decisions about *my* well-being."

Everyone? So it wasn't entirely about me. "That's enough, Rhys. You've made your point and I've apologized."

"Great! Wonderful. Then we can both go on our way and never see each other ever again, because *you* decided that's what's best for me." He spun around and strode off.

"Not just you, Rhys," I muttered. "It was best for me, too."

He turned around and strode back, looking every bit the warrior charging into battle. "Clearly you didn't return for me. So why did you return? Is it the pendant?"

"Giselle thinks—"

"Giselle! Is that why you left Tilting? You took up her offer to be her apprentice?" He swore. "Merdu's blood, Jac! You think *I* make terrible decisions."

I bristled. "I couldn't stay in Tilting forever, pretending to be a boy. I had to grow up at some point and be myself again. I had to think of my future."

"So you thought you'd become an assassin's apprentice? If you wanted more money for spying—"

"It's not about money, Rhys! I had to leave Tilting to...to discover who I am without—" I almost added 'you' but it wasn't fair to blame him for my immaturity. That was my fault for allowing myself to be consumed by him. "I *needed* to grow up," I said again. "I was too naïve."

"You didn't just grow up, Jac. You changed, and not just in appearance." His gaze slowly moved down my length, leaving behind a trail of heat in its wake. It was fortunate he wouldn't be able to see my fierce blush in the night. He cleared his throat. "You never would have argued with me before. Not like this."

I quieted my voice to match his. "That's the problem, Rhys. I *should* have argued with you more. But being around you affected me to the point where I wasn't sure whether the opinions coming out of my mouth were mine or yours."

"Of course they were yours," he scoffed. "You disagreed with me on faith, about the god and goddess, about belonging to the order."

"I never disagreed with you about the order. We had different ideas on religion, that's true, but I never said you should or should not belong to Merdu's Guards. If you think I did, then you're not remembering correctly."

"Oh, right, *you're* the one with the faultless memory, so of course you're always right."

His bitter tone raked over me like nails across skin.

He swore again and dragged his hand down his face. When the hand dropped away, it was as if it removed a mask, revealing a man looking much older than his twenty-eight years. "Sorry," he muttered. "I didn't come here intending to shout at you. I am sorry, Jac."

Tears stung my eyes. His tender apology hurt more than his angry words ever could. I didn't trust myself to speak yet, so merely acknowledged his apology with a lift of my chin.

"Have you killed anyone for her?" he asked.

"Not yet."

"But you plan to."

"That's what she trained me for."

"Then I was right. You have changed. You're not the girl I knew."

"I'm not a girl. I'm a woman."

"You think I haven't noticed?" he rasped.

My throat tightened. I dipped my head so he couldn't see the tears shining in my eyes. His disappointment was like a weight on my chest, pressing down.

"If you're here to assassinate your uncle—"

"We're not. We're not here for work. Giselle wanted to see an ill friend."

"I know you were watching his house earlier. The others told me where they saw you and it's just around the corner from where he lives. Stay away, Jac. Please. He's been looking for you, presumably because the pendant talisman didn't work as he thought it would."

"I'll be fine, Rhys. He wants me alive. He won't hurt me."

"If you think that, then Giselle has taught you the wrong lessons. Be careful. Losing you once was hard enough." His voice cracked. I thought he'd finally give in and hug me, but he must have held on tightly to the last vestiges of his anger because he simply turned and walked away. He did not look back.

I turned away, too, and released a shuddery breath. That was over, thank Hailia. Now that we'd met, we wouldn't speak again. There was no need for our paths to cross, and I wouldn't be in Tilting for long. Our friendship was in tatters and that was how it would remain. It was for the best.

Knowing that didn't make it any easier.

I cried myself to sleep.

* * *

IT FELT SOMEWHAT lazy to use the same method to get into the governor's office as last time, but it really was the easiest and best way. With my hair tied up and tucked under a boy's cap, and my face smeared with soot, I wasn't questioned as I traipsed alongside the cleaners just before dawn. This time I knew which office belonged to my uncle.

I waited for the other cleaners to leave, then opened the same locked casket on the desk where I'd found the document with King Alain's seal. This time it held only money. I doubted Uncle Roderic would have hidden the pendant anywhere else in the office, but I continued to search. It wasn't in the desk drawers, however, including under the false bottom in the lowest one. There were no locked boxes hidden in wall cavities behind the hanging pictures, and nothing up the chimney. I scanned the bookshelves, checking for any sign that one or more of the books were moved more frequently than the others, but the shelves were entirely devoid of dust all the way along. If there was a hiding spot behind them, the only way of knowing would be to remove each one, and my fingers were covered in soot now. They'd leave marks.

One book caught my eye, however. The title on the spine was familiar. I pulled it off the shelf to see the front cover. It was red leather with gold lettering and a sun and moon motif in the center. I'd seen the symbol before on a book in Giselle's collection in Upway.

The gold on the cover glinted in the weak dawn light coming through the window. The city was about to wake. It was time to leave. Time to ask Giselle why she kept me from reading the book each time I showed an interest in it.

Voices drifted along the corridor as two guards stopped for a chat. I listened, waiting for them to continue on their way. More people entered the corridor, however, their footsteps heavy with exhaustion. The dull *clunk* of brooms and mops knocking against full buckets signaled the departure of the cleaners. I needed to leave with them.

I tucked the book into the waistband of my trousers and covered it with my shirt and jerkin, then I cracked open the door and peered out. As the cleaners passed, I stepped in beside them. The two guards at the end of the corridor weren't paying attention and continued to chat as we headed in their direction. They were interrupted by another guard, however. He beckoned them with a crook of his finger. They ceased their chatter and followed him.

I relaxed a little more. It had been an easy morning's work.

The book's hard cover dug into my stomach, but I ignored it. I didn't want to draw attention to it while I was in the open. The punishment for theft was still imprisonment, although my uncle had never got his way and seen to it that thieves were hanged.

I was certain no one followed me after I peeled away from

the other cleaners, or when I walked back through streets touched by dawn's light to the Cat and Mouse. That self-assured certainty was my downfall.

A mere street from the tavern, two men blocked my way. I recognized them. I'd seen them a short while ago in the corridor outside my uncle's office. They still wore their guards' livery. I turned and ran, but another two blocked the exit. As with Giselle's final test in Upway, they were all armed with swords, and all looked capable of using their fists. They were also bigger than me.

But I'd been taught to use my size to my advantage. I had no sword, but I did have a knife. I withdrew it and crouched, ready to spring. They closed in, smiling at the prospect of capturing their quarry.

Heart pounding, I held the knife between my teeth and jumped. I used a nearby barrel to push off and spring higher, somersaulting over the men, then grabbed the edge of the tiled roof. The book fell out of its hiding place as I did so, and one of the men kicked it aside. As two of them came close, I swung my legs and kicked one in the head, sending him toppling against his companion.

Hanging one-handed, I lashed out with my knife and feet at the other two, keeping them at bay. I wouldn't have time to haul myself onto the roof. I had to battle through. With just a knife, I would be no match for skilled swordsmen, but if I could steal one of their swords, I'd be in with a better chance. I quickly studied them all, wanting to choose the slowest as my target. But there wasn't a slow one among them. They held their swords like experts.

There was no more time to waste. I had to act. I swung my body and used the momentum to land some distance from the closest of my attackers. I kicked up a soggy flyer in the gutter and aimed it at him. It was a pathetic projectile and he simply batted it away.

He came at me again, his three companions alongside him. I couldn't fight off all of them at once.

I sank into a recessed doorway and tried the handle at my back. Locked. There was no time to pick it. If safety waited for me beyond the door, I couldn't get to it. I had to take my chances outside.

I changed plans. I would surrender. Tactical surrender, Giselle had called it. Lull them into a false sense of security and use my second hidden weapon to catch them off guard.

The men, however, stopped as a fifth one arrived. Despite being elderly and unarmed, seeing him sent a chill down my spine.

"Good morning, niece." Uncle Roderic's twisted smile contrasted sharply with his casual greeting. "I'm so pleased to see you alive and well, Jacqueline. I'm sure you must be keen to go home. Please. Come with me. We have so much to talk about."

The four guards all pointed their swords at my chest. I dropped my knife and put my hands in the air.

CHAPTER 13

*U*ncle Roderic moved closer. He'd changed little since I'd last seen him. He was still the same small and somewhat nondescript man with slightly stooped shoulders. What set him apart from other elderly men was his sharp gaze as he regarded me.

"You're filthy, Jacqueline. Is that soot?"

My second knife was hidden in my boot. If I could remove it without anyone noticing, I might be able to injure one of the guards and take his sword. Armed with a good weapon, I might be in with a chance of fighting off the other three.

"Come home and have a nice bath," Uncle Roderic went on. "I'll have my cook make you something delicious for breakfast. What do you like?"

"You wouldn't need to ask me that if you'd taken the time to find out when I first went to live with you, instead of locking me in a room and leaving me to die."

He scoffed. "That's a rather dramatic memory you have."

"My memory is faultless."

"True, but that doesn't mean you're not prone to exaggeration. Girls often are."

I tensed. "You can't arrest me without just cause."

"This isn't an arrest. I'm merely a concerned uncle bringing his wayward niece home. As your male relative, I'm within my rights to do so."

"Women can't be forced to stay with their abuser."

"Me? An abuser? No one will believe that. I'm a firm leader, but I don't use force."

"Not in public."

"I admit my housekeeper may have been a little overzealous in carrying out my instructions."

"She did nothing that wasn't by your order." I hoped my plight would appeal to the more kindhearted of the four guards, but none looked like they cared enough about the young woman defying the man who paid their wages. I'd get no help from them.

Uncle Roderic ordered them to take me to the end of the street where his carriage was waiting. When I didn't move, one of the swordsmen poked me with the point of his blade.

"I'll never give you what you want," I said as I walked. "I can't. I don't know how to make the pendant perform magic any more than you do."

"Quiet," he hissed. "We'll talk later."

The sword poked into my back, forcing me forward. Up ahead, the carriage rolled into view at the end of the street. Another guard opened the door. I wouldn't be able to escape that way. My best chance lay in the narrow street with its over-hanging roofs that were almost within my reach. All I needed was to find a way to get onto the roof, or somehow use it to my advantage. But there were no barrels or crates in that part of the street to push myself higher, and I wasn't tall enough to simply jump up and grab onto the overhanging tiles without leverage. I wished I'd learned to use the wall as Rhys had, but it wasn't a skill Giselle covered in training.

My window of opportunity shrank rapidly as we drew closer to the carriage. I needed to act fast.

I glanced over my shoulder as if to say something to my

uncle, then pretended to stumble over my own feet. As I fell, I removed the knife from my boot and struck one of the guards in the thigh. As his step faltered, and before the others had time to react, I slashed him across the back of his hand. He instinctively released his sword. I grabbed it before it hit the cobblestones and rolled out of the way as one of the other guards plunged his blade down.

"Get her!" my uncle shouted.

One of the other three guards had already reacted, however, and charged at me without a moment's hesitation or thought. He underestimated me. Just as Giselle said most men would, he assumed I couldn't wield a sword, so he didn't put any effort into coming up with a strategy. He thought one blow would disarm me.

I easily parried it, and the next. When he realized I was trained, he fell back, keeping his distance. My advantage of surprise had vanished. The uninjured guards regrouped, preparing to attack together. I could fend off two moderately skillful swordsmen, but not three well-trained ones.

While two kept me busy, the other came at me from the side. I saw him out of the corner of my eye and just had time to leap backward. The blade sliced through my flesh, but the cut was shallow. Even so, I sucked air between my teeth at the sting.

"I want her alive," my uncle reminded them. "Don't kill her. Cut her face instead."

The three swordsmen came at me. I scrambled backward until I slammed into the wall. The breath left my body and my vision blurred, but I could still see the three blades rushing toward me, this time aimed at my face. I squeezed my eyes shut against the terror consuming me like a fire. I would not give my uncle the satisfaction of seeing my fear.

The sound of booted feet running on cobblestones preceded the whine of a steel blade being unsheathed. I opened my eyes just in time to see Rhys tackling all three swordsmen. He'd come from the other end of the street from the carriage.

One guard fell, knocking his head on the cobblestones. The second also fell but couldn't get up with Rhys's boot pinning him there while he dispatched the third with an effortless strike to the throat. The fourth man, the one I'd disarmed and injured, had retrieved the dead guard's sword and now came at Rhys. He met a quick end, too.

My uncle shouted at the guard standing by the carriage to come to the aid of his fallen comrades. I pushed off from the wall, picked up a sword, and ran toward him. I expected Rhys to command me to stop, but he didn't utter a word as I dashed to the side just in time to avoid the guard's strike. While his momentum overbalanced him, I struck the back of his leg. He fell to his knees, shouting in pain.

"This is a private matter!" my uncle snarled at Rhys. "It's nothing to do with Merdu's Guards."

Rhys ignored him. He spoke to the guard beneath his boot. "If you try anything, I will kill you."

The guard quickly nodded.

Rhys stepped away. He looked at me, frowning with concern. "You're hurt."

"A little cut," I said, touching my side. My fingers came away sticky with blood.

Rhys strode toward me.

"You're lovers!" Uncle Roderic snarled.

"No," I said. "Just friends."

My uncle pointed at Rhys. "Wait until your order hears how you betrayed them. The brothers won't want you as master after I tell them you break your vows while they suffer a life of deprivation."

"It's me you want! I'll come with you if you promise to leave Rhys out of this." I stepped toward my uncle, but my legs buckled and my head spun. My steps faltered.

Rhys caught me before I hit the ground. With arm wrapped around me and his other hand clutching his sword, he helped me out of the street, past my uncle's carriage.

Uncle Roderic's cry of "Stop him!" was ignored. No guards came for us.

Once we were safe, Rhys sheathed his sword and scooped me up in his arms. I closed my eyes and rested my head against his shoulder. The vein in his throat throbbed rapidly but steadily, and the familiar scent of him surrounded me. I relaxed. I was safe.

Either I fell asleep or slipped into unconsciousness because we seemed to arrive quickly at his secret room. I didn't even notice if we'd been seen. He set me down on the armchair and crouched before me. He tore open my shirt at my side.

"Jac," he said, pressing his hand against the wound. "Jac, stay with me."

"I'm fine. It's just a small cut."

"Then why did you faint?"

"Because I'm a girl?" It was meant as a joke, but once again it fell flat with Rhys.

"You're not a girl. You're a woman."

I smiled and tried to sit up.

"Don't move. You'll make it worse. Give me your hand." He took my hand and pressed it against the cut. "I'll be back in a moment. Keep the pressure on it."

He left.

That's when the pain truly set in. Where before the cut had stung no worse than a bee sting, it now felt like a blacksmith had set up a forge in my side. It throbbed and burned all at once.

It was a relief when Rhys returned carrying a bowl of water and an armful of supplies. He crouched at my side again and cleaned the wound. Or tried to.

I jerked away. "It really hurts."

"Good."

"Sadist."

The corner of his mouth lifted with his half-smile. "Pain means you're alive and fully conscious. So pain is good."

"No, it bloody well isn't."

He went to clean the wound again, but I moved once more. He scowled at me. "I have to clean it before I can apply the salve. The salve will numb the pain, but until then, I'm afraid it will hurt a little."

"A little! It seems you've become the master of understatement while I was away."

"And you've become dramatic. Didn't you get injured in Giselle's training?"

"I was never cut."

"Then your training wasn't hard enough." When I shrank away for the third time, his voice gentled. "I only need one hand to do this, so hold my other. Squeeze it when the pain becomes too intense."

"Will you stop then?"

"No, but it'll make you feel better to inflict pain on me."

"I don't want to hurt you, Rhys. I never did."

He lowered his gaze. "That may be so, but I deserve it after the way I spoke to you yesterday."

"You were upset and in shock."

"That's no excuse." He took my hand and rubbed his thumb across my knuckles. His gaze lifted and locked with mine. "I'm sorry, Jac."

I sucked in a sharp breath as the pain spiked again. I'd been too distracted by his beautiful eyes to realize it was a tactic. I clenched my back teeth and tried to stay as still as possible. Holding his hand helped. Although it wouldn't make the pain stop entirely, I squeezed anyway.

When he finished, he grunted. "Can you let go now? I need the bones in my left hand sometimes."

I released him. "Now who's being dramatic."

He cleaned his hands in the water then dried them on a second cloth before scooping out a dollop of the herbal salve from a pot. It smelled familiar. "This will be gentler than the cleaning, and once it has soaked in, it will numb the pain."

I watched as he applied it. The creamy mixture tingled a little but was blessedly cool against my burning skin. "Does Mistress Blundle make it?"

"She does, but don't tell anyone or she'll get into trouble."

"Why would she get into trouble? Women can be apothecaries."

"But not give medical advice. She's better than most doctors in this city." He wiped his finger on the cloth and set the pot on the table. "How did you know the salve came from her?"

"I smell herbs whenever I pass her door. I'm surprised the authorities haven't realized yet. The smell isn't subtle."

He picked up the bandage and indicated I should sit forward. He leaned closer to reach behind me and begin wrapping the bandage around my middle, but suddenly sat back. "You can do this on your own." He dropped the bandage on my lap then retreated to the window. He perched on the ledge and looked out over the city.

It would have been easier if he helped me, but I understood why he couldn't. I managed on my own. "How did you know I was in trouble?"

He scratched his beard. "I didn't. I was coming to see you to apologize. I couldn't sleep last night after we talked. I didn't want to leave things that way between us. I felt…" He crossed his arms and shook his head at the sky. "I always take that street to the Cat and Mouse."

"So do I." I lowered my bloodied, tattered shirt over the bandage. "You can turn around now."

He hesitated a moment before looking at me. "How did the governor know you were staying at the Cat?"

"I don't think he did."

"He must have, otherwise why know to position his guards there and lie in wait for you?"

"They followed me." At his arched brows, I steeled myself for the lecture I knew he'd give after learning the truth. "I snuck into his office this morning with the cleaners to look for my pendant. I presume I was spotted and his men followed me.

They saved their encounter for the quietest street where they were least likely to be disturbed."

His lecture never came, but his frown deepened. "Four men followed you without your knowledge?" He shook his head. "Unlikely. What about Giselle?"

"You think *she* told him?"

"No, but she may have been followed if the governor knew you worked for her."

"He doesn't know. Nor does anyone else."

"Where is the ill friend she's been calling on?"

"I don't know," I muttered, my thoughts heading in a different direction. "I took a book from his office. It's one I've seen before, and I think it might be important."

"Important how?"

"I'm not sure. I wanted to read it but dropped it during the fight." I stood and was pleased that my side didn't hurt. That salve was a marvel. "I have to retrieve it."

He stood, too. "You're not going back to the Cat and Mouse, Jac. It's not safe. I'll get the book and bring it to you."

"I don't think I should stay here."

"I won't come in. I'll leave the book at the door and knock once."

"It's not that. I can't hide forever, Rhys."

"I understand, but just for now, while you heal."

"Very well. But you *can* visit me. We can talk."

He gathered the bowl of water, cloths and pot of salve. "I think it's best if I don't. I've said what I wanted to say, and that's the end of it." He didn't look at me as he spoke, but at a spot beyond my right shoulder.

"So…we can't be friends again?"

He paused, one hand on the door handle. "We will be. One day." He opened the door.

"Wait." I cleared my throat. "I have questions."

He closed the door but remained standing in front of it. He

still didn't look directly at me. "I'll try to answer them, but there are some things that are best left unanswered."

"They're not personal questions."

Some of the tension left his shoulders. "Oh. Right."

"Not everything is about you, Rhys."

His gaze narrowed, but at least it finally fell on me. A faint smile touched his lips.

"The city is calmer since I left," I said. "Did my uncle have anything to do with that?"

"Only in that he lost some of his power. Funds were removed from his office and funneled into civil projects instead. Those projects employ a great many people. People with wages tend to have less need to steal basic necessities."

"Did you have anything to do with his corruption being exposed?"

"I thought your questions weren't about me."

"Sometimes they're about you. I heard Merdu's Guards have rounded up the worst offenders and gang members, something the constables couldn't do. I presume that was done on your order."

He shifted his weight. "I was…wandering about the city," he said carefully. "Removing the gangs was an unintended consequence of my…wanderings."

Once Rhys realized my uncle hadn't captured me, he must have searched for me in the dens of known gangs, thinking I'd been taken as some sort of slave. Rhys may have merely threatened my uncle, but I suspected he acted on his threats to get the gang members to talk. Knowing my absence had driven Rhys to such lengths sickened me. Giselle may have explained the reason for not giving him my note, but I couldn't forgive her yet.

Rhys shifted his weight from one foot to the other. "The city should be safer for you to move back, but you need to keep away from your uncle. Even if he is removed from office over his corruption, he is still a threat to you."

"I know he was aggressive today, but he won't kill me while he thinks I can unlock the power he believes the pendant holds."

"And when he realizes you can't? He won't simply release you, Jac."

"I would have escaped by then."

"He found you once. He could find you again. All he has to do is find Giselle and follow her until she leads him to you, *if* you continue working for her."

"I don't think he followed her this time. For one thing, he would need to see her to follow her. When and where did he do that? Secondly, he sent Giselle a letter some time ago, wanting to hire her to find me. That proves he doesn't know I work for her."

"It proves he didn't know *then*."

I sighed heavily. "Rhys, Giselle isn't working for him. She could have tricked me numerous times and handed me over to him. She hasn't."

He turned to go. With a hand on the door handle, he paused, and presented me with his profile. He still couldn't look directly at me. "There's one more thing. You heard the governor threaten to ruin my reputation today, but that's not a new threat. He has been saying that ever since I...made inquiries while looking for you."

"If you want me to speak to the priests in your order and assure them we're just friends, I'll do it."

"It's more than you and me. He has been paying women to say they've been with me. Several have already come forward. He's using them to undermine my authority and have the brothers question my dedication. He's trying to destabilize the order to diminish our power."

"It won't work. The brothers chose you as their leader. They know how dedicated you are to Merdu's Guards. Anyone who knows you can see it."

"I'm dedicated to the order. Not so dedicated to all its rules." His fingers drummed on the door handle. "The problem is, I can

deny some of the women's claims, but not all. I have been with…
a few." He cleared his throat. "Before."

The reminder that he'd taken lovers while in the order
always pinched my heart. He'd been happy to break his vows
for them. Apparently, he wasn't tempted enough by me.

"Jac?"

I looked up and saw that he was watching me with a frown.

"You understand it was some time ago, don't you?"

I nodded. Smiled. Pretended it didn't matter. "Of course."

He studied the door handle before opening the door and
leaving.

It wasn't until later that I wished I'd asked him if my uncle's
efforts to destabilize the order were working.

* * *

I WAITED until nightfall to return to the Cat and Mouse to collect
my things and see Giselle. I took the longer way, staying on the
busier roads as much as possible. I found her surrounded by a
group of men listening intently as she told them a story about
the time she tricked the sheriff of a small Vytill village into
releasing her from prison after she'd been arrested for public
drunkenness. She told the story with such enthusiasm that she
seemed to light up from within.

When she finished, they laughed and clapped her on the
shoulder. Some offered to buy her a drink. She saw me and
shooed them off. "I want to speak to my friend alone."

One man winked at me as he turned away. "Lucky you." His
heated gaze swept my length. "And her."

I rolled my eyes and sat beside Giselle. "You're in a good
mood. Is your friend better?"

The light in her eyes fizzled out. "No, but I've come to
terms with her death. Instead of mourning her passing, I'm
going to celebrate and honor her life. Join me for a drink, Jac."
She took one of the tankards a man had set before her and

handed it to me. She picked up another. "Where have you been?"

"My uncle tried to abduct me."

She lowered the tankard to the table with a thud. "You escaped, I see." She blew out a measured breath. "Well done, Jac."

"Rhys came at the right moment. I wouldn't have escaped without his help."

"Where did it happen?"

"Near here. Rhys was coming to speak to me. His timing was fortunate."

"How did the governor know you were here?"

"His men must have followed me from his office. I was there early this morning in disguise, but his guards must have seen through it."

She frowned and shook her head. "You would have noticed someone follow you."

"I don't have eyes in the back of my head, Giselle."

She sipped her ale, still frowning. When she finished, she wiped her mouth with the back of her hand. "He probably knows you're staying here if the attempted abduction happened nearby. We need to move. Tonight."

"*I'll* move. There's no need for you to leave. Your network is here." I nodded at the publican, a man Giselle trusted to feed information and clients to her.

She cradled the tankard in both hands. "It may be wise to split up. Where will you go? You can't return to your old home. Your uncle knows it."

"Don't worry about me. I have a place."

She arched her brows. "You're not even going to tell me?"

"It's Rhys's place. He swore me to secrecy years ago."

She held up a hand. "Very well. At least I know you'll be safe with him."

"He's not there," I clarified. "He'll be at the order's garrison, as always."

Giselle watched me over the rim of the tankard as she sipped. "There is nothing between Rhys and I," I added.

"I know." She set the tankard down. "But I heard something today. Something that puts Rhys in a predicament. His lovers are coming forward."

"They're not *all* his lovers."

"Are you sure?"

"He told me so. He also told me the governor is paying these women to come forward now. He's using them in the hope it will turn the brothers against Rhys. Hopefully it won't work. His past was known to most, if not all, before he was elected as the new master. Even if there are more women than they realized, it won't change the fact that Rhys is an excellent leader."

Giselle's gaze narrowed as she watched me. "Apparently the high priest is furious with him."

"I'm sure he was already aware of Rhys's past, too."

"Most likely, but that was when the women kept the details to themselves. Splashing it all over the city is not merely embarrassing, it undermines the high priest's authority. If he lets it go unpunished, it looks as though he condones priests breaking their vows."

She had a point. The high priest would have to punish Rhys, perhaps via a public apology and a renewal of his vows.

Giselle leaned forward. "Jac, don't get tangled up in Rhys's mess. He is not your concern. I know you care for him, and nothing I say will change that, but he has chosen the order. He has chosen the life he wants. You now have an identity wholly separate from his. Protect it and you will blossom."

Having an independence from Rhys was something Giselle had wanted for me from the moment she'd offered me a position as her apprentice. Seeing her holding court with several men listening enraptured to her every word, wanting to be with her and within her orbit, I knew she wanted that for me, too. It was why she'd chosen not to give Rhys my message the day we'd left Tilting. As much as it still angered me, I understood her motive.

She was right about this, too. I *had* forged an identity for myself that was separate from Rhys. I needed to continue on the path I was already on if I was to have a fulfilling future.

Tomorrow, I would find somewhere else to live. Somewhere separate from Rhys and from Giselle, too. Somewhere that was mine.

"Where will I find you when I need you?" she asked.

"Light a candle in the window of your room here at the Cat. I'll come past every night, and if I see the candle, I know it means you have a task for me. But I'm not returning to Upway with you, Giselle. Tilting is my home. I plan to stay. My uncle is quite old and can't live forever, but while he lives, I'll stay hidden."

She lifted her tankard in salute. "I approve of your plan, because it's yours, Jac. I don't necessarily think it's wise to stay, but I respect your decision."

* * *

WHEN I ARRIVED BACK at Rhys's secret room, the book was leaning against the door, a rolled-up pallet beside it. I placed the book on the small table, then laid the pallet on the floor. I must have fallen asleep instantly.

When I awoke in the morning, the cut in my side had begun to throb again. To distract myself, I went in search of food at the market. As much as I wanted one of Mistress Lowey's pies, I avoided her husband's stall. I didn't want to cause them any problems.

I kept my hood up as I ate a rather ordinary sausage wrapped in flat bread, regretting that I hadn't agreed to the sauce the butcher recommended. Today would be a good day to find new accommodation, but first, I wanted to sneak into my uncle's house while he was at his office and search for my pendant.

There would be staff to avoid, but I knew he retained only a few, and all his personal guards would be with him, not at the house. If I was careful, no one would see me. Hopefully my injury wouldn't hinder me too much.

The way to his house took me near the temple of Merdu's Guards, although not directly past it. I'd had no intention of getting any closer, but changed my mind when I saw the high priest's carriage heading in that direction. A glimpse of the high priest's angry profile through the window worried me.

I gave my sausage and bread to a homeless man huddled in a doorway and ran. Instead of using the main roads, I took a shorter way, careful not to overexert myself and make the wound in my side bleed again. I reached the temple as the main gates opened to let the high priest's carriage through.

Beyond the open gates, I could just make out the courtyard where the brothers gathered, standing in rows, waiting. It seemed to be all of them, and they weren't training. They were lined up as if to hear a speech or have a meeting.

I made sure no one saw me enter the quiet street alongside the temple, or pick the lock of the old tower door. I climbed the stairs then crouched low at the crenellated parapet so as not to be seen from below.

I counted over fifty brothers in the courtyard. Rhys stood facing them, while the high priest alighted from his carriage. He moved to stand beside Rhys and signaled to his guards.

That's when I noticed one of them carried a length of rope. Rhys put out his hands, wrists together. He was going to be tied up!

"Is this necessary?" Andreas barked. He, Vizah and Rufus stood in the front row. None of them were armed. Nor were the other brothers.

Rhys said something I couldn't hear. Whatever it was made Andreas shake his head, but he didn't interject again. They all fell silent as Rhys's hands were bound in front him.

One of the guards placed a set of low steps in front of the high priest. He climbed to the top step and put out his hands, as if calling for calm, but the brothers were already silent. The hush felt wrong in that place of masculinity and athleticism, where I'd previously heard sounds of clashing steel, grunts of effort, teasing words and even raucous laughter.

"Brothers of Merdu's Guards!" the high priest began. "We gather here for the trial of your master, Rhys Mayhew."

Trial!

The high priest accepted a document from one of his guards and read. "These women have come forth to claim sexual relations with Master Rhys, after he joined the order. Tatiana Plummer. Cath Goodes."

Vizah stepped forward, only to be halted by one of the high priest's guards who pointed a sword at his chest. Vizah scowled. "Those women are from years ago, well before Rhys became master."

"When the *incidents* occurred is irrelevant. He belonged to this order at the time." The high priest resumed reading out names.

"Is this necessary?" Rufus asked.

The high priest ignored him and continued to read from the list.

Throughout it all, Rhys remained very still. He looked composed, as if he were merely standing there looking out at a pleasant scene, his hands loosely clasped in front of him. If I couldn't see the rope, the guards' swords or the brothers growing angrier with the announcement of each name, I'd have thought nothing was amiss.

The high priest continued down the list, stopping when he got to the end. He hadn't finished, however. He'd merely got to a name he was reluctant to read out. He adjusted his grip on the list and began to roll it up. "And Jacqueline Trenchant."

Hearing my full name read out was confirmation the list of names was drawn up by my uncle.

"Not her," Rhys said as some of the brothers pointed out that the governor's niece died years ago.

While the priests seemed to accept his correction, it didn't dampen their ire or disappointment. Some hissed at Rhys, others shook their heads sadly. Some openly called him a betrayer and oath breaker.

The high priest ordered them to calm down. "Do you deny the testimony of the other women, Master Rhys?" He slapped his hand against the paper.

"It's not testimony," Rufus cried. "It's a list of names! They could be anyone."

"I have verified most. Are you questioning me, Brother Rufus?"

"Enough!" Rhys shouted. "Let's get this over with. It's true I was with some of those women years ago. I was young, foolish, stubborn, and lacked discipline. Those are not excuses, they are facts. It is also a fact that I broke the sacred oath of celibacy. For that, I want to apologize to all of you. What I did wasn't fair on every brother who keeps his oath. The high priest is right to hold this trial. I am guilty. I'm ready for my punishment."

"Rhys!" Rufus cried.

"Twenty lashes!" the high priest announced.

Lashes! They were going to whip him! I pressed my forehead to the parapet, but the stone didn't cool the rage swelling within me, or soothe the ache in my chest. I felt hopeless and weak. The skills Giselle had taught me couldn't help me fight against so many powerful men, even if they weren't armed.

There was nothing I could do to stop them torturing Rhys.

CHAPTER 14

"*A*re you going to simply accept this?" Rufus shouted at his friend.

Rhys held out his bound hands and one of the guards untied them. He went to help Rhys remove his tunic, but Rhys did it himself. Naked from the waist up, he walked past the high priest and several guards to a post at the far side of the courtyard. I'd seen it before and presumed it was used to tie horses to. Rhys stood facing it and circled his arms around it.

The guard with the rope tied Rhys's hands together again.

"That's not necessary," Rufus growled.

"It's protocol," the high priest said.

"Bollocks to protocol!"

The high priest bristled.

Rhys shook his head at his friends in warning. "If you can't accept my punishment then leave. You're within your rights to do so."

"Rights," Rufus snarled. "This is a farce. If you're being punished for being with these women, then so should most of them!" He pointed at his fellow brothers in a sweeping arc. "How many of you can say you've kept the oath of celibacy, or the vow of poverty?"

"Go!" Rhys growled.

Rufus stormed off to the garrison, shaking his head. Vizah followed, but not before casting a forlorn look back at Rhys, tied to the post. He, too, shook his head before disappearing inside.

Andreas stayed. He moved up to be closer to Rhys, but without his sword, he couldn't fight off the high priest's guards to free Rhys. Indeed, I doubted he wanted to. Rhys wouldn't want him to, either.

The biggest of the guards retrieved a leather strap from a box. He pulled hard on the ends as he moved up behind Rhys. The crack of the leather was loud in the courtyard. He struck the first blow across Rhys's bare back before I was even ready.

Rhys wasn't ready either, if his grunt was any indication. A red welt striped his back, but the blow hadn't drawn blood.

I bit my tongue to stop myself crying out. Being discovered wouldn't help Rhys. It would only make them think I was indeed one of his lovers, just as the high priest's list claimed. There was nothing to do except endure.

I wanted to turn my face away and block my ears to the sounds of the whip flaying flesh, but I forced myself to watch. Rhys had to endure it. So could I.

After the tenth lash, tears were rolling uncontrollably down my cheeks. By the twentieth, blood oozed from the wounds on Rhys's back. Apart from the first blow, Rhys had remained silent as each lash of the strap struck.

The moment the last one had been inflicted, Andreas rushed forward and untied his hands. Rhys stepped away from the post, rolled his shoulders and tilted his head from side to side, stretching his neck muscles.

Then he slowly turned around. His face was impassive, with not a hint of pain on it. He thanked the guard who'd whipped him, as if the man had done Rhys a favor. The guard nodded, respectful.

I pressed a hand to my chest over my heart. It ached. My throat was tight and my tears still flowed. It felt as though I'd never be able to stop crying. I desperately wanted to speak to Rhys and tend to his wounds as he'd so gently tended to mine.

But he remained in the courtyard. Even if he entered the garrison, how would I get in there without being seen?

He addressed the high priest. "If your business is concluded, Your Eminence, the men need to train."

"Of course." The high priest stepped down from his platform and did something I didn't expect. He embraced Rhys, careful not to touch the wounds on his back. "My son, I am sorry, but it is the law of Merdu's Guards."

"I know."

"You took your punishment with courage and fortitude. You have admitted the faults of your past." He drew in a breath. It was difficult to tell from a distance, but it looked as though his eyes glistened with unshed tears. "You embody every quality that a master of Merdu's Guards needs to possess. I support you as master, if you say you are committed."

"I am."

Was it a tactic? Was the entire thing a show, put on by the high priest to appease those who were angry with Rhys for breaking his vow? He'd just proved to them all how strong Rhys was, how brave. These men respected courage, pride and the physical embodiment of masculinity, and the high priest knew that whipping Rhys in front of them was the best way to prove to them that he possessed those qualities in abundance.

Had Rhys known?

"Good," the high priest declared. "Now, we vote."

"Vote?" Andreas asked. "For what?"

"For Rhys to remain as master of the order of Merdu's Guards."

Andreas and the other brothers looked confused. The high priest merely repeated the question.

"A show of hands. Who wishes to keep Rhys as master of the order of Merdu's Guards?"

Hands went up all over the courtyard. I quickly counted.

There wasn't quite enough. Andreas shouted for Vizah and Rufus to come back out. Moments later, when they understood the situation, they both raised their hands. Rufus glowered at the high priest the entire time.

Their votes were enough to keep Rhys as master, but the near-even split meant he clung to the position by his fingernails. It was what Uncle Roderic wanted, a destabilizing of the order, and of Rhys's authority in particular.

The high priest had done his best to reinstate respect for Rhys with that display at the whipping post. It had worked. Several priests who'd been vocal in condemning Rhys as the list of names was read out had voted in Rhys's favor. The high priest had gambled and won. It was the outcome he'd wanted after my uncle's efforts created discord.

Rhys had become a key component in the game between two powerful men, both using him for their own ends. It was unfair, but there was nothing to be done now. Hopefully this was the end.

"You have voted," the high priest declared. "Rhys remains as master. I know he will lead you all with humility and courage. You should be proud to have him as your leader. I've never seen another like him in my lifetime. Nor had Master Tomaj. Remember, Rhys was *his* choice because Rhys is the best choice."

Rhys thanked him for his words with a nod. "I will not let you down again. None of you. I'll pray to Merdu for forgiveness, but it is your forgiveness I now seek. I promise to be a better priest in future."

It was Rhys's promise that got more heads nodding, even some who'd voted against him. The speech from the high priest had been good, but Rhys's had been the one they needed to hear.

Not all were swayed, however. A few walked off, disgusted.

I was relieved to see Rhys return to the garrison after the high priest left. The brothers began their training session, but none of Rhys's close friends joined in. Hopefully they were tending to his wounds.

Despite every fiber of my being wanting to see him, I knew I couldn't. His position as master was too precarious and the presence of a woman in the temple complex would undermine his authority further.

I continued on my way to Uncle Roderic's house. I knew the layout well, and the staff routines. The cook would be in the kitchen, her assistant most likely shopping at the market. The housemaids would be cleaning, while the male staff would be in the service rooms doing their chores. The outdoor staff were the most likely to see me, especially since I needed to cross the garden, but it was the housekeeper I wanted to avoid above all others. The dragon had been the one to lock me in, the one who'd slapped my cheek when I'd cried, and deprived me of food. From the way her eyes shone as she called me names, she'd enjoyed being jailor of my sixteen-year-old self.

After checking that no one was about, I climbed a large tree on the street side, and crawled along a branch, dropping down onto the stone wall surrounding the property. From the high vantage point, it was easy to see if the gardeners were about. Only one was visible as he trimmed a hedge in the formal garden. Once I was on the ground, he wouldn't be able to see me, nor me him.

I lowered myself to the ground and tiptoed from tree to hedge to bush, then quickly crossed to the doors that opened onto the covered porch at the rear of the house. They were locked but I had them open with my picking tools in a moment. I slipped inside, into the large salon used to receive guests. I'd intended to search it first, before moving to another room, but my uncle's voice stopped me in my tracks.

It came from his study, located next to the salon, but I couldn't make out any of his words or who he was with. If he was at home, then I'd have to come back later. I wouldn't risk searching the house with him present. His guards were most likely stationed at the front door and the door to his study.

My patience was rewarded when I heard a door open and his

voice became clearer. But his only words were to tell his visitor to keep him informed. The visitor didn't speak.

The front door opened and closed, presumably sending the visitor on his way, then my uncle informed the staff that he was leaving, too. A short while later, I heard the carriage roll up on the gravel then depart again.

The house fell silent, the staff presumably having retreated to the service areas. I slipped out of the salon and crouched at the door to my uncle's study. I picked the lock then entered and closed the door behind me.

I sniffed. Sniffed again. Two familiar scents mingled in the air. I expected my uncle's, but not the other.

Giselle.

I leaned back against the door and tried to sift through my scrambled thoughts. But out of all the possibilities, one was the most likely—if Giselle was here, it meant she'd taken on Uncle Roderic as a client. She intended to capture me for him after all.

She was going to betray me.

Had that been her plan all along? Surely not. Surely I hadn't been so dreadfully wrong about her these last months. I had believed her intentions for me were precisely as she claimed—she wanted to teach me everything she knew. Somewhere, at some point, that had changed.

Was it today? Or was it when she received Uncle Roderic's letter in Upway?

Was that why she brought me to Tilting before I was fully ready? I'd come to realize that I wasn't as skillful as she claimed. I was good, but not great. I had a lot to learn and required more rigorous training. Had she brought me to Tilting too soon so that I'd be easier to capture?

Did she even have a dying friend here at all?

Too many questions, and this was not the time and place to think them through. I had my own mission to complete.

I searched my uncle's study and bedchamber but didn't find

the pendant. I left his house empty-handed, now certain he kept it on his person for safekeeping.

I returned to Rhys's secret room and sat in the armchair. I stayed there a long time, thinking. It took a while for the fog of shock to clear and my mind to work properly, but once it did, I realized my first instinct must be correct.

I couldn't trust Giselle.

The growl of my stomach reminded me I needed to eat. I was about to leave when I spotted the book with the red cover on the table. I looked at the symbol of the sun and moon, tracing the shapes with my fingertips. The title—*Cult and Culture in the Land of Zemaya*—gave no clues as to why Giselle had been particular about stopping me from reading it.

I tucked it under my arm and headed out to a tavern I'd never frequented before. I settled in to read as I ate a hearty stew, but had to finish the bowl quicker than I intended. The other patrons, all men, wouldn't leave me alone, and the final straw came when one offered me a pouch full of ells to be his mistress.

I stood, picked up the pouch, opened it and tipped the coins onto the table. "You insult me," I said, tucking the book under my arm.

"You want more?" he asked, hopeful. "I have more."

I rolled my eyes and pushed past him. I hurried home, in case he or one of the others followed me. I'd been a fool to think I could frequent a tavern where I wasn't known. Giselle might be good at frightening men away with a mere glare, but I wasn't. It was another reminder that we were not alike. I wasn't ready.

I would probably never be ready to be an assassin.

The knowledge didn't concern me in the least.

It was dark when I reached the room. I lit a candle and placed it on the windowsill. I desperately wanted to know how Rhys fared after his punishment, and I needed to speak to him, too. He'd been right all along not to trust Giselle. I should have listened to him.

I settled into the armchair and read the book. My eyes were

growing weary, and I'd slumped down when I reached a chapter that made me sit up straight. I angled the book to the candlelight and reread the paragraph mentioning the story about the talisman. Just as my mother and our female ancestors claimed, the book stated that there was an old Zemayan legend about the sorcerer placing power into a talisman.

But the talisman wasn't my pendant, and the power was not magical.

I closed the book and hugged it to my chest. I stared at nothing in particular until my eyes stung from exhaustion, then lay down on the pallet. At some point, the candle had burned down and extinguished. My good memory served me well as I recalled incidents from my past, going back to my earliest memories of happy times with my parents. It was painful to think of them again. My childhood had been idyllic, and I'd loved them both dearly. Their loss had been a wrench. My mother's loss in particular had preceded the most frightening and lonely time of my life.

It was late. Rhys wasn't coming. I desperately needed to talk to him, however, and I resolved to get word to him in the morning.

But it was Rhys who got word to me. When I returned from my breakfast at the market, I found a note from him under the door, stating that he needed to see me away from prying eyes and that the secret room was no longer a safe place. He asked me to meet him at the ruined fort at noon then signed it with his signature of a bold, sharp R.

I quickly crossed to the balcony doors and stepped out. I peered down at the street below and watched as folk went about their business in the spring sunshine, not lingering in front of this rather ordinary building. If someone was watching it, they were well hidden.

The delightful smells of Mistress Blundle's herbal concoctions filled my lungs as I breathed in deeply. With a wry smile and a glance in the direction of the temple of Merdu's Guards, I made up my mind.

* * *

A LITTLE WHILE LATER, I took the northern road out of Tilting. The old fort was some distance out of the city and it took time to reach it. Although built by the ancients to keep the Barbarian hordes out, the wild folk from the Margin had never ended up crossing the river into Glancia, so the fort had fallen into ruin hundreds of years ago. Only sections of the stone walls were still in place, the rest having disappeared over time. Long grass licked at the ruins' foundations and yellow wildflowers swayed in the light breeze, their fragrance pungent after being recently crushed underfoot.

The high temple's bell chimed in the distance as I arrived. I was right on time, but I wasn't alone.

"Jac?" Giselle had been lazing on a large fallen stone worked into a smooth block when she suddenly sat up as I approached. Her horse grazed at the edge of the clearing, the reins loosely tethered to a tree stump. "What are you doing here?"

"I was summoned. Why are you here?"

"I received a note from Rhys asking to meet me." She looked around and shrugged. "Why here?"

"Because it's out of the way." The fort was located on a disused track that had been abandoned along with the building many years ago. It was a good place for a rendezvous. Carriages couldn't navigate the rough track and the fort couldn't be seen from the busier northern road. No one would come here if they didn't have to.

"Why does he want to meet us in an out-of-the-way place?" Giselle asked. "Jac, what's going on?"

"Stop the games, Giselle. I know you wrote the note, not Rhys."

She made a scoffing sound. "Me? That's absurd. Why would I write myself a note? And you, for that matter?"

"You didn't write yourself one, and you signed mine with Rhys's signature."

"Are you implying it wasn't his signature? Was it forged?"

"It was forged, by you, and it was a very good forgery. I wouldn't have guessed it was fake except for one thing."

Curiosity got the better of her. She no longer denied having written the note. "What thing?"

"Whenever Rhys leaves me a note at our meeting place, he has never signed it. Not once. Why would he bother when no one else would leave me a note there? How did you know that's where we met?"

Her gaze flicked to the track. "He'll be on his way to rescue you."

"I didn't tell him or send for him," I said. "Rhys is indisposed at the moment. This is between you and me, Giselle, and it ends here. I know you're working for my uncle. I know you lured me here so you could capture me and take me to him. Did he offer you more money this time to get you to change your mind? Or did you in fact agree months ago after you received his letter in Upway?"

"Ah, Jac. Sweet, innocent girl. Rhys has turned your head and got you believing I'm your enemy. I'm not. I'm your friend, your mentor. I swear on everything I hold dear that your uncle didn't hire me to capture you."

"Bollocks! For one thing, you hold nothing dear. For another, I know you met my uncle this morning. Don't deny it. I smelled your scent in his study."

"I don't have a scent. I stopped using the orange blossom a while ago. I told you that. I don't use anything made with a scent anymore."

"Because you don't want me to detect you. I know. But you didn't realize that everyone has a unique scent. In fact, in a rather ironic twist, by not using the orange blossom soap anymore, I was able to get to know your true odor. I'm quite familiar with it after living with you for a while."

She scoffed. "That's absurd. No one can smell a person's unique scent unless they sweat, and then it's all the same."

"Most people can't detect a difference, but I can." I removed the book from the waistband at the back of my trousers and tossed it to her.

She caught it deftly. "You stole my book!"

"I stole my uncle's copy. It's rather amusing to think if he'd just read all of the books he owned, he would have realized a long time ago that the talisman isn't my pendant. The stone doesn't hold any power. I do. The talisman is me."

She showed no surprise, and didn't deny it. She'd given up on the ruse altogether. She watched me carefully, as if she expected me to draw a weapon at any moment.

"Thanks to you, I'm better trained at fighting," I said. "Adding that to my good memory and heightened senses, I'll make a good assassin. When did you realize I was the talisman? Before you hired me? Or in Upway?"

She laughed softly and set the book down on the stone she'd been sitting on. "Unlike your uncle, I've read all the books I own." She tapped the cover. "This one stated the sorcerer gave a talisman in *human form* the power of superior senses plus a memory that forgot nothing. One human per generation— always a woman from the same family. When I first read it, I assumed it was just a story and thought nothing of it. Then I met you. I soon realized you fit the description. *You* were the talisman. I also realized that no one else knew, not even you. You're right in that I thought you'd make an excellent assassin, Jac. Unfortunately you showed no aptitude for the most important part. The killing itself."

"We can't all be as coldhearted as you."

"So I've learned over the years," she said, with a wry twist of her lips.

"What happens now?" I asked. "Shall we fight? Do we see if my superior senses can win over your experience?"

She glanced along the track again. "We wait."

"I told you, Rhys isn't coming. I haven't sent for him."

"But I have."

It was my turn to glance along the track, but there was no one there. "What do you mean?"

"I sent him a message telling him if he wanted to see you alive, he should come."

"Alive?" I shook my head. She wasn't making any sense. "Why do you want Rhys here at all? You might be able to defeat me, but you certainly can't beat him."

Giselle removed a knife from the sheath strapped to her belt. "Because of your brilliant memory, you think you're cleverer than everyone else, but you have it quite wrong. I don't want to capture you and deliver you to the governor alive. I want to kill you and blame your death on Rhys."

The breath left my body in a rush, as if she'd punched me, winding me. I didn't understand. When had she wanted me dead? Not in the beginning, I was sure of it. But some time before coming back to Tilting, she'd changed her mind and decided to abandon the scheme of training me as her apprentice and kill me instead. I stared at her, trying to catch my breath and reconcile the two versions of her. But I could not. The woman who'd been my friend and mentor now looked at me as if I'd meant nothing to her at all.

"You made up the dying friend to bring us both back here," I murmured.

"I didn't make up the dying friend, Jac. *You* are she."

I recalled her words in Upway, that she needed to 'be there for her in the end.' She was talking about me. She'd been saddened at the thought of my death. I didn't think that part was a lie. Apparently I did mean something to her, after all, just not enough to reject the fee and let me live.

"Why is it important I die here?"

"My client is in Tilting and I need to prove you're dead by producing a body. Also, Rhys is here and I want him to take the blame. Not that my client knows that part, but I'll be fulfilling his agreement so he'll have to pay me."

"No one will believe Rhys killed me."

"They will when they find the evidence I've planted. You see, he's going to kill you because he can't have you and doesn't want anyone else to, either. Men," she bit off. "Some are such passionate lovers, but when their love turns sour, that passion turns into violence."

I barked a hollow laugh. "That's a stupid motive. No one will believe it of Rhys."

"I think they will. Celibacy can drive a man mad." She tapped her temple. "Denying a man this basic need makes him act out of character, particularly when he thinks he's in love."

I removed the knife from the sheath at my belt, and moved into a better fighting position, with open space at my back so as not to be trapped against a ruined wall of the fort.

Giselle circled, too. "You're right about one thing, Jac. I can beat *you* in a fight, but not Rhys. I'll kill you a few moments before he gets here, then I'll leave before his arrival. There are some constables stationed not far from here who'll get a visit from a concerned elderly citizen with Dreen features who witnessed a horrific murder at the fort ruins. They'll find Rhys with your body. He'll deny killing you, of course, but once the constables conduct a search of the vicinity, they will find the murder weapon." She opened her palm to reveal the bone handle of the knife etched with the sun and dagger symbol of Merdu's Guards. "The warrior priests all carry one of these."

She lunged toward me, but I was ready for her and danced out of the way, kicking her in the hip as she passed me. She stumbled but didn't fall. Instead of immediately coming for me again, she settled her feet apart. It was then that I realized I no longer had the open space at my back. The fort was behind me.

Her tactic had been to gain the more advantageous position and I'd fallen for it.

"Why are you doing this?" I asked. "If my uncle isn't your client, who is?"

"Ah. This is the brilliant part. I kill two birds with one stone, if you'll pardon the pun. You see, your uncle *does* want you dead after I told him this morning that *you* possess the sorcerer's magic, not the pendant. When he realized he couldn't control you and use the power for himself, he gave up altogether on the idea of capturing you. You should have seen him. It quite broke him to learn that he'd been carrying nothing more than a pretty rock in his pocket. I offered to kill you, and he agreed, although he didn't know I was already going to kill you, on the instruction of my other client. As I was talking to the governor, I realized I could give him Rhys's head on a platter, too, by blaming him for your murder. So he's paying me twice, once for your death, and the second time for planting evidence that points to Rhys being your killer. He detests Rhys and the notion appealed to him. My first client won't like that Rhys is blamed, but that's too bad. By the time he realizes, I'll have collected my fee from him for killing you and will have left Tilting. It's rather a large sum, by the way. You should be pleased."

"Who is it? Who's your first client?"

"The man I stole this knife from. The high priest."

I gasped.

"Shocking isn't it. Imagine a man dedicated to a religion that preaches kindness stooping to murder. Well, murder by proxy." She whipped out a letter from her pocket. "He wrote to me in Upway." She tucked the letter away again and patted the pocket. "Insurance."

"Why does he want me dead?"

"Because you are an obstacle to the stability of Merdu's Guards, and Rhys's position as master, in particular. You're the reason Rhys has never fully committed to the order."

"He *has* committed!"

"No, Jac. He has been one step away from leaving ever since meeting you, so the high priest told me. Master Tomaj talked Rhys into staying on many occasions, but after he died, Rhys once again considered leaving."

"Not for me. He would have told me he..." I swallowed the lump in my throat.

"That he loved you?" She snorted. "Does he? Perhaps he thinks he does. Or perhaps he just wanted to have his way with you in that secret room without feeling guilty about breaking an oath. The room isn't so secret, by the way. I've known about it for years."

The words were barely out of her mouth when she threw a dagger at me. I dodged out of the way as it whizzed past my ear, thanks to my keen sense of sight, which had picked up the slight movement of her hand in time.

The maneuver saved my life but unbalanced me. Giselle took advantage and swiftly attacked. I managed to move just beyond the point of her blade as she struck but couldn't counterattack quickly enough. All of my energy went into defending myself and delaying my death. If Rhys received Giselle's message, he would come whether I wanted him to or not. Even with the wounds on his back from the whipping, he could beat her. I just needed to stay alive until then.

I ran through the ruins, keeping distance and pieces of wall between us. She threw another dagger at my head but once again I managed to dodge it, only to realize she'd used the moment of my preoccupation to close the gap between us. She was fast—faster than me—and fearless. She gave me no time to think through my reactions. My mind seized. I stumbled backward, tripped over a stone, and fell onto the grass.

Giselle loomed above me. "Your memory isn't so perfect when you panic, otherwise your instincts would have taken over by now."

"I didn't train long enough to develop instincts for every

attack. You saw to that. You brought me back to Tilting before I was ready."

"Why do the terrible students always blame the teacher? The truth is, you don't have the strength of character for this. It takes more than a few keen senses and a good memory to win against someone like me."

Before the final words were out of her mouth, she lunged. I just managed to roll out of the way of her descending blade, cutting her shoulder with my knife as I did so. But it must have been a mere scratch, because it didn't stop her. With a dagger in each hand now, she came at me from above. Rolling out of the way of one blade would bring me into the path of the other. She sat on my legs and bore her weight down, ensuring I couldn't wriggle free.

I was trapped. She was right. My keen senses couldn't save me.

CHAPTER 15

y tactic to delay death until Rhys arrived wasn't working. Despite my efforts, I couldn't buck Giselle off. Although I still clutched a knife, she had two. And they were about to cut my throat.

Until then, I could still use my voice. "I'll pay you!" Her hesitation encouraged me. "I'll pay you more than both your clients."

She snorted. "You can't afford me."

"I can steal the money. You know I'm a good thief. My uncle is rich and I know his house well. I'll get you the fee by the end of the week."

"Tempting but no."

"Then it's not about money, is it?"

"I thought it was, but now...for some reason, your offer is not appealing enough for me to let you go." She huffed a humorless laugh as if the realization surprised her.

I looked past her shoulder and gasped. "Thank Hailia."

"You think I'll fall for that?"

"My keen sense of hearing can pick up sounds well before you. I can determine how many approach when I hear footsteps, or hoofbeats. In this case, there are four horses just beyond the clearing." Giselle's eyes hardened. Her muscles tensed. "You summoned Rhys," I went on, "but I suspected you were up to something when I received your note, so I summoned his friends before I came here."

Her gaze flickered as she finally heard the horses. That moment of distraction was enough for me to thrust my knife toward her. She deflected the strike before the blade sank into her shoulder, but I was able to use the distraction to punch her in the side with my left fist.

With the horses drawing closer, she realized she had little time left. She abandoned her plan to kill me and ran for her horse. She rode off in the opposite direction to the four approaching warrior priests.

I stood just as Rhys leapt down from the saddle. "That way!" I shouted, pointing in the direction Giselle had gone.

Vizah, Rufus, and Andreas went after her.

Rhys cupped my face in his hands. "Jac! Are you all right? Are you hurt?"

"I'm fine." I shook like a leaf in a breeze, but I wasn't harmed.

Rhys drew me into a fierce hug, one hand buried in my hair, the other at my back. I almost threw my arms around him but remembered his wounds and instead rested my hands at his waist. I leaned into him and soaked in the comforting rhythm of his heartbeat and familiar scent.

After a moment, he drew in a deep breath and pulled away. "I'm sorry I didn't get here earlier. Neither your message nor Giselle's reached us until after training."

"Your timing was perfect. I'll have to thank Mistress Blundle." I'd given the apothecary a note to deliver to Rufus, Vizah or Andreas at the temple before I left to meet Giselle. I'd told them *not* to inform Rhys. I hadn't wanted him involved at all—his wounds were too fresh. At that point, I'd simply thought Giselle wanted to kidnap me. I hadn't known her true intention or that she'd sent a note to Rhys summoning him here just as she'd summoned me.

"You should have waited for them," Rhys told me. "You shouldn't have come alone. Merdu and Hailia, Jac, when I received Giselle's note and realized what she intended to do..." He scrubbed his bearded jaw and looked in the direction his friends had gone through the trees. "I thought we wouldn't make it."

"What did Giselle's message say?" I asked him.

"She demanded money for your release or she'd hand you over to the governor."

"Ah."

"Ah?"

"That was a trick to ensure you weren't prepared for what you saw when you got here. Her real plan wasn't to kidnap me."

He touched my chin, forcing my gaze to meet his. "What was her plan?" he asked, voice as dark as a moonless night.

The return of his friends stopped me from answering. "She got away," Andreas said as he dismounted.

"Are you all right, Jac?" Rufus asked.

"I'm unharmed, thank you."

"She was trying to kill you, wasn't she?" Vizah asked, proving he wasn't a fool.

I nodded. "She planned on blaming my murder on Rhys. That's why she wanted to lure him here, too."

Rhys frowned. "No one would believe I'd kill you."

"She planned to let the constables think you loved me but were tortured by the oath you'd taken."

None of the men met Rhys's gaze. "No one would believe it," Rhys said, somewhat forcefully.

"She was going to leave behind evidence. She had a knife engraved with the symbol of Merdu's Guards."

"She wouldn't have one in her possession," Vizah said. "Would she?"

Rhys absently scrubbed his chin through his beard then suddenly stopped. "No. No, no, no."

"What?" Andreas asked.

Rhys tipped his head back and groaned. "Master Tomaj's knife went missing after his death. It wasn't on his body."

"How did Giselle get her hands on it?"

Rhys looked to me. He knew me so well that he could tell when something troubled me. "Jac?"

It was the moment I was dreading. Giselle's betrayal was upsetting, but the high priest's betrayal would be a brutal blow for Rhys and his friends. "Giselle said she stole it from the high priest. He's her client."

Vizah scoffed. Rufus and Andreas cast grave glances at Rhys.

Rhys took a step back as if he'd been shoved. "Jac, what are you saying?"

"She told me the high priest hired her to kill me."

"Why?" Rufus asked.

Rhys paled. "The high priest wants to kill you," he murmured. "Because of *me*?"

"He thinks I'm a distraction for you. He thinks I make you want to leave the order."

He bent forward as if he was going to throw up, but rested his hands on his knees instead. He groaned, a low sound that came from deep within.

I crouched in front of him and cupped his face as he'd done mine moments before. I stroked his beard with my thumbs. "Rhys, you have to tell him he's wrong. Tell him you have no intention of leaving the order. Reassure him."

He straightened. "I have told him, numerous times."

"Then he doesn't believe you."

Rufus grunted and crossed his arms. "Clearly."

"Rhys," I went on. "Tell him again. Otherwise I have to leave Tilting forever. I can't stay here."

"No," Rhys said heavily. "You cannot." He strode past me, and gathered his horse's reins.

"You can't confront him," Rufus pointed out. "It's her word against his."

"I believe Jac."

"So do I, but he'll claim she's lying. Who will believe a young woman over the high priest, aside from us?"

"I can't let him get away with it," Rhys growled.

"There's more," I said. "The high priest hired Giselle to kill me, but not to frame you for it, Rhys. He's unaware of that part of Giselle's plan. My uncle hired her for that after she told him she was going to assassinate me."

He frowned. "But he wants you alive."

"Not anymore. Not since she told him my pendant isn't a talisman containing the sorcerer's magic."

"I could have told him that," Andreas muttered.

"He wouldn't believe you," I said. "But he believed her because she had the proof. In fact, he had the proof in his bookshelves, too, but neither knew it. There's a text on Zemayan culture that says the sorcerer placed magic into a *person* a long time ago, not an object. The person—a woman from a generation of the same family—is the talisman."

"What magic?" Vizah asked.

"There's no such thing as magic," Rufus snapped at him.

Andreas stepped toward me. "Jac?"

I kept my gaze on Rhys. "The magic takes the form of heightened senses and the ability to recall things perfectly."

Rhys blinked slowly at me, as if he was disoriented after waking from a vivid dream.

"Senses?" Vizah asked.

"Sight, sound, smell, hearing and touch," Rufus rattled off. "Jac, there's no such thing as magic. If someone has heightened senses, it's just the way they were born."

I continued to watch Rhys. He stared back at me, but I didn't think he quite saw me. I suspected he was recalling moments when I'd seen something in the poor light that he couldn't see or heard something before he did.

He suddenly blinked again, snapping to attention. "It's you," he murmured. "*You're* the talisman."

I nodded. "Giselle realized soon after meeting me. I think it was when I recognized her at a distance from her scent alone."

Vizah sniffed his armpit. "Not everyone has a scent."

"I don't need superior senses to smell yours," Andreas told him.

Rufus, however, shook his head vigorously. "This is absurd. Jac can't smell people from a distance. Rhys, you should know better. Magic doesn't exist. The sorcerer is just a Zemayan myth. There is only one faith, and that's the one we serve."

Rhys nodded, but he wasn't agreeing with Rufus. I doubted he even heard his friend. "You always knew when it was me coming up the stairs."

"You have a distinctive rhythm," I said. "Everyone does."

"That's why you were so good at spying. You overheard conversations from a distance, which meant you could stay hidden. I thought you got in close and I worried you'd be caught, but you were able to stay far away. Further than I could."

"She's small," Rufus pointed out. "She can hide better than you or I. Or she can read lips."

"In the dark?" Rhys asked.

I pointed to a large tree in the woods some distance away. "Stand behind that tree and say something."

One hand on his sword hilt, Rufus strode into the woods and stepped behind the tree. "Vizah has a fungal infection on his big toe," he said.

I smiled. "Vizah, apparently you need to see Mistress Blundle about the fungus on your toe. I'm sure she'll have an ointment for it."

Vizah clamped his hands on his hips. "That's private business!" he shouted at the tree.

Rufus returned to us. "I only heard Vizah."

"She told me to see Mistress Blundle for a cure for my toe. It's not a fungus, it's just an interesting color."

Rufus folded his arms over his chest. "So Jac's senses may be acute, but that doesn't prove the existence of the sorcerer."

Andreas clapped his friend on the shoulder. "No one's asking you to believe it, but you can't stop others from thinking differently to you."

Rufus arched his brows at Rhys, challenging.

Rhys patted the saddle on his horse. "Climb up, Jac. I'll take you somewhere safe."

Rufus moved to block my way. "She can ride with me. I can protect her equally as well as you. Probably better at the moment, considering your injured back."

Rhys glanced sharply at me. When I showed no surprise at Rufus's words, he tilted his head to the side, questioning.

"I'm a very good spy," I said.

"And nosy." He led his horse to Rufus and placed a hand on his friend's shoulder. "While Jac's life is in danger, she rides with me. I won't risk your life or anyone else's. That's an order."

"Bloody stupid one," Rufus muttered, stepping aside.

"Then you shouldn't have voted for me to lead you." Rhys clutched Rufus's arm. "But thank you. I'm glad you did."

He helped me into the saddle as the other three mounted.

"Want us to warn the sheriff about Giselle?" Andreas asked.

"No. He may still be in the governor's pocket. The power may have shifted, but we can't be sure if we can trust him yet."

Rhys settled behind me on the horse and took the reins in one hand, resting his other on the hilt of his sword. Thanks to our closeness, and perhaps my heightened sense of touch, I detected a bandage wrapped around his torso as my back bumped against him. I could also feel the tensing of muscles in his legs as he directed the horse to move. His warm familiar scent was mixed with the herbal smell of a salve that had been applied to his wounds. Being near Rhys had always been a heady, all-consuming experience, but now I knew why. My senses were filled to the brim with him.

It could be a wonderful, deeply satisfying place to be. Or it could be dangerous if our enemies knew how he affected me.

Rhys was thinking about my senses, too. "I understand how heightened hearing, sight and smell manifest. But what about touch and taste?"

"I'm able to detect individual ingredients in a complicated dish, which I realized once I ate Mistress Lowey's pies. She used to comment on how remarkable my sense of taste was. Before that, I thought everyone was like me. I also dislike boring food."

"You made that clear when you refused to eat the meals I brought from the order. Even when you were starving, you would barely touch it."

"If I had my way, your cook would be exiled from Glancia for the crime of cooking bland food."

He laughed softly, his breath ruffling my hair. "And touch?" He released the sword hilt and lightly stroked my thigh with his thumb. My blood responded with a resounding thud and my cheeks flushed with heat.

I blew out a shuddery breath. "I feel everything, everywhere. The touch of something soft and smooth can be pleasurable, making all my nerve endings hum in delight. But pain...it hurts more than just at the source. I can feel it in my bones, my teeth, my scalp..."

"Merdu's blood, Jac," he whispered. "The cut in your side...I thought you were being dramatic when I cleaned it."

"Once my shock and the numbness that went with it wore off, the pain was rather intense."

"I should have been gentler. Next time—"

"There won't be a next time, Rhys. We both know that."

We rode in silence for a while, every part of me tuned to him, so I felt him tense the moment before he spoke. "I'm sorry, Jac. Everything's a mess. If I hadn't been tempted—"

"Don't. Self-recrimination will only make you feel worse." I laid a hand over his on the reins. Even though I couldn't see his face, I heard the soft hitch in his breath.

The track widened, and Rufus rode up alongside us. "Next time you send a note, Jac, you should wait for assistance."

I bristled. "I would if the situation was right, but I had to catch Giselle in the act otherwise she would never stop." I turned in the saddle to appeal to Rhys.

"I will never believe it's a good idea for you to confront a dangerous killer without me," he said.

"There was a good reason—"

"There is *never* a good reason."

"There is," I said testily. "We'll confront my uncle with what we know and tell him we'll go to the councillors if anything happens to me. You can confront the high priest. They'll both deny it, of course, but they'll be forced to withhold their payments to Giselle, otherwise they risk public exposure."

"That may neutralize their involvement, but she isn't doing it for the money, Jac. She must have other reasons to do this to you."

"You're right," I said darkly. "She admitted as much."

"She won't stop until you're dead."

The steel in Rhys's voice put me on edge. I suspected that was why he spoke so harshly. He wanted me to be worried, and therefore alert.

Rufus leaned toward us in the saddle. "At the risk of being stabbed by Rhys's glare, I urge you to leave Tilting, Jac. For good."

Behind me, Rhys swallowed heavily.

"I'll go," I agreed. "I'll leave as soon as possible."

* * *

RUFUS DIDN'T WANT to leave Rhys alone with me at the inn, but Vizah and Andreas moved up alongside his horse, grabbed the reins, and led him away. Rufus tried reasoning with his friends until they turned the corner. He must have thought I couldn't hear him at that point because he reminded them of what Rhys had already suffered by breaking his vow of celibacy in the past.

"That's not why we're walking away," Andreas said.

"It isn't?" Vizah asked.

"No. We're leaving them alone so they can say proper good-byes this time. This way it'll be final."

One of them gave a grudging grunt. I suspected it was Rufus when he said, "Very well."

"It's a good point," Vizah added, his tone thoughtful. "We need to avoid the madness of last time. Maybe he'll get rid of that beard now."

One look at Rhys made it clear he hadn't heard them. He led the way inside and asked the innkeeper for a room, being particular to point out that I was a cousin staying in the city for the first time. Once upstairs, Rhys inspected the crate of firewood. "There's enough here to keep you warm for one night. There's a jug of water and a basin. Both look clean."

"I can see that, thank you."

He crossed to the other side of the room and rearranged the straw pallet to be closer to the fireplace. "It's very basic. My apologies, I'd forgotten how cheap this place was."

"You've stayed here before?"

"When I was younger."

I wondered if he'd brought women here, then pushed the thought away.

"There are some blankets and cushions in that trunk," he went on.

"I presumed as much."

He lifted the trunk's lid and pulled them out. "They're clean." He set about laying the blanket on the pallet. "I'll ask the innkeeper to bring up something for you to eat so you don't have to go downstairs."

"Thank you, Rhys."

He moved the cushion from one end of the pallet to the other then back again. "I think you should put your head at this end.

That way you can see the door." He shifted the pallet closer to the fireplace. "It won't get too cold tonight, but you might find it more comfortable here."

"Rhys."

He straightened and studied the arrangement, then shifted the pallet back. "On second thoughts, you'll feel too hot that close to the fire considering you're sensitive to extreme temperatures."

"Rhys," I said, louder. "Thank you. I can manage."

He sniffed the air. "Does it smell musty? Should I open the window?"

I moved to block his path to the window. "Rhys, be calm."

"I am calm."

"You're wound up tighter than a cat stalking a bird."

He finally looked at me. "Your acute senses telling you that?"

"No, my acute knowledge of you." Perhaps it wasn't a wise thing to admit, but my sharpened senses didn't include the ability to know when to keep quiet. "Rhys, are you all right? The wounds on your back…"

"I'm fine. They're nothing. I can't even feel them."

"That's because you've applied Mistress Blundle's numbing salve and have a bandage to protect them from the coarse fabric of the shirt beneath your tunic." I plucked at his sleeve.

He crossed his arms, breaking the flimsy connection between us. "I feel fine. Thanks for asking."

"You *let* the high priest do it, didn't you?"

He looked away, confirming my suspicion.

"Did you two plan it?" I persisted.

"I wasn't aware of his plan beforehand. Not until he arrived at the temple and informed me he had an idea to secure my role as leader. When his guards led me to the whipping post, I realized what he had in mind."

"It was too late to stop him by then," I said. "He *forced* it upon you."

"It wasn't too late. There were only two guards. The others were further away. My friends would have taken care of them."

"The guards were armed with swords and none of you were."

He merely shrugged, as if that were irrelevant.

"How can you be so nonchalant? Rhys, they could have inflicted more damage to your back, not to mention what affect the experience could have on your sense of self after being punished like that in front of your men."

He smiled wryly. "Some would say I need to be brought down a peg or two."

"Don't make light of this!" I felt tears rushing to my eyes, but I couldn't stop them. "Seeing you like that…it was sickening."

"There's a reason it wasn't meant for public viewing."

"Is that your way of telling me I shouldn't have snuck into the tower to watch?" I buried my face in my hands for a moment before confronting him again. "I snuck in because I was worried. I sensed something was wrong when I saw the high priest. You can try to tell me I shouldn't have worried, but it will do no good. I will always worry about you, Rhys, even after I leave Tilting." I went to thump his arm because I wouldn't allow myself to hold him.

He caught my fist and enclosed it in both of his hands. "As I will always worry about you, Jac. It seems there's nothing that can be done about it. We'll always feel this way. So we must acknowledge it." He lightly kissed my knuckles. "Then we move on." He released me and turned away. One hand on the mantelpiece, he drew in a measured breath as he stared into the empty fireplace. "I don't regret going along with the high priest's scheme in the temple yard. It was necessary to regain the respect I'd lost. The vote that followed was needed to reconfirm my position as leader. Don't tell Andreas, Vizah and Rufus. They won't like that I willingly played my part. Especially now, in light of the high priest's actions against you. By hiring Giselle, he has proved himself unworthy."

I wiped my damp cheeks and pressed a hand to my rapidly beating heart. "The doubters don't deserve you if it was necessary for you to go to such lengths to prove your honor and loyalty. Anyone who knows you knows you're dedicated to the order, that you love your brothers and your life there."

The hand on the mantel closed into a fist. He thumped it then turned around. He looked much like the first time I'd seen him upon my return to Tilting, as if he hadn't slept in days. "Jac, the order is not my only love, but it demands that it is."

The muscles in my jaw ached as I tried to hold back my tears.

"But this is bigger than me," Rhys went on. "Merdu's Guards needs stability now more than ever, and a master they can all rally behind if we're to oust the high priest from his position. Someone willing to go to great lengths to ensure justice is served."

I huffed a laugh. "How ironic that the high priest's failure to get rid of me is the very thing that reaffirms your reason to stay on as master."

"Please don't make this any harder than it is already," he whispered.

I bit my lower lip and turned away. I drew in a fortifying breath and slowly released it. It gave me time to consider how to proceed. I turned back to face him again. "I'm coming to the high temple with you to confront him."

"No, you're not." He rested a hand on the hilt of his sword. "Your presence might provoke him to finish the job that Giselle couldn't. I can't risk that."

"Why not confront him publicly? It's the best way to force him to resign, and he won't attack either of us in public." When he didn't answer, I forged on. "He doesn't deserve the dignity you're affording him."

Rhys went to push past me to the door but stopped. "When this is over, I'll make sure the governor is brought to justice, too."

"How?"

His gaze searched my face, as if taking in my features all over again. "Whatever happens, stay here. Giselle will be looking for you."

"But Rhys—"

"No, Jac. Nothing you say will stop me, so let's not part in anger." He removed his glove and caressed my jawline with his thumb . He smiled sadly. "I'll see that your pendant is returned to you, but we won't be seeing one another again."

I watched him go with an ache in my chest so fierce that I felt like I was suffocating. I collapsed onto the pallet and drew up my knees. I hugged them and cried for Hailia knew how long. The last time I left Tilting having not said goodbye to Rhys in person had hung over me like a cloud, and a part of me had known I'd return to right that wrong.

But this time he had said goodbye. This time he'd made it clear we wouldn't be seeing one another again. He'd made his choice to stay in the order, and I couldn't sway him from that path.

I wasn't enough.

When my body ran dry of tears, I lay down and stared up at the ceiling. As much as I didn't want to go over our final conversation in my head, I couldn't set it aside yet. I replayed every word in my head, recalled every crease of his brow, and felt intense pain in my heart all over again.

Then I suddenly sat up.

This is bigger than me, Rhys had claimed. It was something people said when they sacrificed themselves for a greater good. I'd thought Rhys meant he was sacrificing himself by staying leader of Merdu's Guards when he didn't want to. Taken on its own, his words gave me no reason to think otherwise.

But when added to his lack of a response when I suggested he confront the high priest publicly, and when he hadn't answered my question about how he planned to bring my uncle to justice, it might have meant something else altogether.

Perhaps he wasn't going to force either man to resign or have them arrested. Perhaps he was going to kill them.

And he didn't expect to get away with it. Knowing Rhys, he intended to turn himself in afterward—if he lived.

CHAPTER 16

$\mathcal{T}$he rule that dictated women weren't allowed into the temple complex of Merdu's Guards meant I had to remain at the gate while one of the brothers fetched Rufus, Vizah and Andreas. Impatience made me pace back and forth, but wariness kept me alert for signs of Giselle. I employed every sense I possessed, even after the three warrior priests joined me.

They immediately knew something was wrong, but Rufus's words weren't what I expected. "I suspected there was a problem when I read his note."

"What note?" I asked.

"He must have sent it from the inn." He fished it out of his pocket and handed it to me. This time I was in no doubt that it was written by Rhys. Giselle wouldn't have encouraged Rufus to step into his role as master. It was the core of Rhys's message, however.

"I thought it meant he'd decided to leave the order for you," Rufus said as he tucked the letter back into his pocket.

"He wants to bring the high priest to justice," I told them. "My uncle, too."

"Merdu's Guards aren't a vengeful order," Vizah said. "If he can't force them to resign or turn themselves in, he'll give up and come back." Not even he seemed to believe his own words, however.

"The high priest won't let him leave the high temple," Andreas said. "He likes Rhys, but he likes his own power more. He'll make sure his guards don't let Rhys escape."

Rufus turned and ran back through the gate, Andreas and Vizah at his heels. I followed. The priest at the gate tried to stop me, but I shoved him away with both hands. No one was going to keep me from helping Rhys.

The priests working in the stables prepared horses, including one for me. It had been years since I'd ridden on my own, but I was determined to do it. Getting on the back of a horse with one of the others would only slow them down and take them longer to get to Rhys.

It meant I fell behind the moment we exited the gate, however. The three warrior priests had already turned the corner, heading in the direction of the high temple, when Giselle dropped onto me from a tree branch as I passed beneath it.

Despite my shock, I managed to twist as we fell and land on the ground beside her instead of under. It meant I didn't have the full force of her weight pinning me and was able to scramble to my feet. My hip and shoulder ached but I forced myself to focus on Giselle, not the pain.

We squared up to one another, slowly circling. Neither of us had drawn weapons.

"I thought I'd find you here," she sneered. "You can't leave him alone, can you? You always come back. Has he agreed to leave the order for you yet? No?" She clicked her tongue in mock disappointment. "So sad. The grand love story that never was."

In the edges of my vision, I saw that my horse had returned home and the priest guarding the gate held its reins. Behind him, the gate was open. Some brothers emerged. Realizing what was happening, they stepped toward us.

I put up a hand. "Stay back. This is between Giselle and me."

They murmured amongst themselves, questioning whether

they should intervene anyway. One even went so far as to suggest it's what Rhys would want.

"No, he wouldn't," I called out, louder than the volume at which they spoke so they could hear. "He wants this resolved. Those are his orders."

"Eavesdropping again?" Giselle asked. "It's rather a rude habit."

"But a useful one."

"Do you really think you can beat me?"

"I'm not sure, but a wise person taught me a lesson today. He said some things are bigger than the individual. Sometimes you have to sacrifice yourself for the greater good."

"Ugh. Typical Rhys. So righteous. Defeatist, too. Where's your positivity, Jac? Or did it leave you along with the man who refused to be your lover?"

"It's only defeatist if I plan on dying while capturing you. I assure you, I do not."

Her brittle chuckle raked my nerves. "It seems you didn't learn the lesson *I* taught *you* today. Time for a revision class." Instead of lunging at me, she reached behind the tree trunk and produced a sword she'd stashed there.

I leapt back as the blade sliced through the air, then leapt back again and again to avoid being cut to ribbons.

I heard the whine of a sword being drawn from its scabbard and held out a hand to receive it from the priest.

Giselle smirked. "They're not going to help you, Jac. They loathe you. You're the one who took Rhys away from them. They want you dead as much as the high priest does."

The sword was thrown perfectly, and I caught it easily by the hilt. Giselle's face dropped as she realized her plan to get away with killing me looked less likely with witnesses on my side rather than hers. She must have been relying on them hating me to get away with murdering me and escaping. She'd misjudged them badly.

I pointed the sword at her, my feet a little apart, my other hand ready to withdraw my dagger. She lunged toward me. I parried and engaged her. The fight was even, each of us parrying the other's strikes or getting out of the way before being cut. If we continued to fight only with swords, the winner wouldn't be determined by skill but by whoever could outlast the other.

But I didn't want to win. I wanted a confession in front of witnesses. It might be the only way to save Rhys, if he wasn't already dead.

I removed my dagger and threw it. It missed her. I didn't give her time to gloat, however. I rushed forward and engaged her once again in a sword fight. We didn't stand still and parry one another's strikes. We circled around, moved back and forth, and jumped over the other's blade when it was slashed in a low arc. She used the tree trunk and branch to hang from, while I employed the somersaults and flips I'd perfected during training.

"Impressive," she said after I did three backflips in a row to avoid her thrashing sword. "But you're tiring."

She was right. But I wasn't the only one. Her smile and quick footwork were an act. My keen sight noticed her sword arm drop as the weight of the weapon sapped her strength. Her breathing became labored, and a bright flush colored her cheeks as beads of sweat dampened her hairline. She wouldn't last much longer.

I ran at her, sword pointed at her chest, teeth bared in an angry last-ditch effort.

She sidestepped out of the way, kicked me in the behind, and sent me tumbling into the dust. I dropped my sword as I fell, just catching myself before I landed face down in the dirt. I hissed in pain as layers of skin on both palms scraped off.

I flipped onto my back, but it was too late to scramble away. Giselle stood above me, sword pointed at my throat. She smiled through her heaving breaths.

"I give up!" I cried. "You beat me."

My gamble paid off. The opportunity to gloat, to be viewed

as a winner in front of dozens of warriors, gave Giselle pause. She wasn't ready to kill me. She wanted to soak in her success a little longer with an audience looking on. Ending my life would end her euphoria. "You put up a good fight, Jac, but you don't have what it takes. Almost, but not quite."

"By defeating me you defeat Rhys, too," I said. "He failed to protect me." I worried it was a little too thick, exposing my tactic, but Giselle nodded enthusiastically.

Whispers and murmurs rippled around the group of warrior priests, but Giselle didn't seem to hear them. "I suppose I have. If you'd trusted in yourself and not relied on a man to rescue you, this outcome could have been different."

"Is that why you want Rhys to take the blame for killing me? To thoroughly defeat him?"

The murmurs grew. Some of the warrior priests stepped toward us, but others held them back. Giselle did notice their reaction this time. The first flicker of uncertainty passed across her face. She had two choices—deny it but risk not being believed, or admit the truth and justify her actions.

She chose the latter. "I don't want to kill you, Jac. The high priest does. *He* hired me."

The murmurs grew louder. Some of the warrior priests shouted denials and others whipped out their swords to challenge her.

"It's true!" she shouted back, her gaze and sword point still on me. "He knew Jac was a threat to Rhys's loyalty to the order and would remain so while she lived. He hired me to assassinate her so Rhys could continue as your master without distraction."

"That's a lie!" one warrior priest snarled.

"Our faith forbids taking a life unless in battle," growled another.

"The high priest is above suspicion," added a third.

Giselle's lips thinned, her nostrils flared. The point of her blade bit into my neck. I smelled blood.

She could kill me before anyone could stop her. My gamble

would fail. Except I remembered something she'd forgotten in the heat of the moment.

"You can prove it to them," I urged her. "The letter."

She removed the piece of paper she'd shown me earlier at the ruins. "The high priest wrote to me. It's all in here." She thrust the letter in the direction of the group of warriors.

And in so doing, she was distracted for the briefest of moments.

I batted the blade away from my throat, cutting my hand in the process. I winced but there was no time to wallow in the pain. I rolled out of the way and collected my sword then rose onto my knees just in time to parry Giselle's blade before it removed my head from my shoulders.

My training had taught me how to fight off someone whilst on my knees and I employed every one of the moves Giselle had taught me in Upway. Just as she'd said then, my excellent memory bolstered my instincts. It meant I could predict her every move, but her experience meant she could predict mine. We moved as one, two dancers whose steps were choreographed by a masterful teacher. It was predictable for both of us.

Until it wasn't.

When her moves started to precede mine by the barest margin, I changed course and attacked in a way she didn't expect. I parried her sword then bent to remove the dagger hidden in my boot. The usual course of action when presented with that move was to kick the opponent in the head before they could use the knife. I wouldn't recover from such a blow quickly enough to counterattack. I might never recover from a hard knock to the head.

But predicting that kick meant I had just enough time to leap to the side. Her boot missed my head only to slam into my shoulder. Pain exploded like a firework in my bones. I fell, landing with a cry.

Giselle fell, too, screaming as she clutched the back of her knee. Blood oozed between her fingers and dripped onto the dust.

My fingers ached around the handle of my bloodied dagger.

Giselle's screams of pain changed to shouted curses at me, calling me some colorful names I'd not heard since my days living on the streets. She spat at the warrior priests who came to disarm her, but when she realized that wouldn't work, she tried to reason with them again.

"Jac is stealing your master from you!"

"That doesn't justify murder," one said.

"She's a whore. She's everything you loathe about women."

The same priest stood over her and shook his head sadly. "You misunderstand us. We don't hate women of any description."

I pushed to my feet, clutching my shoulder as the pain ripped through it again. I closed my eyes only to open them again at the sound of horses approaching. A lot of horses, and a carriage, too.

Rhys rode in the lead. He was unharmed, thank the goddess. Relief filled me, pushing aside the pain and the fear that had festered within me ever since we parted. He jumped down from the saddle and scooped me into his arms, only to aggravate my shoulder.

He sprang back at my cry of pain. "You're hurt."

I clutched my shoulder. "I think it's dislocated."

"Merdu, you're white as a sheet." He signaled to one of the warriors. "Brother James is a healer. He sees these sorts of injuries all the time."

Brother James spoke reassuringly as he gently felt my shoulder. "It's definitely dislocated. Now, this will hurt. On the count of three, I'll put the shoulder back. Are you ready?"

He didn't give me a chance to nod. He pushed my shoulder back into place. I cried out, only to have it smothered by Rhys's chest. He held me, stroking my hair, until I realized the burning spike had become a dull ache.

I pulled away. "Thank you, Brother James."

The healer nodded. "Make sure you rest it. No lifting anything heavy for a few days."

Giselle snorted. "What about me?"

Brother James bent to inspect her wound. She sucked air between her teeth but unlike me, she didn't cry out. "Get your needle and thread, Brother. I can cope with the pain. Unlike some."

While the healer returned to the temple to get his medical kit, I took in the newcomers. Rhys was accompanied by Vizah, Rufus and Andreas, still on horseback, as well as several of the high priest's guards, either on horseback or riding on the carriage itself. The high priest sat inside, his face stony as he glared at Giselle.

She glared back from where she sat on the ground. "You idiot! You let him catch you. Why didn't your men protect you?"

The high priest turned his face away without answering.

"Because they trained in the order of Merdu's Guards," Rhys said. "They're loyal to the faith, not to any single man. Not even him. Once I explained the situation, they agreed to let me confront him. By the time Andreas, Vizah and Rufus arrived, it was clear he was guilty."

"There's proof," said one of the warrior priests. He handed Rhys the letter Giselle had dropped.

"You think I'll make it easier for you?" she snarled at Rhys. "Merdu, you two make me sick. I wish I'd killed you while you slept, Jac."

"She would have heard you entering the room," Rhys said, as calm as can be.

Vizah peered over Rhys's shoulder to read the letter. He whistled. "That's a large sum of money. The orders who feed and clothe the poor could do a lot with that."

"It wasn't about the money for Giselle," Rhys said. "She wanted Jac dead because she's jealous of her."

Giselle barked a humorless laugh. "Jealous? I don't love you, you arrogant prick. I never have."

"It's nothing to do with me. You're jealous of Jac because she's better than you and you loathe that."

"She's not better than me. She's good, but more practice would have made her better. Years more. She was lucky today, that's all."

"You're right," I said. "I do need more training. I knew I wasn't ready when we left Upway, and I remember telling you as much. But it's more than that. I also lack the quality you have, the hunger to kill or the desire to be the best fighter. But it wasn't luck that helped me beat you, Giselle. It was your own arrogance. You think being better than everyone means they're less than you, and when you believe that then you stop noticing them. You thought the warrior priests would support you in murdering me because it's what their high priest wanted, but you misunderstood them. You misjudge people because you don't get to know them. You don't value friendship, loyalty and honor, but they do, as does Rhys. Your downfall was isolating yourself from friendship even when it was offered to you." I tapped my chest. "I'm sorry for you, Giselle. You brought this on yourself."

Giselle spat on the ground. "Self-righteous bitch. You two are perfect for one another."

Brother James returned with his medical kit, but Rhys hadn't finished extracting a confession from Giselle. Once her wound was stitched, he ordered his men to help her to her feet then search her.

They found the dagger she stole from the high priest, but Rhys seemed disappointed. He must have wanted a note from my uncle too. Without evidence, we had no proof. Giselle might no longer be able to assassinate me, but he could hire another, if he still wanted to get rid of me.

Rhys hadn't yet given up, however. "The governor hired you, too, didn't he?"

Her smile was twisted. "He did, but he'll get away with it. There's no proof." She shrugged, unconcerned.

"His guards followed you after you met with him upon your return to Tilting. He knew if he found where you were staying that Jac would be there, too. He realized she was working for you, and he wanted to kill her without paying you. That's the sort of person you do business with."

"What does it matter now?" she sneered. "I still can't produce proof from thin air. You'll have to take my word for it."

We both knew it wouldn't be enough.

The sheriff arrived with several constables in tow and demanded to know why he'd been summoned. Rhys spoke quietly with him, but not so quietly that I couldn't hear what they were saying. Even if I couldn't, it would have been clear from the direction of the sheriff's gaze. It flew to Giselle, held prisoner between Vizah and another warrior, then shifted to the high priest, still seated with an expression of regal arrogance in his carriage. He cut a lonely figure, isolated even from his guards. I doubted any of the warrior priests, or indeed the priests and priestesses from the other orders, would stand by his side now. He'd brought shame on them and on their faith by breaking the oath to not take a life. He wasn't the man they wanted representing the Glancian-based orders.

The sheriff directed some of his constables to accompany the high priest and Giselle to the holding cells. The warrior priests lined the side of the street and hissed or jeered as the high priest's carriage drove past.

Rhys turned his back and joined me. He tucked my hair behind my ear and smiled wanly. He looked weary in both body and heart. "All right?"

I nodded. "The shoulder is still a little sore."

He touched my cheek. "You disobeyed my order," he said without any heat in his voice.

"I thought you went to kill the high priest in revenge, which would have given the sheriff a reason to arrest you, if the guards didn't kill you first."

"I suspected the guards would come to my side once I explained, but if they didn't, I was prepared to face the worst outcome. I judged them correctly, though. They trust me."

My heart lifted at the echo of the words I'd said to Giselle, pointing out that her unwillingness to accept friendship had led to her ignoring people and ultimately misunderstanding them. "And the risk of arrest, if it came to that? How were you going to avoid it?"

"Charm and wit."

I laughed. I couldn't help it. It was wonderful seeing a flash of the old, carefree Rhys again. I'd missed that side of him more than I realized. "What happens now?" I asked.

"The high priest and Giselle will face trial. The supreme priest in Vytill will need to be notified. I'll write to him tonight. But first, there's other business to be concluded. I'm paying the governor a visit."

"You can't!"

"I won't be alone." He nodded at his three friends, hovering nearby.

Another warrior priest joined them. "I'll come with you."

"As will I," said a second.

More men joined, then soon the entire cohort of Merdu's Guards stood behind Vizah, Andreas and Rufus, and several of the high priest's guards, too. Dozens of large, muscular men in prime fighting condition were a powerful sight. Only yesterday, he'd had the support of just over half. Today, he had them all waiting for his order. It was a reminder of why Master Tomaj and the high priest had so much faith in him becoming the leader at such a young age. He was a natural.

As the men all repeated their oath to follow him, Rhys put up his hands for silence. "I only need some of you. But there are two things you need to know before you support me."

I walked off to visibly separate myself from him. I didn't want my presence to dilute their support.

"First, we have no proof the governor hired Giselle," he continued. "Nor is he likely to confess. I don't yet know how we'll bring him to justice, but we will. I won't let him hunt Jac any longer."

I slipped past the sheriff, who was listening to Rhys's speech with two constables at his side. He gave no inclination of his thoughts, but at least he didn't demand Rhys stop his pursuit of my uncle. I doubted Rhys would stop for anyone, anyway. Even me.

"Secondly," Rhys went on. "You need to know that I'm resigning."

The warrior priests murmured amongst themselves. More than one asked the same question. "Then who'll be master?"

"Whoever you vote for. If it matters, I endorse Rufus."

"Me?" Rufus said.

"You're everything the order needs in a leader. Devout, dedicated, honorable, steady."

"You make me sound dull."

Vizah clapped his friend on the shoulder. "Sometimes dull is good."

Andreas clapped his other shoulder. "You're serious, not dull."

"I never had the right temperament," Rhys went on. "But you do, Rufus. You'll make an excellent leader."

I tried to listen in to the conversations within the group of warrior priests, but they overlapped and blended together, making it difficult to pick out the individual threads. They distracted me, however, and I didn't notice Rhys approach until he touched my elbow.

"Where are you going?" he asked.

"I don't know. I'm just walking around." I shrugged but that made the pain in my shoulder flare. "Ow."

He rubbed my arm just below my shoulder. He had an odd

look in his eye as he watched me. For once, I couldn't decipher it. "Is there something you want to say to me?"

I nodded. "I want to come with you when you confront my uncle."

The sheriff had overheard me and joined us. "I think that's fair, but we should leave immediately. I don't want him getting wind of this and leaving the city."

"You believe us?" I asked. "You'll arrest him?"

"Not without evidence, but I want to hear what he has to say."

"I thought you and he were friends."

"Acquaintances." He cleared his throat. "I've, uh, suspected he was corrupt for some time but there's been no proof. If he took public money for himself, he covered his tracks well."

Rhys crossed his arms and arched his brows. "That's convenient for those complicit in his schemes."

The sheriff stiffened. "Show me evidence that he committed a crime, and I *will* arrest him."

Rhys indicated the horses. "After you, Sheriff." As I went to follow, he took my hand. "Jac? Is something wrong?"

"I'm not looking forward to this."

"I won't leave your side."

I gave him a flat smile. "Thank you, Rhys."

* * *

UNCLE RODERIC'S power had diminished while I was in Upway. His dwindling authority meant he couldn't siphon off funds intended for the city, and it was clear in the lack of staff he now kept. The sheriff had instructed them to join us in the same salon where I'd listened to my uncle speaking to Giselle in the adjoining study. They now lined up according to rank, with the lowest maid at the very end. I didn't recognize her or some of the others, but I did recognize the older ones, including the housekeeper who'd been my jailor when I first arrived at the house years ago.

My uncle's power wasn't the only thing that had diminished. He looked frail in the vast room without his guards surrounding him. The shock of seeing me alive drained his face of color and he leaned heavily on a walking stick.

"Dearest niece," he said, smiling that slick smile of his. "I am so glad you've returned home. Your room is just—"

"Enough," I growled. "No one here believes you care for anyone other than yourself."

He folded both hands on the head of the walking stick. "See how she is, Sheriff? Disobedient to her menfolk, disrespectful of her elders."

"She claims you hired an assassin to kill her and frame Master Rhys for it," the sheriff said.

"Absurd." Uncle Roderic's hand fluttered near his doublet pocket. "Why would I want to kill my own niece? She's my only family."

I strode up to him. He swatted my hand away as I reached into his pocket, so I swatted back, harder. I withdrew the pendant and stepped back before he could snatch it off me. "When I moved in here after my mother died, you imprisoned me with the help of your staff and stole this from me."

Out of the corner of my eye, I saw the housekeeper tilt her chin, defiant. Others in the staff lineup shifted their weight from foot to foot.

"That's a family heirloom," Uncle Roderic said. "It's rightfully mine. Everything you own is mine."

"My mother gifted it to me. By law, personal gifts are mine to keep. But you took it. I stole it back and escaped. You thought I'd died, but that didn't stop you searching for this pendant."

The sheriff asked to look at it. I handed it to him, and he held it up to the light. "It matches your eyes, Miss Trenchant, but it's just a stone, not a precious gem. I doubt it's worth much. Certainly not worth all this trouble."

"Family legend said it held magic that would make the wielder powerful."

The sheriff scoffed. "Preposterous."

"Not to him. He believed it."

The sheriff laughed. Uncle Roderic bristled, indignant.

"For some time after I escaped, he thought I was dead," I went on. "Then he saw me. He came for me and stole the pendant again. He was at the height of his powers, and I couldn't stop him. Not then. I bided my time. His influence waned, and it became clear this pendant held no power. He thought I could unlock it, that my mother had passed on the secret to releasing the sorcerer's magic. He hired Giselle to find me and bring me to him. She declined. He hadn't offered her enough money to give up the apprentice she was investing her time and energy into training. You see, she'd read about the talisman being a *person,* and realized it was me, not that pendant."

The sheriff turned to face me fully, his gaze raking over me.

"It's not as interesting as it sounds," I said. "I have heightened senses—sight, sound, touch, smell and taste."

The sheriff looked disappointed. "I thought the high priest hired Giselle to kill you."

"He did. He offered her a lot more than the governor did to merely find me, and by then she'd become worried about being supplanted by her apprentice. She accepted his contract. But she got greedy. She saw a way to have two clients for the same job. She convinced my uncle that I was a threat to him while alive, and that she could get rid of me and blame Rhys for it. My uncle despises Rhys. He once vowed to expose Rhys as a liar and oath breaker to the brothers of Merdu's Guards. By going along with Giselle's plan, he'd fulfill his vow after his earlier attempt to discredit Rhys failed to oust him from the leadership role. My uncle and Giselle came to an agreement in this room."

Uncle Roderic scoffed. "A nice story, but you can't prove any of it."

"No. But by declaring it and exposing you in front of witnesses, I have neutralized the threat you posed. If anything happens to me, everyone will blame you."

"And I will come for you," Rhys added. "And I will be very, very angry."

"Guards!" Uncle Roderic's shout was as thin and weak as his physical appearance. "Guards!"

"They can't help you," Rhys said. "Three of Merdu's finest warriors are keeping them occupied."

Uncle Roderic swallowed. "Unless you're going to arrest me, Sheriff, I'd like you all to leave my house."

The sheriff gave me an apologetic look. "He has every right to throw us out of his own home."

"I'll go," I said. "But I want you to know that I'm not afraid of you anymore, Uncle. I pity you. You're at a time of your life when a man needs his family. I would have cared for you in your dotage if you'd just loved me as an uncle should. But now you have no one."

"I have the servants."

I glanced at them. The younger ones blinked wide-eyed at me. They would never have witnessed anyone speak to their employer that way. Perhaps they'd even feared him. Some of the older servants wouldn't meet my gaze. They clearly remembered me. Only the housekeeper who'd locked me in my room and taken away the key glared at me, defiant. Challenging.

I turned back to my uncle. "If you believe they're taking good care of you then I really do pity you. Your clothes are wrinkled, your hair needs a trim, and you don't look like you're eating properly. That's not loving care. That's doing the bare minimum."

The mention of the servants gave the sheriff an idea. "Did any of you see the woman known as Giselle meet him here at the house?"

Most lowered their heads. One of the young maids looked at her colleagues, but none would meet her gaze.

"If you remember anything, it could be important," he went on. "I only need one witness to place her here. Alongside her confession, that's enough to convict them both."

Still no one came forward.

The sheriff sighed and dismissed them, then he directed Rhys and me to leave the room ahead of him. I walked out, not bothering to look back at my uncle. He wasn't worthy of a second glance.

We rejoined Rufus, Andreas and Vizah in the next room, standing with the guards, ensuring they didn't try to save my uncle. Going by their sheathed swords, the guards were no threat.

"Do you want me to put it on you?" Rhys asked.

"Hmmm?" I looked at the pendant in my hand. "Oh. Please." I handed it to him and turned, lifting my hair to expose my neck.

"Are you all right?" he murmured.

"I am. Better than I thought I'd be without an arrest. He's weak now. I truly do pity him."

"So do I." He finished fastening the necklace and let the pendant fall into place. His fingers skimmed the skin at my neck, leaving little tingles in their wake. "Jac—"

"Shhhh." I put up a hand to silence him and listened. Voices came from the service stairs behind the wall. The servants had been exchanging words ever since dispersing, but I'd blocked out their chatter. This conversation caught my attention, however.

I was about to open the hidden service door in the wall paneling when someone on the other side screamed.

CHAPTER 17

I barged through the service door into the cavity beyond. I knew the house's layout from the night I'd escaped, so was ready for the short landing. I managed to stop before plunging down the narrow staircase. The young maid on the second step screamed again.

The housekeeper slapped the girl across the mouth. "Shut it."

The maid started to cry.

The housekeeper raised her hand again, but I grasped her wrist.

"No," I snapped. "You'll never intimidate a young woman again."

The housekeeper's top lip curled with her sneer. "There was always something different about you, something *wrong*. I told him he should kill you before you caused trouble. He'll regret not listening to me now."

"You terrified me once, but I'm not afraid of you anymore."

"Because you have him protecting you." She jerked her head at Rhys.

"Because I'm stronger than I was then. And it's true, I have friends that give me confidence, who support me when I need it."

She tried to wrench free, but I shoved her back against the wall. Whether she hit her head, or whether the change in me from the time I'd lived there shocked her, I didn't know, but she stared at me, wide-eyed.

"I believe assault is a crime," I said. "Fortunately, the sheriff is still here and there are witnesses."

"I was just calming the girl down. You scared her when you burst in unexpected."

"She screamed before we came in." I glanced at the entrance. Someone had given Rhys a cup, which he was now handing to the shaking maid. She drank the entire contents in one gulp. "Did the housekeeper threaten you?" I asked her.

She clasped the cup in both hands and chewed her lower lip. She was too terrified of the housekeeper to disobey her.

Rhys indicated we should swap positions. I released the housekeeper then smiled gently at the young maid. "What's your name?"

"Bella."

"It's nice to meet you, Bella. I'm Jac. I used to live here. You heard in the salon that the housekeeper helped my uncle imprison me?"

She clutched the cup to her chest. Her gaze flicked to the housekeeper then back to me. She nodded.

"You also know that I was born with excellent hearing. While I was out there, I overheard you telling the housekeeper in here that you wanted to speak to the sheriff. She tried to dissuade you, but you insisted. That was brave of you, Bella."

She glanced at the housekeeper again. Others had crowded at the entrance, including the sheriff, while some of the servants looked up from the bottom of the staircase below. The housekeeper was outnumbered.

Seeing the support bolstered Bella's confidence. She lifted her chin. "She ordered me not to say anything. She said if I told anyone what I'd seen, she'd kill me. She hit me across the face. That's when I screamed the first time."

"And what did you see? What did she not want you to tell the sheriff?"

"That Dreen woman came here, the one who wears trousers. She met the governor in his study. I was on the porch outside, throwing dust from my pan into the garden and the window was open. I heard them. He wanted her to bring you to him. She said there was no point because you couldn't make his pendant work." She shrugged. "I didn't understand what she meant. I understood the next bit, though. She said she'd kill you, and make sure Master Rhys was blamed. The governor agreed to pay her for that."

The sheriff disappeared.

"Stupid girl," the housekeeper hissed. "You don't bite the hand that feeds you."

Bella shrank back against the wall.

"You did the right thing," I assured her.

"I should have said something earlier, but she ordered me not to. She said I'd lose my position here, and I've got nowhere to go."

Rhys marched the housekeeper out of the stairwell and handed her over to one of the constables. Two others emerged from an adjoining room, Uncle Roderic between them. Two weren't necessary. He posed no threat, frail as he was. Indeed, the constables were there more for support, since he didn't have his walking stick.

The sheriff followed. "Found him cowering in his bedchamber." He ordered his constables to escort my uncle and the housekeeper to the holding cells.

A heavy weight lifted from my shoulders as I watched them go. "When will his trial commence?" I asked the sheriff.

"That's up to the magistrate, but no more than two or three days from now."

"I'll visit him before I leave Tilting." I almost told him I was leaving because there were too many memories here, haunting me at every turn, but then I'd have to admit they were memories of Rhys and the wonderful times we'd spent together, not of my uncle's treatment. I was able to push those aside. I wasn't able to forget Rhys.

"He doesn't deserve your kindness, Miss Trenchant."

"He's still my uncle, my only family."

Rhys's hand touched my lower back, reassuring.

I stepped forward, breaking the connection.

The sheriff followed his men, taking the remaining constables with him. My uncle's guards asked if they were free to go, and Rufus nodded. They, too, left.

Rufus looked past my shoulder at Rhys. "Until there's a vote, you're still master. You're needed at the temple, but I understand if you want to stay with Jac."

Rhys's answer was simply to push past me and stride out.

I watched him leave, my throat tight, my chest aching. It would be the last time I saw him. It had to be, for both our sakes. He may have resigned from the role of master, but he was still dedicated to the order. I couldn't live in the same city as him. Tilting was too small. I didn't want to bump into him when I turned a corner, or worse, *hope* that I did. I was tired of waiting and being hopeful that we had a future together. It was time to move on.

He'd made his decision, and I had made mine.

"He looks terrible," Andreas said, giving me a pointed look.

"It's the beard," Vizah told him.

"It is not the beard."

Rufus put his arm around his friend. "Come on, idiot."

"Am I an idiot?" Vizah mused. "Or am I smarter than all of you?"

Rufus and Andreas exchanged glances. "You're an idiot," they both said.

* * *

I COULD HAVE STAYED on at the house. My uncle had never thrown me out and had in fact told me I could have my old room back. But I didn't want to stay somewhere I couldn't trust all of the staff. I returned to the inn. Although I had nothing to pack, the room was paid for and it was growing dark. I needed somewhere to stay overnight.

I ordered bread and cheese to eat in the room. I couldn't stomach a single bite, however, and set the plate aside. Sitting cross-legged on the pallet, I stared into the low flickering flames in the fireplace and tried to think about my future.

The knock on the door startled me. Rhys's voice startled me even more. "Jac, it's me. Can I come in?"

My heart thundered in my chest.

I opened the door and stepped back. "You shaved off the beard." The sight of his handsome face did nothing to steady my erratic heartbeat or the rush of blood to my head.

He rubbed his smooth jaw. "A number of people told me it didn't suit me." He stepped inside and closed the door behind him. "But there was one opinion in particular that swayed me."

"Don't, Rhys. I can't do this anymore. It's too hard."

"I know."

"Then why are you here?"

"Because I don't want you to leave."

"I have to. It'll be easier for both of us to move on if I go."

He'd been advancing toward me, that odd look in his eye once again. With every one of his steps, I'd taken one back.

"Stay there, Rhys. Come no closer."

He stopped. "I can't kiss you from here."

"So you'll kiss me but not sleep with me?"

He frowned. "What are you talking about?"

"You broke your oath of celibacy for Giselle, and others. Many others, apparently. Yet not for me."

The frown cleared. "You may have an incredible sense of sight, yet you can't see the obvious."

"And now you insult me."

He took another step closer. I stepped back again, almost tripping over the pallet on the floor. "I broke my vow before meeting you because it changed nothing. With them, there was no temptation to leave the order. But you're different. I knew if I bedded you, I'd never go back, and I wasn't ready to give up being a warrior priest then."

I'd never doubted my hearing. Not once. Until now. I shook my head, confused.

He stepped closer. "I want to be with you, Jac."

I moved back again, bumping into the wall. "You think I'll let you break your vow after all these years of denial? You think I want to wake up beside you and see the regret on your face?" I pointed at the door. "Go. Now. Before it's too late."

One side of his mouth tilted up in that mischievous smile I'd not seen in a long time. "I'm not breaking any vows."

"I don't understand."

"I resigned."

"I know, I was there."

"Not just as master. I've resigned from the order. I'm no longer a priest in Merdu's Guards."

I stilled. "You're wearing your priest's tunic."

He looked down at his clothes. "I own nothing else."

"But... Are you sure, Rhys?"

"For someone with excellent hearing, you're not listening," he murmured under his breath.

"I heard that."

"Show off." He flashed a grin. It was precisely what I needed to see. I'd not seen him smile like that since before he became master. "I'm sure, Jac." His voice purred, and his gaze melted me.

Now that I wanted him to come to me, he stayed still. "The brothers must be devastated," I said.

"I've made many sacrifices for the order," he went on. "Now it's time they make the sacrifice and let me go."

"They'll blame me."

"I've explained that I want to leave. This is my choice. You recall when I told you the order was the right place for me, that I wanted to be there."

I nodded, even though it wasn't a question. He knew I remembered.

"That was true then, but it's no longer true. Now it feels right to leave. Do you remember what I said outside the temple gates earlier, when I resigned?"

"When you resigned as master?"

"When I resigned from the *order*."

I thought back to his announcement, trying to pinpoint how I'd misunderstood his full intention. "You said 'You need to know that I'm resigning.' The brothers all spoke among themselves, then asked you who should be master. You told them it was up to them to vote but you endorsed Rufus. You rattled off a number of qualities he possessed that—"

He closed the gap between us and placed a finger to my lips. "Not that part." He caressed my top lip with his thumb. My skin responded with a rush of tingles as it always did when he touched me. "The part about not having the right temperament," he murmured.

Being so close to him wasn't very helpful for my concentration, but my excellent memory wouldn't allow me to forget.

"You said you didn't have the right temperament to be master."

"Not master. To be a priest. I was resigning from Merdu's Guards because being a priest is not for me. There are too many restrictions. I needed the order when I was younger. It was my home. The brothers were my family. They still are and always will be. But it is time for me to leave home and begin a new life with someone else." He cupped my jaw and searched my face. "With you, Jac. If you'll still have me."

"Ohhh," I said on a breath. It seemed to be all I could manage.

His hand dropped away. "I've changed. I'm not the man I used to be when we first met. I'm not as easygoing—"

It was my turn to stop him with a finger to his lips. "I've changed too, Rhys, and this version of me loves this version of you even more."

His chest swelled. His lips twitched with a tentative smile.

I stroked them with my thumb, as he'd done mine. "I'm glad to see your smiles again. I've missed them."

"I love you, Jac."

"I love you too, Rhys."

He kissed me. It was not like the drunken kiss we'd shared a lifetime ago. It was tender and honest, and filled with the sweetness of longing we'd both tried to suppress.

The kiss soon changed, however. It became earnest. I wasn't sure which one of us deepened the kiss, but it didn't matter. We tugged at and untied each other's clothes. My fingers fumbled, but I managed to get his tunic and shirt over his head, while he was a little gentler with me, careful of my injured shoulder and the cuts and bruises. It was frustratingly slow.

It became even more frustrating when he stepped away, out of my reach. He dragged his hand through his hair and cursed under his breath.

My gaze lowered to his magnificent chest, rising and falling with his ragged breaths. It was bare, without bandaging. "Is it the wounds on your back? Do they pain you?"

He shook his head.

"Then...have you forgotten how to...you know?"

It was meant as a joke, but he didn't smile. "I won't take your virtue, Jac. Not until we're married."

I ground my back teeth together to stop myself snapping at him in frustration. "Very well. What about when we're engaged?"

He considered it, then nodded. "All right."

"Then I accept."

"But I haven't proposed yet."

I tilted my head to the side and arched my brows.

"Right." He cleared his throat. "It's not how I imagined it, but Jac, will you marry me?"

I grinned. "I will." I hooked a finger into the waistband of his trousers. "Now, show me what I've been waiting to see all these years."

* * *

WE STAYED in the room all the next day. The day after that, we borrowed clothes for Rhys from the innkeeper then headed to the sheriff's office. The holding cells behind the office kept the prisoners locked up until their trial was held, but we didn't get that far.

"I'm afraid he died overnight," the sheriff said. "I am sorry, Miss Trenchant."

Rhys circled his arm around my waist. I leaned into him. Not because I was so shocked at the news and needed support, but simply because I liked to be near him. Hearing about my uncle's death didn't affect me.

"The magistrate has yet to complete the formalities, but no one will object if you wish to move in immediately, Miss Trenchant," the sheriff went on.

I frowned. "Move in where?"

"To your uncle's house. It's yours. Or it will be soon."

"But I'm a woman. The house and all my uncle's property and belongings go to his nearest male relative."

"There aren't any. You're the only surviving relative he had. The magistrate will ensure the property deeds are amended and your name added." He waved a hand at Rhys. "You may want to tell the magistrate what name you want to use if you plan to marry soon."

"Oh. You mean the property will be given to Rhys, as my husband."

"No, Miss Trenchant. The law recently changed. Women can

inherit property in their own right now. I'm simply asking if the magistrate writes Jacqueline Trenchant or Jacqueline Mayhew."

I was going to be the owner of a house? Just me?

"We haven't settled on a date," Rhys said when I didn't respond. "Ask the magistrate to write Trenchant for now. We'll have it changed later."

I left the sheriff's office still feeling somewhat numb. "What should I do with such a large house?"

"You could live in it," Rhys said. "Or if the memories are too painful, you could sell it."

"I think I will sell it. It's too large, too ostentatious. Besides, I want us to choose where we live together."

He drew me against his side and kissed the top of my head. "We've both lived in one room for a long time. We deserve something bigger, but I agree. Something a little more modest is probably more suited to us."

We discussed where in the city we wanted to live while we walked to the temple of Merdu's Guards. The bell of the high temple on top of the hill chimed midday, just as it had done every day since the bell tower was built. Just as it would for years to come, whether the high priest was in residence or not. A new high priest would be appointed soon, and everything would continue on as it always had.

Merdu's Guards would continue, too, but without Rhys. His name would be remembered, however, etched in stone in their small temple beneath Master Tomaj's. I suspected it would be remembered in many other ways, too. He would be the charismatic warrior priest, the charming young man who'd broken a few vows along the way to becoming master, and finally given it all up for a woman.

I couldn't enter the temple complex. Nothing had changed there. Women still weren't allowed in. Rhys fetched his friends and brought them out to me. We stood under the tree where I'd once hidden and listened to the high priest's conversation with Master Tomaj and Rhys, and where Giselle had hidden before attacking me a mere two days earlier. The day was warm, and the shade was welcome.

I thought seeing Rhys's friends would be awkward. I thought they'd blame me for taking Rhys away. But they all embraced me, none more fiercely than Rufus, the serious new master of the order.

Rhys stood close behind me, one hand on my hip. "Is all well here?"

Rufus nodded as he glanced back at the gate. "The vote happened last night. I'm master."

"Congratulations," I said. "Any news on the high priest?"

"The *former* high priest. He's awaiting trial. The sheriff thinks there's enough evidence to convict him and Giselle. The crime of conspiracy to murder isn't punishable by death, but they could be sent to the prison mines in Freedland."

It sounded awful, but the alternative was rotting in jail, and that sounded worse.

"Let's discuss happier things," Andreas said. "When will you two marry?"

"Very soon." Rhys's voice rumbled through his chest against my back.

I told them about my uncle's death and inheriting his house, and that we'd decided to sell it and find a cottage, perhaps on the river. Rufus and Andreas offered suggestions for streets where we should make inquiries, but Vizah didn't seem to be listening.

He must miss having Rhys around. I wondered if he was having second thoughts about staying in the order too. Like Rhys, he'd come to Merdu's Guards as a youth in desperate need of a father figure. Master Tomaj had provided that. But being brought into the comforting fold of the order at such a young age meant they hadn't fully understood what they were giving up for a future as a warrior priest. Now, as men, the life they wanted for themselves was becoming clearer. They understood the consequences of their choice.

For Rhys, what he wanted for his future had changed altogether.

"Are you all right, Vizah?" I asked gently.

"At the governor's house, I overheard you telling him that you would have cared for him in his old age, but he'd rejected you and chosen to be alone. It was one of the saddest things I'd ever heard."

I threw my arms around him and hugged him. "You'll always have Rhys. And me. We're your family, Vizah."

Andreas gently punched Vizah in the arm. "As are we," he said with a nod at Rufus.

Rufus threw his arm around Vizah. "We don't abandon our brothers." He gave Rhys a flat smile. "Even the ones who no longer sleep in the next room."

Vizah sniffed and turned his face away.

"Are you crying?" Andreas asked.

"It's the pollen in the air today," Vizah said, wiping his nose on his sleeve.

Rhys drew the bigger man into a hug. "Don't worry. Jac and I won't move too far away."

"What will you do for work?" Rufus asked him.

"I haven't decided. I'll find something."

"I hear the position of governor is open."

Rhys laughed.

No one else did.

"You'd have to start as a councillor first," Andreas said. "Knowing you, you'd move up the ranks quickly. Running the city will be easy after running this place." He jerked his thumb at the temple gates.

Rhys pressed his fingers into his forehead and groaned. "I have no money. I don't even own these clothes. We can't live without money, Jac."

I cupped his face with both hands. "Take a breath, Rhys."

He drew in a breath and released it slowly.

"You have time to think about your future," I went on. "I

inherited my uncle's property *and* his wealth. It will buy us more than enough time."

"Right. Of course. I forgot about that." He circled his arms around my waist. "If we have too much, do you want to set up an orphanage? Or a school?"

"I would like that very much."

He kissed me lightly and the world disappeared. In that moment, it was just us.

Until Rufus cleared his throat. "I think it costs a lot of money to run an orphanage, but we can help build it. It'll give the brothers something to do."

Rhys clasped his arm. "Thank you."

"How much money is needed to set up an orphanage?" Andreas asked.

We all shrugged.

"I don't even know how much it costs to buy a candle," Vizah said.

Rufus indicated to his friends that they should go. "Let's leave these two to plan their wedding, new home, orphanage, and children."

"About that," Vizah said. "Can I put in a request?"

"For us to have children?" Rhys asked, sounding amused. "Do you have a particular number in mind?"

"Three. All boys. I want you to name one after me."

"Vizah's a good name," I said, trying not to laugh. "We'll consider it."

Vizah grinned. "Then you can name your second one Rufus and your third Andreas."

"Why am I third?" Andreas asked.

"I should be first," Rufus said. "I am the master of the order now."

Andreas rolled his eyes. "I was wondering how long it would take before you brought that up."

Rhys put his arm around me again as his friends walked back to the gates. "What if we have girls?"

"I'll think of some girl names," Vizah called back. "Don't worry, Jac. Leave it to me. You won't have to worry about a thing."

Andreas thumped Vizah's shoulder again. "She'll be the one birthing them."

Vizah placed his hands over his ears, earning another thump from each of his friends.

Rhys steered me away. "I've never noticed how immature they are."

"Says the man who encourages them."

He grinned that boyish, charming grin I'd missed. Without the burden of responsibility for something he no longer felt committed to, he was back to being his old self, with a few modifications that came with maturity.

I tilted my head up, intending simply to look at him and allow myself to be steered along by his body. But he stopped and faced me. His gaze searched mine.

"You have the most remarkable eyes, Jac. They're like nothing I've ever seen."

I pulled the pendant out from beneath my shirt. "They're the same color as this stone."

"The color is the same, it's true, but your eyes have a depth and warmth that a mere stone can't match." He bent his head and kissed me lightly, teasingly. "Have I told you how much I love you?"

"Not since this morning."

"Then I love you, Jac. I may not have much, but I have that. I give it all to you."

"It's enough, Rhys. More than enough. I'll cherish it, always."

AUTHOR'S NOTE:

WHILE THE WARRIOR PRIEST is intended to be read as a standalone story, it's actually a spin-off of the AFTER THE RIFT series. To avoid spoiling that series for those who haven't read it, I had to be careful not to give away too much in this book. It means those of you who haven't read the AFTER THE RIFT books may have questions about the broader world events, and what happened to King Leon in particular. If you want to deepen your understanding beyond Jac and Rhys's experiences in the city of Tilting, you should start with book 1, THE PALACE OF LOST MEMORIES. It begins just after King Leon moves to his mysterious new palace outside Mull. Over the course of the six-book series, you will learn what happened in Glancia while Jac was being trained by Giselle in Dreen and get a glimpse of how Rhys fared in her absence. It was when writing those scenes a few years ago that I realized there was more to his story. Unable to forget such a compelling character, I eventually found time to revisit that world for THE WARRIOR PRIEST. To go back to where it all began, turn the page to read the description of THE PALACE OF LOST MEMORIES, book 1 in the AFTER THE RIFT series.

~ C.J. Archer

ABOUT: THE PALACE OF LOST MEMORIES

BOOK 1 OF THE AFTER THE RIFT SERIES

The king's magnificent palace was built in a matter of weeks. No one saw the builders, no villagers are allowed beyond the gilded gate, and only one servant has ever left. The haunted look in her eyes as she was recaptured by the palace guards is something Josie, daughter of the village healer, has never forgotten.

For Josie, the palace is a mystery that grows more intriguing after she meets the captain of the guards, a man known only as Hammer, as mysterious and captivating as the palace itself. Whispers of magic fuel Josie's desire to uncover the truth, but an ordinary girl like her can only dream of ever being invited inside.

When the king decides to take a wife from among the eligible daughters of the noble families, the palace gates are finally thrown open and the kingdom's elite pour in. In a court where old rivalries and new jealousies collide, the king's favorite is poisoned, and the healer is summoned. As her father's assistant, Josie finally sees inside the lavish walls, but she soon learns the palace won't surrender its secrets easily, for not a single resident, from the lowest servant to the king himself, has a memory from before the palace existed.

In her quest to help the servants, Josie becomes embroiled in courtly intrigues alongside the enigmatic captain. As their feelings for each other grow, the hopelessness of their situation becomes apparent. How can she love a man who doesn't know his own past?

To make matters worse, they discover that ending the enchantment will shake the very foundations of the kingdom, and destroy everything Josie holds dear.

THE PALACE OF LOST MEMORIES is available now from all bookstores. Or read an excerpt on CJ's website:

WWW.CJARCHER.COM

ALSO BY C.J. ARCHER

SERIES WITH 2 OR MORE BOOKS

The Glass Library

Cleopatra Fox Mysteries

After The Rift

Glass and Steele

The Ministry of Curiosities Series

The Emily Chambers Spirit Medium Trilogy

The 1st Freak House Trilogy

The 2nd Freak House Trilogy

The 3rd Freak House Trilogy

The Assassins Guild Series

Lord Hawkesbury's Players Series

Witch Born

SINGLE TITLES

The Warrior Priest

Courting His Countess

Surrender

Redemption

The Mercenary's Price

ABOUT C.J. ARCHER

C.J. Archer has loved history and books for as long as she can remember and feels fortunate that she found a way to combine the two. She spent her early childhood in the dramatic beauty of outback Queensland, Australia, but now lives in suburban Melbourne with her husband, two children and a mischievous black & white cat named Coco.

Subscribe to C.J.'s newsletter through her website to be notified when she releases a new book, as well as get access to exclusive content and subscriber-only giveaways. Her website also contains up to date details on all her books: http://cjarcher.com Follow her on social media to get the latest news:

facebook.com/CJArcherAuthorPage
instagram.com/authorcjarcher

www.ingramcontent.com/pod-product-compliance
Lightning Source LLC
LaVergne TN
LVHW030550260825
819565LV00025BA/2262